A LITTLE WHITE LIE . . .

"You don't read, do you, Miss Alexander?" Sean asked softly.

Corinne refused to be cowed by this particular shortcoming. "That's right, sir. I guess I've labeled myself wrongly when I say *governess*. But I'm very good with children. I take good care, and I like them very much."

"Yes, I believe you do."

"I would like to have a . . . postin' . . . here, sir. I would take very good care of your little girl."

"My Kenny?"

"Yes, sir. Your . . . Kenny," she said.

And the hint of sadness in her tone did not go undetected.

Sean got to his feet and walked to a cabinet in a corner of the room. "I don't know that I have a need of you, however," he said. "My wife is perfectly capable—"

"Oh! But you have no . . ." Corinne groaned as she realized her mistake.

"I'm afraid you've tipped the game board in my favor, Miss Alexander. I have no wife and you knew that."

Diamond Books by Jill Metcalf

SPRING BLOSSOM
AUTUMN LEAVES

Autumn Leaves

Jill Metcalf

DIAMOND BOOKS, NEW YORK

This book is a Diamond original edition,
and has never been previously published.

AUTUMN LEAVES

A Diamond Book / published by arrangement with
the author

PRINTING HISTORY
Diamond edition / May 1993

ISBN: 1-55773-892-0

Diamond Books are published by The Berkley Publishing Group,
200 Madison Avenue, New York, NY 10016.
The name "DIAMOND" and its logo
are trademarks belonging to Charter Communications, Inc.

PRINTED IN THE UNITED STATES OF AMERICA

10 9 8 7 6 5 4 3 2 1

DEDICATED TO

BETTY

You're always there with friendship, love, and a helping hand!

This one's for you, Mom.

Love,
Jill

Chapter 1

Natchez, Mississippi
1844

"Now, remember, Kenny," Corinne whispered. "Don't talk when he gets here. Just let him look a bit and think things over."

Five-year-old McKenna frowned up at her much taller sister. "I don't want to live with him," she said unhappily.

"Yes, you do," the older girl said. "You'll see. But first we've got to get him to take you."

"No," the girl returned with mutinous determination.

"Kenny, so help me," Corinne muttered. "We've been plannin' this for weeks." She stood to her full height then and frowned down. "You want to eat good, don't you? You want nice things, don't you?"

"I want to stay with you," Kenny said, having firmly made up her young mind.

"We've already been through this, sweetie. Once you're livin' here, I'll be watchin' and I'll come see you when I can." And she would not have the fragile girl subjected to the hardships of their life any longer. Winter was coming and Kenny needed a warm place to live. Corinne couldn't give her that. "You know I've been watchin' this man," she said kindly, kneeling down and smiling as she smoothed her sister's faded cotton dress. The poor garment was hopelessly wrinkled. "He doesn't seem stuck-up like the other swells I've been followin'. I told you that. His house is small, but I bet it's clean and warm inside. You could live nice there, Kenny. And if he isn't too smart, maybe I can find a way to come and live there, too."

McKenna's large blue eyes stared into her sister's hazel ones. "You'll try, won't you, Corie? You'll make a plan so's we can be together?"

"You know I will, baby," Corinne whispered and then feigned a bright smile. "But first we've got to get him feelin' sorry for you. Don't forget, don't talk too much, and you haven't got any family. You forget about mama and me when you're talkin' with him."

The girl merely nodded. Now that they were here, McKenna was genuinely afraid. But Corie usually made good plans.

"Now, you go across the street and sit on his steps and you wait," Corinne instructed. "I'm goin' to be watchin' from here behind the trees."

McKenna nodded again and turned to go, but Corinne pulled her back around and hugged her fiercely. "And it's okay to smile at him, baby," she whispered. "Men like little girls who smile."

McKenna's small, slim arms squeezed about Corinne's neck, and then she let loose, turned, and ran barefoot across the street.

Corinne stood and tucked herself behind the spiny hedge where she had hidden for long hours, day after day for the past weeks. Her hazel eyes darted briefly toward the sky, judging the time. . . . He would be coming soon.

She looked back across the street in time to see her sister plant herself on the second step of four and smooth her skirt over her knees. Corinne wished again that Kenny could have worn something better, but there was nothing else. Still, her pride hurt to see the girl dressed in rags.

Curiously, Corinne worried more about her sister's poverty than her own. The tall, slim seventeen-year-old was dressed little better. In addition, her prospects were certainly more grim. But Kenny would have a chance . . . with luck.

The small brick house near the corner of Pearl and Jefferson streets was unpretentious when compared to some of the mansions in the neighborhood. That was precisely why Corinne had chosen the place. The house *and* the man. He seemed unpretentious, too, and his house and gardens were meticulously kept. The small front porch and two square-cut columns that supported the porch roof were gleaming white, as were all the window frames. The shutters were painted black, however, and shone so brightly that one could believe the paint was still wet.

The street was lined with combinations of holly hedges, giant oaks, and crepe myrtles draped with Spanish moss that fluttered in the autumn breeze like lacy gray petticoats hung to dry. The oaks were shedding their leaves now, gently blanketing the streets, while acorns dropped dramatically upon unwary passersby.

It was a good street; far enough away from Silver Street that led to Natchez Under-the-Hill to suit her. Corinne was quite pleased with Kenny's new home.

She smiled softly as she watched Kenny twist her slender fingers together while she dutifully watched up the street for the man she had seen from a distance many, many times. She wondered if the child was nearly as frightened as her big sister was at this moment. Probably not. Kenny had not experienced too much harshness as of yet. That's what Corinne wanted to save her from. Corinne wanted her sister to have a home, but she prayed it would be a *good* home.

And then she saw him. Corinne's neck strained around the base of the bushes for a good view as she attempted to remain well hidden.

He walked confidently, with long-legged strides that seemed to eat up the distance effortlessly. He was immaculately dressed, as was usual, and she loved the way his tall hat seemed to tip a bit arrogantly on his head. His slim, gray trousers fit snugly over muscular thighs, and his dark long coat, cut away at the waist, accentuated a flat stomach. The man was exceptionally handsome and in fine physical condition to Corinne's way of thinking. That might have put her off if she had not seen him smile only the day before. His smile was too beautiful to be sported by an arrogant, pompous man. It was important that the man be sensible and humane. . . . Kenny would not take kindly to a swell.

His name was Sean Garrick.

The day had been long, and Sean Garrick wanted only to get home to his supper and spend a quiet evening alone for a change. Faye had been excessively demanding of late, and between keeping his mistress happy and dealing with the demands of his work, Sean was feeling unusually weary.

That was why he frowned fiercely at the waif planted on his doorstep. He stopped a few feet away, staring in astonishment at the child, who simply looked up at him a bit doubtfully. She was a wretched little thing with her dress badly wrinkled and her hair wildly knotted. It appeared as if someone had attempted to clean the child's clothing, but he had other thoughts about the actual cleanliness of the girl herself.

He watched one slender, filthy foot curl over its mate, and when his eyes roamed upward to her face she smiled.

Sean was certain that one stern, unhappy frown would send the child scampering, but all she did was liken her own expression to his. Bold little urchin, he thought.

He moved a step closer. "What are you doing here, then?" he asked, and the girl tipped her head back farther so she could see his face.

"Waitin'," she said.

"Waiting? For what?"

"You."

His dark brows shot upward. "I don't know you."

The girl shrugged bony shoulders. "My name's Kenny," she said softly.

"Kenny?" A *girl*? "Where do you belong, Kenny?" he asked quietly. And when she did not respond immediately, he questioned, "Where do you live?"

"Here," she said boldly.

"Oh, no," he said, shaking his head as he wandered in front of her. Then he turned to look at the waif from a different angle. . . . She looked equally as bad from all sides. He tapped the silver head of his walking stick lightly against his chin while he studied the girl. Well, whatever she was after, he did not have room in his life to provide it. "I think you'd best be off about your business now," he said not unkindly.

The child did not move.

Sean studied her a moment longer and then decided that he would simply leave her there. She would tire and wander off eventually.

"I must go in now," he said and watched her eyes follow. When he reached the top step, she pivoted and continued to watch. Sean Garrick felt that child's deep blue eyes burning into his back as he opened the door and disappeared inside.

Across the street Corinne cursed softly, woefully dropping her head forward on her chest as her eyes drifted closed. The man had no heart. The plan had failed.

Corinne told herself she should not have been surprised. She knew many men, but none possessed the kind of *heart* it would take to give an unknown child a home. She had hoped it would be different up here, above the Hill.

She had hoped Sean Garrick would be different.

She waited for several long, painful moments while Kenny continued to sit on the step in abject misery. She waited until she could no longer stand the sight of the sorrowful child sitting there alone. The man was not going to come out of his home.

She whistled softly.

Kenny heard the signal and was instantly alert. She scampered down from the steps and raced across the street, happy to be joining her sister even though it would mean going back down the Hill.

Concealed behind the fine grosgrain draperies that covered the front windows of his townhouse, Sean Garrick watched the moppet dive behind a cedar hedge.

Chapter 2

Corinne held tightly to Kenny's hand as they made their way along the crowded boardwalk until they reached the brick structure known as Tim's Place. They moved quickly along the front of the building—as frequently a male body or two had been known to literally sail through the open door. It was not a place where even the women of Natchez Under-the-Hill were wont to go. It was a man's world in Tim's Place, and women were best off to respect that.

Corinne and Kenny both understood that.

It was almost dark as the two girls made their way up the rickety, wooden stairs on the outside of the building. Everything was either bleached by the sun or darkened by water. They climbed the twenty-three steps to the small landing. Once there they paused for a moment. When familiar sounds came from within, Corinne frowned down at the small girl by her side. "We'll have to go to the storeroom," she whispered, and Kenny turned mutinous once again.

7

"I want to see Mama," she whined.

Her older sister tugged on her hand and started back down the steps. "Mama's busy," she said bluntly as a familiar pang of resentment caused knots in her stomach.

Constance Alexander had been entertaining men for as long as Corinne could remember. She understood that her mother took money in exchange for favors, and while she was not certain what "favors" entailed, she believed that what her mother was doing was degrading and demoralizing. She believed these things because her mother frequently cried over cups of rum-laced tea. Eighteen years ago the woman had been abandoned by her lover, Corinne's father, and had never recovered.

The fine, well-educated, young Constance Alexander had become lost in a totally unfamiliar world . . . Natchez Under-the-Hill.

The money Constance made seldom found its way to do good for her two daughters. She would throw it away on gaudy clothes, cheap liquor, or reckless chances for making a fortune. But she was so easily duped or cheated that the *fortune* never materialized.

Though Corinne hated what her mother did, she felt compassion for her. Constance was a gentle person who had continuously chosen badly when it came to men, and that had not been any different when she had chosen Corinne's father. The pattern of one unworthy man after another had developed over the years, but Corinne was determined not to follow in her mother's steps—she would choose carefully when it came time to select a mate. And it would be a permanent venture. She had seen women above the Hill strolling along, arm-in-arm with their gentlemen, and that was what she would have . . . one man and only one. For the rest of her life.

If she ever got out from Under-the-Hill.

At the bottom of the stairs Corinne turned to her right, gently pulling the weary Kenny along in her wake. They made their way to the back of the building and entered an open doorway into a narrow, darkened hall.

"I'm hungry, Corie," Kenny whined.

Her sister turned to her abruptly, bending low. "Sssh! You know to be quiet here, baby. I'll get us some food once I've seen Tim." Looking hastily along the length of the hall, Corinne determined that they were alone. "You wait here and I'll be back with the key."

Kenny hated waiting in that dark place and pressed her back against the wall of unfinished stones as she watched her sister disappear toward the lighted entrance. She did not like staying in Tim's Place, and they stayed there a lot. Perhaps she should have tried harder to make the man above the Hill like her.

Corinne was also in the habit of hugging the wall as she peeked around the doorless entrance to the barroom, hoping she could catch Tim's eye without having to enter the place. The room was huge, the air blue with smoke, and the noise level almost unbearable. And each and every time she went in there, she managed to draw the attention of one or more disreputable characters. It mattered little that she wore boys' britches and shirts. Any woman who dared to enter was fair game, and it was difficult to convince some of these men that their attentions were unwanted. In some cases it was damned near impossible.

Tim was there behind the bar, busy pouring hard, dark rum into heavy glasses. She stared at his profile intently, hoping he would eventually sense that she was there.

"You want the key, Corie?" a male voice asked, and her head snapped to her right.

A slow smile spread across her pretty mouth, and she nodded. "Would you ask Tim for me, Peter?"

"Sure thing," he said, and the tall, lanky youth walked across her path and went directly behind the bar to the owner's side.

Corinne had known Peter Kemper most of her life. He was close to nineteen now, she supposed, and he had been a good friend. He was tall and slim but muscular from his trade, and he never failed to offer her a kindness. He was a thief, like his father before him, but he possessed a strange code of honor when it came to her. And it had been that way since they were children running in the streets Under-the-Hill together. He liked his rum and he liked his women, but there had been many times in the past when she had been glad that he had been about. Corinne did not know what she and Kenny would do if they did not have Peter and Tim as friends.

Peter smiled as he returned to her, his body blocking any view of her from the others in the room. "Tim says he put another cat in the storeroom today. The rats are kind of bad in there, Corie," he added with concern. "You could stay in the cave, if you'd rather."

Peter and his father had dug one of many caves in the steep hillside above the town's few buildings where they hid their stolen goods. But Corinne found the caves more frightening than the rats in Tim's storeroom. During her lifetime there had been landslides up on the hill, and goods had been buried in the caves . . . She did not want that happening to Kenny and herself.

She smiled at her friend. "It's all right, Peter, thanks. Kenny can sleep for a bit, and we'll go upstairs later."

In other words, she would watch over her sister and sleep when she could. He understood that. He did not like it, but he understood. And there was no use making her feel bad by mentioning that he hated the way she had to live. Corie did what she had to do to survive. They all did. "Is Kenny hungry, Corie?" he asked, when what he really wanted to do was make some scathing remark about her mother. "I can get you some food."

She nodded once again. "Thanks, Peter."

She was always grateful, and she was always sweet. Peter failed to understand how she had remained that way. Corinne was an exceptional girl, and he could easily love her in a way that was not at all brotherly. In fact, he had long ago reached a level of desire that would frighten Corie if she knew about his feelings. And loving her caused a dilemma for Peter. As much as he wanted her, he also wanted to see her get out from Under-the-Hill. Although few of them ever did.

"You go along to the room," he said quietly. "I'll be back."

Corinne moved quickly along the dark corridor until she reached her sister. "I've got the key, baby," she said cheerfully, as if they were about to spend the night in some swank hotel. "And Peter's gettin' us some supper." It was all very ordinary. It was all very familiar. And it was all horrid.

"What's he goin' to bring us, Corie?" Kenny whispered while she waited in the hall for her sister to light the single lamp on the shelf near the door.

"I don't know, honey," she said. "We'll have to wait and see."

"My tummy's growlin' at me."

"Just as long as your growlin' doesn't scare off the cats," Corie murmured.

"What?"

"Nothing, baby. Come inside now so I can lock the door."

Kenny pattered across the room to where an old cot stood wedged between boxes of supplies and barrels of rum. "I should've tried harder to make that man like me," she said unhappily.

Corinne turned abruptly to face her. "You did just fine, Kenny." She walked across the room and sat on the edge of the cot beside the girl. Corie had already decided that they would take a second shot at Mr. Garrick. "I think maybe it might take a few days for him to understand, you know? He probably wouldn't want to take somebody's little girl away from her family," she added thoughtfully and watched a black-and-white cat dive behind a sack in the opposite corner. Corinne shuddered as the cat squealed in triumph. "We have to make him understand you have no home."

"But I live upstairs," McKenna returned logically, and Corinne smiled, hugging the girl close to her side for warmth.

That was no home, she thought. That was shelter, but rarely. "You'll have to fib a little, Kenny," she instructed quietly. "The man won't let you live in his house if he thinks you already have a place."

McKenna stared wide-eyed at her sister. "But it's a sin to lie," she breathed. "Mama said so."

"Sweetheart," Corinne said fondly, "I think God will forgive us this time."

*   *   *

Sean Garrick had abandoned the work he had intended to complete before morning and now sat in his study, staring reflectively at the dancing flames of the small fire he had just started. The night air was damp and chill, and he wondered if the waif who had been sitting on his stoop could enjoy the luxury of any form of heat. The shy smile and large blue eyes seemed to have been burned into his memory. He kept seeing her and the filth of her!

The child was no concern of his, of course. But that did not mean he could remain unmoved by her suffering. Some people abused the privilege of having children, he decided. And he fully believed that having children was a God-given *privilege*. He had been delighted when his wife of four years had told him she was pregnant. That had been five years ago, and he was convinced he and Marie would have made exceptionally good parents. But he had lost her . . . Marie and the tiny son she had wanted so very much. The boy had died even as he killed his mother.

He had lost them both.

Needless to say, Sean was not surprised when he returned home the following evening and found Kenny awaiting him. Clearly the tall, slim girl he had seen across the street the previous day had planned something, and this small moppet was the pawn. He was just a little bit curious as to what they wanted from him.

And very wary.

"You're back, are you, moppet?" he asked as he planted one booted foot on the lower step and stared down at the girl.

McKenna smiled up at him. "My name's Kenny," she chirped.

He smiled. "Yes. I remember."

"Do you like girls?" she asked.

He laughed lightly. "Very much."

"I'm a girl," she said softly and waited. Her heart began to make her chest hurt.

Sean studied the silver head of his walking stick. "Where do you live, Kenny?"

She had a little problem with that one. Even though Corinne said it was all right this once, it was difficult for her to lie. "I'm hungry," she said, avoiding the issue.

Sean's dark eyes looked down at her then. "Are you?"

The girl nodded her head adamantly. But when he did not move and continued to stare, McKenna began to feel a little unsettled. Fidgeting, her fingers knotting, she smiled worriedly. "I'm sorry, sir," she said softly. "I'm not to ask for food, I know."

"Why not, if you're hungry?" he asked.

"Beggars have no pride," she quoted.

Sean's dark brows arched upward. "Indeed? Who told you that?"

"Corie," she said, before remembering she was supposed to forget.

"And who is Corie?"

Because she had not done as she was told, Kenny looked decidedly worried as she muttered, "I forget."

Sean laughed softly and straightened. "I doubt there's much you *forget*, my young friend," he said and walked around the girl, up the steps. Opening the door, he called, "Mrs. Pringle? Could I see you out here for a moment?"

Suddenly McKenna was truly frightened, and she

stood up, whirling around to face the door. "I'm real sorry," she blurted. "I have to go now."

Although thoughts of touching the girl were distasteful, Sean recognized her fear and reached out and gently grasped her shoulder. "It's all right, Kenny. Mrs. Pringle is a fine woman. You needn't be afraid."

McKenna's eyes widened as a tall, slim woman dressed totally in black appeared at the door.

"Ah, Mrs. Pringle," Sean said. "Our young friend here says she is hungry. Is there something we might offer?"

Normally a kind, happy soul, Mrs. Pringle was, however, unused to children, and she wondered where Mr. Garrick had managed to find such a creature. "Sir, should you be touching that?" she asked, and Sean grinned, knowing the woman well.

"*That* is a little girl, Mrs. P.," he said jovially. "A hungry little girl."

Jane Pringle thought for a moment. The last time Mr. Garrick had done something like this, she had been stuck with a monster of a dog who now resided in the house. "Sir, if you give a kitten rich cream, it will keep coming back for more."

"It seems to me we have plenty in this house to share," he said firmly but not unkindly.

The woman turned silently and disappeared inside the house.

"Is she your wife?" the girl asked, and Sean laughed heartily. Mrs. P. was old enough to be his mother.

"No, moppet. Mrs. Pringle is my housekeeper."

Kenny looked confused by that.

"It means she keeps my house clean and cooks for me."

The girl's eyes rounded, and she frowned up at him.

"Is she a slave?" she asked with obvious disappointment.

"Do you know about slaves, Kenny?"

"It's bad to have slaves," she said seriously.

"Yes, it is." And he hoped she did not say *that* to just anyone. Words like those landed even small people in trouble. "But Mrs. Pringle is not a slave. I pay her wages and provide her a small cottage in exchange for her work."

A cottage?

"I could work," she returned cheerfully.

"Could you?" he asked softly. "And what would you do?"

That was a troublesome question. Kenny sometimes had trouble helping Corie make up the cot. And she sure could not cook!

"Never mind, Kenny," he said. "One day, perhaps."

Mrs. Pringle returned then with bread and some cold sliced lamb wrapped in a cloth. But she did not smile when she bent at the waist and gave the bundle over to the girl.

"Thank you," Kenny murmured politely.

Sean watched her for a moment, frowning as she clutched the white cloth and its contents to her thin chest. It was a curious thing, this; the child was clearly an urchin, yet someone had taught her some manners. The same *someone* who had instructed the girl to sit on his stoop? Why *his* stoop? "Are you going to come and sit here every day, Kenny?" he asked, suspecting the child was too young to carefully guard her responses.

Kenny looked confused but nodded.

"Why? Why would you sit here?"

Fidgeting under his direct stare and worried about

all his questions, Kenny said simply, "You have a nice house."

"But there are other, finer houses in Natchez."

Scratching behind her left ear, Kenny squinted at him. "You mean the big houses?"

"Any house," he said pointedly.

"But them's rich people in the big houses, and rich people aren't nice. You're nice."

Sean laughed at the backhanded compliment. "You haven't told me why you're sitting on my stoop."

Kenny was in big trouble now; Corie hadn't told her if she should tell. But if she didn't answer his question, how would he know? It was too big a decision for a five-year-old, and Kenny had been taught to be forthright. "So's you'll let me live with you," she said softly.

His suspicions confirmed, Sean frowned and moved away from the child. "You'd best take your food on home now," he said quietly, steeling himself for her response.

But Kenny did not respond. She continued to shy away from lying to him. She simply could not say she did not have a home when she did. In place of an answer she nodded and whispered another thank you.

Taking a last look at the girl, Sean entered his house.

Kenny promptly sat back down on the steps, still clutching her bundle and awaiting a signal from across the way. She would like to peek inside the cloth and see what the lady had given her, but she was saving the surprise to share with Corie.

It was almost dark before she heard the soft whistle.

Chapter 3

Sean could not get Kenny out of his mind all of the following day. And that, he supposed, was what the young woman had planned. Although he still was not certain what they wanted from him, it was more than clear that he had been singled out and targeted. Still, the plight of an undernourished child was difficult to ignore.

And the more he thought about Kenny, the more he began to feel that something must be done for her. He found it difficult to understand a mind that would use a child to achieve an end . . . any end. Additionally, he found it deplorable that the child could be kept in such a state.

He left his office early that day, having decided that perhaps Faye could offer a suggestion or two. He had no idea how his current mistress felt about children, but she was, after all, a woman. And women had instincts about these things, didn't they?

He had sent a boy around to Faye Doherty's home, requesting her assistance with a small problem. Sean

19

had gone round to fetch her by hansom later in the day, allowing enough time to endure the usual wait that Faye habitually imposed and still reach his home at the customary hour.

And, as usual, she was worth the wait. Faye was a woman any man would be proud to escort. She was beautiful and always impeccably dressed. Her auburn hair was perhaps a bit too bright to be natural, but the sausage curls on either side of her face were perfectly formed. The rest of her abundant hair was pulled back and arranged in myriad tiny curls bound up by a ribbon that matched her green-and-white striped silk day dress. The gown fit her snugly, accentuating her narrow waist and ample bosom. A matching parasol and white kid gloves added the finishing touches to this vision of perfection.

Sean knew Faye had powerful friends in the city—a legacy from her late husband—and traveled in wealthy circles. But these were not things that influenced his relationship with her. . . . Faye was a consummate snob, but she also suited his purposes.

"Hello, darling," she drawled as she breezed into the parlor where he waited.

Sean smiled and got to his feet, holding his arms aloft as she sailed into them, pressing her fingertips lightly against his chest while raising her cheek for a light peck from him. He could tumble her about in bed, but God forbid he should muss a single hair once she was dressed.

"Thank you for agreeing to come," he said, stepping back and smiling down at her. "I have a hansom waiting," he added as he took her elbow and escorted her toward the foyer and the main door to the street.

"This is all very mysterious, Sean, really," she said as they paused outside the door while he adjusted his silk hat. "Could you not simply *tell* me your problem so I could offer an opinion?"

Sean grinned lopsidedly. "I believe my *problem* will have more of an impact if you see for yourself."

"Impact" understated Faye's reaction when they drove up to his house a few moments later.

Faye's eyes were turned in the direction of the townhouse as they rounded the corner.

"See?" he asked simply.

Her small turned-up nose crinkled as she looked about. "I see your house, Sean," she said impatiently.

"On the steps," he directed.

The corners of Faye's pretty mouth turned down in distaste. "An urchin," she said. "A particularly filthy one," she added as Sean signaled the driver to halt.

"A little girl," he said softly as they continued to study the tyke. "An undernourished child."

Faye's head snapped around, and she frowned at him. "*This* is your problem, darling?"

Sean's eyes raised slowly to hers.

She laughed as his silence answered her question. "You must be joking, Sean," she said, as if she had never been quite so scandalized.

"She waits for me every evening."

"Well, shoo her away, darling," she said lightly.

Sean's dark brows dipped dangerously over his eyes. "We're not talking about flies here, my dear. This is a child."

"Well, I can see that," she returned, her head turning briefly toward Kenny and then back to stare at him. Faye did not want anyone else competing for Sean's attentions. It mattered little that her rival would be someone's filthy brat.

Sean stepped carefully over his companions skirts and descended from the cab, turning and reaching into his pocket for coins to pay the driver. "Come down and meet her," he said to Faye as he conducted his search.

"Don't pay the driver," Faye said flatly. "I don't believe I can stay long."

Sean frowned but eventually shrugged and reached up a hand, then paid the fare while asking the driver to wait. When he turned back to his mistress, it was to see her staring at Kenny with obvious distaste.

"She is probably infested or infected, Sean," she said. "Possibly both." She squinted up at him. "Do you have any idea where she comes from?"

Sean shook his head even as he smiled down at the child. "Hello, Kenny," he said. "I want you to meet my friend."

Kenny smiled brightly as her eyes roamed from one adult to the other.

Faye certainly had no intention of acknowledging *this* introduction. "What are you planning, darling?"

Sean ignored her bad manners and said quietly, "I was hoping you might know of someone who could take her in."

Faye was visibly shocked. "Darling, what has gotten into you? Who on earth would take such a filthy creature? Certainly not anyone *I* know."

"Perhaps *that* is the problem," he said.

"I don't understand."

"I don't suppose you would, Faye." Now that he thought about it, he had seen this lack of caring in her in the past: he had simply chosen to ignore it. But today her lack of sensitivity was grating on him.

"Sean, there are some very good orphanages in the city," she said, backtracking just a bit. "Perhaps I could make inquiries for you."

Again that dark head was shaking. "I'd not see my dog sent to one of those places."

Faye could now see that he was quite serious about this particular child and decided she must tread more carefully. "What would you like to do for her, darling?"

"As I said, I was hoping you might know some couple who would enjoy having a little girl," he said reasonably, trying desperately to set his previous impatience with her aside. "We could clean her up. Possibly purchase a dress and shoes. I'm certain she's quite a cute little thing under all of that dirt."

How could anyone possibly tell? Fay wondered. "But she must have a home, Sean. A family?"

There was *someone*, right enough, but he was not certain if the tall, slim girl was family to Kenny. To Faye he said only, "Kenny says no to both."

Faye was becoming increasingly peevish again. "She seems to be faring well enough," she offered.

"We've been feeding her," he said, smiling at Kenny again. "Mrs. P. and I."

Standing on the street and staring at this urchin was making Faye feel quite uncomfortable. And wasn't this just a bit of *déjà vu*? Sean had acquired his wretched stray dog in much the same manner as it seemed he was about to acquire a wretched stray child. "I can inquire about, Sean. But I would not get my hopes up, were I you."

He wouldn't. It was now clearly understood that Faye would die before she would ask any of her friends to house this child.

He nodded and turned to assist Faye back into the hansom, whether she was ready to depart or not. "I thank you for coming, anyway," he said flatly.

Faye turned and gracefully dropped down onto the

cushioned seat. She had the terrible feeling that this afternoon would cost her dearly. "You won't forget the Delecroix ball, darling?" she asked with a pretty smile. "It's Thursday evening, if you recall."

"I shall be in touch, Faye," he said, sounding weary. With a last dark look he signaled the driver once again. The hansom turned about in the street, and Sean raised a hand in response to his mistress's wave as she sped by and away.

He silently watched the cab until it disappeared around the corner. Faye Doherty was four years his senior, and while she had been married for upward of fifteen years, and had no doubt been intimate with men other than himself, she had never had a child. He had thought perhaps she was barren, but now he understood.

The afternoon was proving to be quite an education.

He turned now and smiled down at the child who sat patiently. "You should not frown so, Kenny," he said lightly. "You're far too pretty to frown."

"Is she your wife?"

Sean chuckled. "No, my pet. I don't have a wife."

"She didn't seem very friendly," Kenny complained.

"No, I suppose she didn't."

"Her clothes was pretty," she offered, having decided she should be saying only nice things so this man would like her.

"*Were* pretty," he corrected distractedly. "Her clothes *were* pretty."

A long silence followed, and eventually Kenny began to squirm under his scrutiny.

Finally Kenny could stand the silence no longer. "Did you have a nice day?" she chirped.

Sean threw back his head and laughed. "What am I going to do with you?" he asked.

"If you wanted to pay me a cottage, I could work," she said, beaming up at him as he laughed again.

He would not be able to afford to "pay" her a cottage if what he had in mind transpired. Mrs. Pringle would negotiate a raise in pay, and he would not deny her.

"I'll make a deal with you," he said, propping a foot next to her hip and dropping elbow to knee. "If you promise to take a bath, I'll let you live in my house until I can find a proper home for you."

The girl's eyes rounded as her expression changed from elation to consternation. "But I already . . ." Kenny immediately stuck a dirty fist into her mouth.

"Don't put *that* in your mouth," he said, reaching out to lightly touch her wrist. "You already what?"

"I think *your* house is proper," she muttered.

"Wouldn't you like to live with a nice couple?" When she looked puzzled, he clarified. "Wouldn't you like to have a mother and a father?"

Kenny thought about that for a moment. She already had a mother . . . nobody needed two. And if he sent her to live with a *couple*, Corinne might lose track of her. "I think living with just you would be nice," she offered shyly.

Of course she thought that way. The child had been coached. And this plan of his could be risky if this child were a pawn in some lethal game. He had yet to understand why he had been singled out by this tiny imp and her tall, slim friend, and it was entirely possible he was playing right into more dangerous hands.

Still, he could not seem to help himself.

*   *   *

Corinne could hardly believe their luck. She watched the man guide Kenny up the steps and through his front door. She stayed and watched for interminable hours, always mindful that they might simply feed the child and then turn her out.

But Kenny did not appear.

When darkness descended and the street grew quiet, Corinne dropped her head forward on her knees. In the shelter of her hiding place she cried with equal measures of relief and sadness.

The loneliness would follow.

Inside the small house on Pearl Street there was an uproar.

Mrs. Pringle felt Mr. Garrick should have more concern for her sensibilities before thrusting the care of a child of questionable background upon her.

Kenny, having the uncanny ability of most children to sense displeasure in others, felt she might be happier in Tim's storeroom than with this stern woman.

Sean felt he should rethink his high opinion of females.

Sitting at the round table in the kitchen, Sean had watched the woman and the girl literally stalk each other around the room for the past twenty minutes. Meanwhile, Kenny's bathwater was growing cold, and the child was still fully clothed.

"Mrs. P.," he said at last. "Perhaps we should alter our tactics. If you would be good enough to go to the shops and see about some clothes for the girl, I will assist her with the bath."

Mrs. Pringle stopped dead in her tracks and frowned in complete shock. "Sir! You cannot do that!"

There was little doubt about her meaning. "She's a little girl, for heaven's sake. If I were her father, you would not think such a thing as shocking," he said reasonably.

"You are not her father," the woman said, as if the very thought could not be tolerated.

"Mrs. P."—he sighed—"it looks as though I might become just that . . . by acclamation."

Jane Pringle continued to look astonished that he could even consider such a thing. But then her eyes turned on the child. Someone had to help the poor wee mite, and until she and Kenny could achieve some form of harmony, it appeared as if Mr. Garrick would be the vanguard of this unorthodox crusade. She would, however, never understand why he had felt duty bound to enter into this situation.

Sean could see the woman beginning to soften and smiled his understanding. "Take the household purse, Mrs. P.," he said gently. "I'll replace the coins tomorrow."

Heaving a great, suffering sigh, Mrs. Pringle asked. "What should I purchase, sir?"

"One of everything, I should think. Once we have her decently garbed, we can take Kenny to the shops for proper fitting," he added thoughtfully. "Oh! And a nightdress, I expect."

"Indeed, a nightdress," the woman muttered and tossed an unexpected smile in the girl's direction.

When they were alone, Sean stood and removed his stock, then unfastened the top buttons of his shirt, preparing for battle. "You did promise," he reminded Kenny as he folded back shirtsleeves to the elbow.

"I thought that lady might drowd me," Kenny complained, and he smiled.

"The word is *drown*, my pet, and Mrs. Pringle

would do no such thing. She's not used to little girls, so you must cooperate.''

When he saw her deepening frown, Sean explained. ''If you are nice to Mrs. Pringle, she will be nice to you.''

''I'm nice most of the time,'' Kenny offered.

He laughed, returning to his chair. ''I'm sure you are, moppet,'' he said. ''Now, come here for a moment.'' Sean had already designated one of his hairbrushes to be used for the child, although he fancied it would have to be thoroughly cleaned after this usage. When Kenny approached he took her between his wide-spread knees and turned her away from him. ''If you don't do something about this, my girl, it will be impossible to deal with once it is wet.''

There followed a deluge of squeals and cries as Sean tried his best to brush out the horrid mess of knots the child was sporting. ''I really hope you're not infested, Kenny,'' he muttered. Even though he tried to be gentle, he knew he was hurting. ''I'm sorry, moppet,'' he murmured, separating another hank of hair before applying the brush. ''I'm really not too practiced at this.''

''It hurts!'' she cried, stomping a small foot and digging ten little fingers into his knees.

''We're finished!'' he said at last and turned her about to face him. ''You're a brave girl,'' he added as he brushed a tear or two away from her cheeks. ''How would you like something pretty-smelling in your bath?''

Kenny felt she had been abused enough at this point and longed to be back at Tim's, but she nodded her head woefully.

''That's my girl,'' he said and swung a long leg over the child's head as he stood and moved toward the bath. He tested the water first and, finding it cool as he had suspected, poured more hot from the kettle on the cast-iron stove. When he straightened from the chore, he surveyed the soap and bottles Mrs. Pringle had left on a small stool beside the copper tub. "What do you think, Kenny?" he asked, trying to entice her in. "Which would you like?"

The girl shuffled to his side and eyed the two small bottles, one green and one brown. "Are they yours?" she asked, peering up at him.

Sean smiled. "I think they must be Mrs. Pringle's. But I'm certain she left them here for you to use."

"Me?" she asked, clearly amazed.

"Of course. See which smells nicest."

Dirty little fingers reached out, removed one stopper after the other, and then held the brown bottle up to him. "This one!" she chirped.

"This one it is," he said and dropped a portion into the warm water. Immediately the entire kitchen took on the scent of violets.

"Pretty!" Kenny crowed.

"Pretty, indeed," Sean echoed as his nose began to twitch. "Off with that dress, now," he ordered lightly.

Without hesitation Kenny reached for the tattered hem and drew the cloth up and over her head. Nothing shy about this one, Sean thought as he picked up the discarded garment and took it outside. He left it on the porch, deciding it could be burned later.

When he returned to the kitchen, Kenny was hovering over the edge of the tub. "Let me help you." He caught her about the waist, lifting and then lowering her gently into the water; it was like lifting a large package that was empty inside, so slight was she. And her weightlessness made Sean very unhappy.

"Have you eaten today?" he asked conversationally as he dropped to his knees and began to lather a cloth with scented soap.

"I saved some cheese that Mrs. P. gave me yesterday," she said.

Sean winced. "I think you had best call her Mrs. Pringle, moppet."

"You don't."

"I'm older."

"Everybody tells me that."

"That's because everybody *is* older," he teased. And then he frowned thoughtfully. "Who do you mean when you say *everybody*, Kenny?"

"Oh, Corie and Tim and Peter," she said, slapping her hands together under the water.

Sean made a dive for one of her hands and raised her arm for a scrubbing. "Who are they?"

Kenny realized she should not have said Corie's name and sputtered, "Friends."

"Where do your friends live?"

Kenny was concerned about all these questions, but she could not see that he could cause any trouble. "Near the water," she said softly.

"Under-the-Hill, Kenny?" he asked, not really wanting to know *that*. "Is that where your friends live?"

The girl nodded. "By the water."

Sean briefly closed his eyes to obliterate the distaste of this child knowing the people down there. "Is that where you were living, too?" he asked softly and almost groaned when the girl nodded her head. "I'm glad you found me, then, sweetheart," he whispered.

Chapter 4

Time began to drag for Corie after that day. She no longer had Kenny to watch over and to feed. Once again she was alone, as she had been before her sister's birth. Once again she could dart amongst the back alleys, seeking any little treasure she could find. Or any trinket she could steal and sell.

Corinne had only herself to care for now.

When it was vacant, she returned to the room above Tim's Place to sleep a little. When it was not, she hid in Tim's storeroom with the cats and the other creatures she preferred not to think about.

There was a sameness to it all, a familiarity, as shabby as her existence might be. But there was *aloneness* now, too. For the first time in her life, Corinne felt lost.

And she felt drawn to the house on Pearl Street.

Sean had spied the slim girl with the auburn hair on more than one occasion. Either she was coming more often to her hiding place across the street or she was becoming careless in exposing herself. His curiosity had more than peaked by now. Kenny had been with him for several days and still nothing untoward had occurred. He was wary and more careful, of course, knowing the child was being used as a pawn by the auburn-haired creature and possibly by others. But he had not guessed, as yet, what game they could be after. The only thing that was clear to him was that Kenny's appearance in his life must be part of a larger scheme. One just did not plant a five-year-old child on someone's stoop with good intentions.

Still, he could not regret befriending Kenny. She was a sweet, good-natured little thing, full of giggles and nonsensical chatter. Because of her, and for the first time since losing his wife, Sean found himself eager for his days to end so that he could get home. He knew, also, that the child had come dangerously close to his heart.

If only he knew why Kenny and her accomplice had chosen *him* as their pigeon.

He turned away from the window, contemplating a number of avenues for drawing the tall girl in, if indeed she had some ulterior motive.

Kenny was meticulously scrutinizing slices of ham on a platter when he returned to his place at the head of the table.

"You may have more if you wish, moppet," he said.

Kenny's hand streaked toward the platter.

Sean caught the delicate wrist before her fingers could dive into the meat. "Fork, please," he said and immediately thought better of it. "Perhaps I should help."

He picked up the meat fork. "This one?"

"The little one," she said, "I'm gettin' kind o' full."

"I began to doubt I'd ever hear you say that, Kenny," he said, placing the meat on her plate.

She smiled winningly. "I never had *ham* before."

Sean poured more coffee from the silver carafe, settled back in his chair, and carefully concentrated on filling his pipe as he spoke. "What *are* you used to eating, Kenny?" he asked casually.

Kenny spoke around a mouthful of meat. "I eat lots of things now," she returned happily.

"But before. What kinds of things did you eat before you came here?"

The child speared another piece of meat but thought about his question before putting it into her mouth. "Cheese and bread . . . and sometimes Peter would bring us some chicken." She popped the meat into her mouth and stared out the dining room window as she continued to think. "And sometimes we could pinch an apple or an orange from the fruit man," she added proudly.

Sean winced but let the point on stealing slip by as he held a taper to the bowl of his pipe. "Who's Peter?"

"He's a friend. He always does nice things for us."

"You and your mama?" he asked, watching her carefully.

The girl's eyes dropped to her plate, and she slowly set her fork down. "I don't think I can eat any more."

"All right, sweetheart," he said, dismayed by her discomfort. "But drink your milk."

The girl did as she was told, eagerly—the cool milk was wonderful and drinking it with every meal was no hardship.

"Do you remember your mama?" he asked and drew deeply on the stem of his pipe.

Kenny carefully placed the glass back on the table. "I remember," she said quietly, but she refused to look at him.

"Do you remember where she lives?"

"I like that stuff you put in there." She pointed at the pipe, ignoring his question. "It doesn't smell awful like cigars."

Sean's dark brows rose in question. "Do you know about cigars?"

"Lots of men at Tim's Place smoke them," she offered easily and then giggled. "They make the air turn blue."

Sean didn't think he liked the sound of this. "Where is Tim's Place?"

"Near the river."

"Did you live there?"

"Mostly." The careless shrug of her bony shoulders told him he was losing her again, however.

"Did Corie and Peter stay there with you?"

"Peter never," she said, feeling very afraid now. "Can I go outside?"

"You *may* in a minute, moppet," he said not unkindly, leaning toward her. "Tell me, who is Corie?"

Kenny looked everywhere except at him.

"You told me she was your friend."

The small head, wreathed in red-gold curls, nodded warily.

Sean studied the child for a moment, sighed, and sat back again as he frowned at her. Without doubt the girl had been coached, and yet she was far too young to be depended upon not to reveal several truths about

herself. And if he pushed her too far, he would lose
her trust. He didn't want that.

"It's a beautiful Sunday morning, moppet. How
would you like to take a walk with me?"

Kenny smiled, relieved, and nodded eagerly.

"Well, run and get your bonnet, then."

Corinne assumed that Sunday was a quiet day for
the household. Obviously a bad day to have come. She
was beginning to think no one would ever emerge
from the house and was just about to give up her vigil
when Kenny and the man appeared.

Kenny looked wonderful! She was dressed in a
pink-and-white ruffled dress with bows at the elbows
of the puffed sleeves and a larger, similar bow at the
waist. The lace trim of her white pantelets was tiered
all the way down to her slender ankles. She wore a
saucy, deep-crowned pink bonnet, lace-trimmed
around the stiff brim. Corinne experienced an instant
of doubt, wondering if Kenny felt suffocated in all
those trappings. But then she supposed not, for, when
Sean Garrick held out his hand, Kenny tucked her
much smaller one in his and smiled at the man. The
girl seemed at ease with him. Kenny chattered and
plucked at her skirts happily, and Sean Garrick
laughed before turning and walking up the street.

Corinne closed her eyes and let her chin drop to her
chest. A tear made its way past her thick, brown lashes
as she admitted that she had done the right thing for
her sibling. "That's one of us best out of it, Kenny,"
she whispered.

Now if she could only do the same for herself. But
Corinne doubted that would ever happen. . . . Few
ever made it out from Under-the-Hill. Unless it was to

jail they were going or were laid out in a pine box. Her options were hardly numerous.

Still, she was determined not to fall into the same trap that had held her mother prisoner for all these years.

She watched Sean and Kenny disappear around the corner at the next block and wished she could follow. Just to see where they went. Would he perhaps buy the girl some small treat? A sweet? If only she dared . . . but if Kenny should happen to look back and see her following, she would give everything away. Corinne would not risk Kenny's situation now. There would be no chances taken until enough time had passed. Time enough for Sean Garrick to want, to need, the girl in his life for the rest of his days.

"Once he *loves* her," she whispered, for there was no doubt in her mind that Kenny was completely lovable.

"So how's Kenny gettin' on with that swell?" Peter asked as they shared a stolen, roasted chicken.

Even though they were in the storehouse at Tim's Place, Corinne's eyes lit up at his question. "Oh, Peter, you should see her! She's all clean and dressed pretty. And she smiles at Garrick all the time, as if she's real happy."

"She should be happy," he said and then dug his teeth into a wedge of white meat. "She's livin' high, isn't she?"

Corinne frowned, not liking the implication of his remark. "She wouldn't be happy if the man were not good to her, Peter."

Peter laughed at that. "With pretty dresses and bonnets and livin' in a swank place? Most of the women I know wouldn't care if Garrick treated them like shit.''

Corinne hauled back and punched him square in his chest. ''I told you not to use that kind of language around us!''

''Us?'' he questioned, rubbing his chest with the palm of his hand. ''It's only *you* now, Corie.''

Corinne threw a bone on the existing heap of bones. ''Well, don't use it around *me*,'' she said, pouting.

''Aw, you've heard that stuff all your life,'' he muttered and reached between them for more chicken.

''Well, I don't like it.''

''You're getting a bit prissy, girl. I think you're wanderin' above the Hill too much.''

''Never you mind what I do,'' she said and looked around for some scrap of cloth to wipe her fingers.

''Well, I do *mind*,'' he returned, studying the meat his dirty fingers were tearing at. ''I've always watched out for you.''

''I know that.'' She sighed and returned to sit beside him on the narrow cot.

And then he voiced the thought that had been roaming around in his head for days. ''Now that you got Kenny looked after, why don't you come and live with me?''

Corinne's hazel eyes rounded in surprise. ''Peter,'' she breathed.

''Well, you're not surprised,'' he said defensively. ''I've wanted you to come for a long time.''

''But you know I can't.''

''I know you won't,'' he grumbled and threw the last of the chicken on the pile of bones. ''Ah, I know I'm not good enough for you,'' he relented.

''Peter,'' she said softly. ''That's not true. It's this

place. You know I hate this place, and you'll never leave.''

Peter took a deep breath, combed his fingers through his sandy, unkempt hair, and paced across the room. At the door he turned. "We could make a fair go of it, Corie," he said more reasonably. "I'd do my best to take good care of you."

Corinne felt her heart tearing as she turned her eyes from the pleading look he was casting her way. They had grown up together in the streets. He'd been good to her and Kenny, and with the exception of his chosen profession, she believed he was a good man. But he had no ambition to change his lot in life, and Corinne had held on to her dreams for too long.

Corinne decided to step up the next segment of her plan.

Chapter 5

Having washed her face and hair and dressed in borrowed clothes, which she hoped were not too garish, Corinne approached the front door of the townhouse on Pearl Street. She had chosen to visit during the latter part of the evening, hoping Kenny would be in bed; one look of recognition from her sister would ruin everything.

Mrs. Pringle gasped as she opened the door. The creature standing there was like nothing she had ever seen before.

Corinne knew she would have to bluff a far mightier foe than this disgusted-looking woman, so she squared her shoulders and smiled. "Hello. I wish to see Mr. Garrick."

"I . . . huh."

"My name is Corinne Alexander, and I have an offer for him."

Mrs. Pringle almost expired on the spot. "Oh . . . !"

"I'm a governess," Corinne threw in brightly.

Mrs. P. leaned heavily on the doorknob. "A governess?"

"Right!"

The older woman's eyes dropped to the girl's feet and roamed upward. . . . She had never seen a more disgusting costume and could only assume this was a girl of the evening. "I don't believe Mr. Garrick has any need of a governess," she said quietly.

"Well, course he does," she said, as if the woman were completely daft. "He's got a little girl, doesn't he?"

"Yes, well . . ."

"Then would you tell him I'm here, please?"

Mrs. Pringle might have been successful, eventually, in shooing the chit off the front porch had Sean not decided to investigate her reason for remaining at the door for this length of time.

"Who is it, Mrs. P.?" he asked as he walked up behind her.

"A . . . governess," she said ruefully.

"A gov—" Sean looked over the woman's shoulder and broke off his sentence. He recognized her instantly, although the boys' clothes were gone and she had done something dreadful to her hair. But there was no mistaking the girl. "I see," he murmured. The time has come, he thought. Now he would find out what had been planned for him.

The man had obviously been relaxing for the evening. He had set aside his high-collared dress shirt in favor of an open-necked, loose-fitting shirt of fine cambric. Corinne was momentarily dazed by the sight of whorls of dark hair outlined by the V of his shirt; she thought he must be a very hairy man, indeed. Her eyes dropped the length of his fitted dark trousers to the soft leather slippers that had replaced the highly polished black boots she was accustomed to seeing him wear. And as she inspected the length of him, intending to meet him eye for eye, she found herself thinking he was bigger, up close like this. He was big and he was beautiful and she knew she had no right to be standing on this man's stoop, let alone this close to him.

And then, stupidly, she realized he had spoken to her. "What?" she asked, instantly dismayed that her voice did not sound as confident as it should.

"What is your name?" he repeated patiently.

"Oh!" she puffed and then smiled. "Corinne. Corinne Alexander."

"And you are a governess?"

His tone was entirely too disbelieving, and Corie rounded her shoulders back a peg, sticking her nose in the air as she had learned by watching other women in this neighborhood. "Right."

Sean hid a smile behind an index finger as he slowly caressed the corner of his mouth. "Well, I suppose you'd best come in," he said casually. "We can hardly discuss business out here on the stoop, can we?"

"Course not," Corie agreed but hesitated in stepping forward when she caught the frown of disapproval from the woman at his side; she looked as if she had just swallowed a cherry pit and couldn't decide if she should cough it up or not.

Sean turned his head toward the housekeeper in reaction to the girl's sudden confusion. He was not surprised by Mrs. P.'s obvious disapproval, and her feelings probably held some merit. Still, he did not want her spoiling his fun. "I believe Miss Alexander would enjoy a cup of your delightful tea, Mrs. P., if you don't mind,'' he said. There was no question, of course. The woman would do as he asked.

With a stiff, single nod of her head Mrs. Pringle turned on a heel and gladly left Sean to handle the creature as he saw fit.

''I have a small library,'' he said, turning to face the girl even as he stepped to the side of the open door. ''Perhaps we could best talk there.''

Corinne had never been bowed into a house before, but that is exactly what the man did! It was a small bow, just as she stepped past him, but she took it as a polite sign of welcome nonetheless.

Once inside, Corinne stopped and looked about in awe. The foyer was not large, but it was warm and tastefully decorated. Everything gleamed and shone from frequent attention, and the smell of beeswax seemed to combine with the scent of lemon and other herbs she could not clearly identify. A long, narrow rosewood table stood against one wall, and the pale yellow glow of a lamp accentuated the mirror above it. The floors were obviously as well cared for as the furniture, and Corinne thought the place looked as if no one ever touched or walked or dared to move about for fear of dirtying something. Garrick's housekeeper must work harder than a dock hand, she decided.

''This way,'' he was saying as he turned from her and walked toward the back of the house.

Corinne lengthened her stride to keep close behind him. Her head swiveled this way and that as she tried to memorize everything, every nuance of this house, because, if she couldn't achieve her goal, this could be her last view of the place where her sister would grow up. From what she had seen, however, Corinne was very glad she had chosen Sean Garrick for Kenny.

He led her to a room where two walls were lined

with books from floor to ceiling. Two full walls! There was a large desk in one corner, facing the room, and everywhere there were man-things; pens and inkwells, heavy leather-bound books and papers, paintings of horses and hunt scenes, a pipe stand and pipes and large, comfortable-looking chairs. Nowhere was there evidence of a woman's touch in this room.

He motioned her to a grouping of three chairs that surrounded a highly polished round table before the fireplace. "It's a bit chilly," he said, hunkering down to place new logs on the grate.

Corinne sat, gingerly tested the thickly padded seat of the large chair, and settled back, carefully placing her hands in her lap as she watched Sean Garrick go about the business of lighting a fire. He was obviously strong, easily lifting large chunks of wood with one hand. And when he stretched forward, Corie could see the knotted muscles of his upper arm beneath his shirt. The men of the docks were muscled like that from years of heaving crates and barrels. It seemed unlikely to her that a man who made his living from behind a desk should have such apparent strength. She wondered briefly how he got that way.

Once flames crackled about the logs he had placed, Sean stood and turned, then sat in the chair opposite the girl. Having caught her openly staring, he enjoyed the thought that if he knew her better, or at all for that matter, he would advise her never to play poker—the girl's face was expressive enough for a blind man to read.

"Now, then," he said, crossing his legs at the knee and smiling directly into her eyes. "You're looking for a posting, are you?"

Corinne swallowed heavily, realizing she had his full attention and his scrutiny. "What?"

"A job, Miss Alexander. I believe you are here to inquire about a position?"

"Oh! Right!" she said and straightened in her seat, primly smoothing her gaudy yellow gown. "I know you have a girl—"

"How do you know?"

Corinne blinked, startled by his interruption. "What?"

"How do you know I have a child here?"

Corinne studied his expression for a moment, deciding he was not annoyed, as his tone had led her to believe. "Why, I've seen you with her," she said. "Walkin'. And all the folks hereabout know of her."

"Indeed? 'All the folks'?" Sean was thoughtfully conducting his own examination of *her* expressions. "And you've decided the child needs a governess?"

"Well," she drawled, dropping her eyes to study her skirt again. "Most people hereabouts like their children well looked after. And I thought . . . since I'm between . . . postin's, it wouldn't hurt to ask if you'd be needin' some help with the girl."

Sean was biting his lip to keep from laughing at her struggle to present a believable picture. "You've had previous experience, then?"

"Oh, yes, sir!" she piped, looking directly into those all-seeing black eyes of his. "I looked after a girl from the time she was a babe."

And had not done too bad a job of it, he realized, considering she must have had limited resources. Still, once they had scrubbed away all of Kenny's surface dirt, and come to know her, it had become apparent someone had been kind and loving to the child. And he surmised that, simply because of Kenny's sunny, loving nature. But why had she given Kenny up, and why had she chosen him?

"You have references, I assume?" he asked.

Corie's pretty hazel eyes grew large and round. "I can get some," she threw in, her mind momentarily spinning in turmoil as she tried to recall anyone she knew who might know how to write.

"Yes, I would definitely need to see references," he said quietly, and his eyes fell aside to a small table. His hand hovered in the vicinity of his pipe, but then returned to the arm of his chair as Mrs. Pringle entered the room. "Ah, good. Thank you, Mrs. P.," he said as the woman placed a large tray on the table between them.

The housekeeper shot him a frown that spoke of her deepest thoughts, sniffed softly as she passed by Corinne's chair, and exited hurriedly.

Corinne's eyes fell to the silver tray beyond the teapot and the cups and the small plates to an array of pastries the likes of which she had never seen.

"Shall I pour?" Sean asked, sliding forward in his seat as he reached simultaneously for a cup and saucer and the teapot.

Corinne nodded dumbly as she tore her attention away from the tempting sweets.

"Lemon? Cream?"

Corinne swallowed the rush of saliva that suddenly flooded her mouth. . . . If her stomach growled now, she would die! "Cream, please."

Sean placed the cup of tea in front of her and poured the cream, watching her eyes for a signal to stop. When she blinked, he set the cream aside and moved the sugar close at hand. "I'll let you sugar it," he said, returning to his seat before adding lemon to his own tea. The girl seemed to carefully study the movements required to add three teaspoons of sugar to her drink. He winced as she seemed to contemplate adding a fourth. "*Tart*?" he asked pointedly, studying her yellow dress.

"Thank you," she said, having taken the question at face value.

He held the plate of sweets and studied her curiously as she mulled over this weighty decision of which pastry to sample. Corinne and Kenny were different, but this girl's eyes lit up over the sight of sweets just as Kenny's did. And there were other things about this young woman that had him puzzled; such as the curious mix of unschooled diction interspersed with basic manners.

"Thank you," she said politely again once she had made her selection. Corinne wanted to stuff the delicious-looking treat into her mouth but instead forced herself to nibble. Still, the treat quickly disappeared.

"I've been giving some thought to the proper rearing of my Kenny," Sean said conversationally and watched her over the rim of his cup. . . . She did not like his saying "my Kenny." "One wants to do what's best for one's child," he goaded a bit further. "I want her to have proper manners, of course, to dress well and with taste, to meet the right people. And, naturally, she will require an education. Although females do not require as much of that as males. Would you agree, Miss Alexander?"

"Yes, sir," she said again, giving him her full attention. Corinne had the distinct feeling this man possessed more intelligence than she had bargained for.

"Yes, well, I've been pondering over what type of education Kenny should receive." His hand reached to the side and picked up the book that lay beside his pipe. "I wonder if you think something of this nature would be suitable?"

Corinne's heart ceased to beat altogether, and her eyes seemed to view things independently as she reached out to take the book from his extended hand. She ran her fingertips lightly over the leather front of the book and then turned the bound side up, sightlessly staring at words that had no meaning.

Sean watched the color drain from the girl's complexion and took pity; he had his answer to this particular question, and there was no point in tormenting the creature further. "No. I don't suppose *The Pathfinder* is a work a young girl would enjoy," he said quietly and set his cup aside, reaching out and taking the book from her hands. "Although Cooper is a master," he added before placing the book on the side table and out of her sight.

"Yes. Yes, he is," she said lamely.

"You don't read, do you, Miss Alexander?" he asked softly.

Corinne refused to be cowed by this particular shortcoming. "That's right, sir. I guess I've labeled myself wrongly when I say *governess*. But I'm very good with children. I take good care, and I like them very much."

"Yes, I believe you do," he said kindly.

"I would like to have a . . . postin' . . . here, sir. I would take very good care of your little girl."

"My Kenny?"

"Yes, sir. Your . . . Kenny," she said.

And the hint of sadness in her tone did not go undetected.

Sean got to his feet and walked to a cabinet in a corner of the room. "I don't know that I have need of you, however," he said as he drew up the top of the tall chest and withdrew a bottle from its depths. A glass also materialized from within the cavity, and he studied the amount of brandy he poured as he spoke. "My wife is perfectly capable—"

"Oh! But you have no . . ." Corinne groaned as she realized her mistake.

"I'm afraid you've tipped the game board in my favor, Miss Alexander," he said as he returned to his chair. "I have no wife and you knew that."

Still, Corinne was not willing to concede the contest so easily. "Of course I knew," she said firmly, daring to glare at the man. "I always check out the houses where I want to seek work. To make sure they're proper, you understand? It's wide known that you have no wife."

Sean smiled, ceding a partial point. "Well done, Miss Alexander."

Corinne dipped her head in acknowledgment of his compliment. Smiling, she said, "I could start work tomorrow."

Sean raised his glass and savored a draft of brandy before commenting. "If you've *checked* out my household, you must know that Kenny is not my child."

"Right!" she returned victoriously.

"What relation is she to you?"

This time saliva gave over to bile as Corinne realized her hopes had just been effectively squashed by him. So, she had not fooled him for a moment. But it had been worth the try. At least now she knew what sort of place Kenny was living in, and it couldn't come much better, she guessed. But then she had the terrible thought that he might not keep Kenny if he new the whole truth about her.

As regally as any princess, Corinne rose to her feet.

"You've no need of my services, sir, that's plain to see. I'll not waste more of your time."

She whirled around the edge of her chair then and made for the door.

But Sean was quick. He halted her halfway with a large, firm hand clamped onto her upper arm. He whirled her about and stared down at her. She looked so young. Not yet twenty, he guessed, and Kenny was probably close to five. "Is she your daughter?" he asked softly.

Corinne was so utterly stunned it took her a moment to react. "My . . ." She could not even speak the word as the reality of what he was suggesting sank in. "My daughter!" she finally screeched. She reached back with her hand, intending to reward the insult as he deserved, thought better of it, and whirled away from him, wrenching her arm. "Let go, you miserable swamp toad!"

Sean merely laughed at the insult and grasped her other arm to turn her. "Stop struggling. I did not mean to insult you."

"Well, you did," she returned heatedly, glaring up into dark eyes that had lost some of their anger. "I am seventeen and Kenny is five. What would that make me if she were my daughter?"

Sean smiled and offered softly, "I've said I'm sorry and I mean that. Who is Kenny to you?"

Calmed by the softness of his voice and the sincerity of his tone, Corinne said quietly, "My sister. My half-sister."

"Come and sit down."

But when he would have moved with her toward the chairs, Corinne balked.

"I think the least you can do is explain to me what this is all about," he said firmly. "I am now supporting a five-year-old girl, and obviously that is with thanks to you. I believe I have a right to know what else you may have planned.''

Corinne was instantly alerted to the fact that if she did not appease his curiosity and his concerns, Kenny could find herself back on the streets. And that must not happen. "I have nothin' else planned," she said. "And I'll tell you everything if you'll only keep Kenny with you."

Sean frowned at the pleading note in her voice but was wary enough to realize it could be a trick. He tugged gently on her arm, led her back to her chair, and poured her a second cup of tea. When Corinne blatantly eyed the plate of sweets, he smiled and offered her the entire plate. "You're just like Kenny when it comes to those things. She would eat tarts and squares all day if we allowed it."

"We don't get sweets much," Corinne muttered as she made her selection and set the plate aside.

"Do you ever get enough to eat?" he asked.

That stung her pride a bit, and Corinne stiffened in her chair. "We're not starvin', if that's what you think."

That was precisely what he thought, but he remained mute on the point. "It was you who told Kenny to sit on my stoop?"

Corinne nodded.

"Why me?" he asked reasonably, reaching for the remainder of his brandy.

"You're alone here except for the housekeeper."

Sean arched a dark brow in surprise at that. "And because I'm alone, you assumed I would keep the girl? Nothing more than that?"

"Oh, there was much more," she returned bluntly.

"You're not so rich that you don't know how to smile at people."

Sean laughed and shook his head, trying to find the logic in her statement. "I'm afraid you'll have to explain that one."

Corinne settled back in her chair and sipped her tea as she looked at him over the rim of her cup. He seemed easy to talk to, and that was only another point in his favor; Kenny must remain here at any cost. "Rich people are snobs," she said. "It's as simple as that. They would croak before they'd give you a smile hello if you're less than them. And they wouldn't take a girl like Kenny no matter what."

"So you knew I lived alone and you suspected I was not rich? Is that sound enough reason to leave the child with someone you don't know?" he asked. "I could have an unpleasant nature and be abusing the girl. Had you thought of that?"

Corinne nodded her head and set her teacup aside. "But you're a good man and you wouldn't abuse her. I believed that or I wouldn't have brought her here."

"But you didn't *know*," he said, growing exasperated. It had been a foolhardy and dangerous scheme.

"I knew," she said calmly, staring at him directly. "I've been watchin' you for months."

Sean stared at her with absolute amazement. "You dare to tell me that?"

"Picking you was done carefully, for Kenny's sake," she said with a casual shrug that was intended to hide her growing concern about his acceptance of her sister. "Her full name is McKenna," she added, hoping to appeal to his sense of pity. "I think our mother thought that was the name of Kenny's father. But she probably wasn't sure. Anyway, winter is coming on, and Kenny doesn't take well to winter.

She gets colds and fevers a lot. I knew I had to find her a place where she could be warm, and so I started lookin' up here for somebody to take her. I saw you smile at people on the street . . . old ladies or kids, it didn't seem to matter. And I knew you were the one,'' she finished with a casual shrug.

Oh, she was playing this up royally, he thought. She was manipulating him beautifully and he knew it. ''You needn't back me into a corner, young woman,'' he said stiffly.

Momentarily confused by his meaning, Corie commented frankly, ''I'll do whatever I have to do for Kenny to stay.''

Sean studied her closely, wondering what *that* was supposed to mean. And then he looked at her tawdry gown and decided he knew *exactly* what she had meant. And he wanted no part of it. ''Kenny will stay,'' he said, getting up and moving to the cabinet in the corner. As he splashed a bit more brandy in his glass, he said as kindly as possible. ''But your . . . services . . . as governess or anything else will not be required.''

Corinne, again, innocently missed the suggestion capsulized within his statement. She'd spent too much of her lifetime concentrating on staying alive and protecting herself to learn the nuances between men and women. That anyone could possibly associate her with her mother's profession simply had never entered her head.

''I wanted to see that Kenny was all right,'' she said softly. ''That's the only reason I came here.'' It was a blatant lie, of course. She had hoped for something more, much more, but she would not jeopardize Kenny's situation to improve her own. ''You haven't let her out of the house for weeks, not even to take her for a walk with you, and I was afraid she was sick.''

Sean was wandering about the room, sipping brandy occasionally as he battled a number of confused feelings about this girl who had plotted and schemed and was now so damned forthright about it all.

''She has been out,'' he muttered distractedly. ''But not where you could see her.''

Corinne craned her neck as her eyes followed him. ''What?''

He seemed to return his attention to her then, and he stopped, leaning back against the carved mantel. ''I knew you watched her from across the street, and I wanted to know more about all of this nonsense. So I planned to draw you in. I felt that you would come eventually when you did not see her. I just did not know how long it would take.''

Corinne understood then. ''We've both played games,'' she said softly.

''So it would seem.'' There was something about his tone that boded ill.

''Please don't hate her because of me. I did what I had to do, don't you see? Kenny is a good girl. She's very sweet and very smart. She won't give you any trouble.''

''Don't you think I saw that before I took her in?'' he asked, not knowing whether he was more irritated with her for scheming or himself for falling in with her plans.

''Then she can stay?''

Sean saw the light of hopefulness brighten her large hazel eyes and turned away. ''I've already said she would stay,'' he muttered shortly.

Corinne got to her feet and turned to leave. ''I want to thank you,'' she said but turned back before opening the door. "I wonder if I could see her—just for a moment?"

"She's sleeping."

"Oh. Of course." She stared at the closed portal for a moment, and he watched her hesitation before she turned to face him again. "Could I come tomorrow? Just to see her for a moment? I'll come through the back gardens so no one will see."

Sean set aside his glass and walked toward her, his hands shoved deep into the pockets of his trousers. "I want to make one thing perfectly clear, Miss Alexander," he said firmly. "If Kenny is to remain in this house, she will be raised as I see fit and with no interference from you. I've gleaned some inkling of how she has lived, and I want her to forget all of that. She will be fed and clothed and educated as a proper young lady. I care deeply for the child even in this short time, and I suspect you counted on that. But I will brook no interference. Do you understand?"

He could have stabbed her through the middle with a hot poker and the pain would have been less, but Corinne faced him squarely and proudly. "I haven't done bad by her. *Sir.*"

She whirled from him then, flung the door wide, and tramped along the hall toward the door. But before she could exit the house, Corinne felt his hand on her forearm and halted. But she dared not look his way and let him see the moisture that had gathered in her eyes.

"Miss Alexander," he said quietly and searched for a means to soften what had gone before. "I didn't mean to . . . I want you to understand . . ."

"Oh, I understand," she said evenly.

Sean sighed heavily, his thoughts burdened by her. "I don't believe you do," he said with a sudden glimmer of the complexities of this young woman. "Kenny likes to play in the garden when the afternoons are sunny. If tomorrow is such a day, you'll find her there. But I would prefer if you wait until late . . . when I have returned from my office."

She should have been heartily offended that he felt he had to be in attendance to protect Kenny from her own sister. She knew that. But she was too happy at the prospect of seeing the girl to react in any way other than happily. "I'll be here," she said and scooted out the door.

Mrs. Pringle had remained at the entrance to the pantry and now approached slowly, quietly. Sean sensed her presence as he stood in the open doorway and watched the tall, slim girl race across the street.

"They're half-sisters," he said quietly.

"I wondered."

"She mentioned their mother, but I couldn't bring myself to ask what kind of woman she must be."

"I think we both know the answer to that, sir."

Sean smiled sadly over his shoulder. "There are several possibilities. None of them good."

"Agreed," she said, but there was no censure in her tone.

His eyes returned to the street then, and he watched Corinne disappear from view. "Our Kenny's name is McKenna."

"Odd."

"Quite." He closed the door quietly before turning to her with a smile. "I expect by now you're aware of what I plan to do. I hope you're amenable to discussing compensation for the extra duties I'm about to foist upon you, Mrs. P."

The meaning of *extra duties* was more than clear.

"I've not had a great deal of experience with children, sir."

"Then we shall learn together. Are you game?"

Thinking of the pleasant sound of Kenny's laughter ringing through the otherwise quiet house, Jane Pringle nodded her agreement without hesitation.

Chapter 6

Corinne had carefully counted off gardens to be certain she waited at the rear of the correct house. Garrick's house.

She had managed quite nicely to run between hedges and fences in the square block behind the house. There were trees and shrubs in abundance back there, and anyone could easily hide from view of the neighbors. Regardless, Garrick's yard had been made quite private by rows of well-tended holly trees. And there was a pretty cottage set back below the gardens.

She had washed out her boy's shirt and dungarees the evening before and had donned them in the morning despite the fact that they were still damp. Nothing seemed to dry near the river. And while her mother slept, Corinne had managed to wash her hair and take a sponge bath . . . a luxury made even better by the scented bar of soap she had swiped from one of Tim's girls in the neighboring building.

Corinne had lain awake well into the early morning hours thinking about her meeting with Sean Garrick.

She was pleased with the choice she had made for
Kenny, although the man was a bit arrogant. Still, he
seemed a fair sort, and she was confident he was kind
to her sister. At one point during the long night she
had become angry over a remembered slight and had
decided she would defy him. She would arrive at his
home whenever she damned well pleased. But when
she realized he could probably find ways of keeping
her from Kenny altogether, Corinne thought better of
her planned defiance.

The day had been long with her forced wait, and
anticipation had driven her to run the length of the
backyards by early afternoon. Then she had knelt
amongst the thorny bushes . . . waiting.

She thought Garrick must have arrived early from
work this day, for the sun was still warm when she
saw him emerge from the rear of the townhouse with
Kenny in tow. The girl was holding his hand and
smiling and giggling at a huge black dog that ran
circles about them, barking happily as they walked
almost the entire length of the yard. Near the well-
planned gardens he sat on a solitary bench and smiled
at Kenny when she showed him the small pot and
spoon she seemed to treasure.

Corinne thought her sister looked better than she
had ever done; her cheeks were blooming with color
and her hair was clean and shiny. She was wearing a
green dress trimmed with white lace, and a full, frilly
apron covered from her shoulder to hem.

Sean knew she was there. He would have sensed
her presence had he not caught a small flash of red
plaid amongst the green of the bushes. Without a word
he looked directly in Corinne's direction and nodded
once.

Kenny was busy chattering, leaning against Garrick's knee, when Corinne approached from behind the girl. "Hi, Kenny," she said softly, standing a few paces off.

The dog raced in Corinne's direction as Kenny whirled, bumping Sean's leg as she turned to face her sister. But she was not to say Corie's name nor let anyone believe that they knew each other—they'd talked about that a lot. "Come back, Thor!" Kenny hollered at the dog in an attempt to deal with the situation.

Sean was quick to identify that the child's hesitation stemmed from coaching and not from lack of desire to run across the lawn to the young woman who waited. He could feel the tremble of anticipation in the small hand that gripped his knee. Placing his hands gently on Kenny's shoulders, he said softly, "It's all right, Kenny. I know about her."

Still Kenny waited for some sign from Corie as she buried five small fingers into the thick black fur of the dog that stood in front of her. But then Corie was smiling and nodding, and Kenny released her hold on both the man and the dog and raced across the space between them, flinging herself into her sister's arms. "Corie!" she cried with glee. "You came!"

"Of course I did, baby," Corinne murmured.

"I thought you might have forgot," Kenny said bluntly and tightened her stranglehold around Corinne's neck.

"I'd never forget," she whispered. "Never."

Sean reached into his coat pocket and extracted pipe and pouch and a small box of matches. He ran his hand lightly down Thor's shoulder, to keep the animal at his side, before proceeding to fill the pipe bowl with tobacco. He watched the scene between sisters as smoke began to billow around his head. They were a loving pair, it seemed, and it troubled him that Kenny should be so attached to a young woman who could only come to a bad end.

Corinne was kneeling now, her eyes roaming over the pretty little face that had never been so clean. "Are you happy here, Kenny?" she whispered.

The girl nodded. "I eat good, Corie. Mrs. Pringle makes the bestest chicken I bet I ever ate. And I have my own room and new clothes. I got to take baths, though."

Corinne smiled and smoothed back a lock of hair that had run astray of Kenny's braids. "Good chicken, huh?"

"Yup. And this pot and spoon is mine to dig in the garden. But I can only dig in one little corner," she added in a whisper. "There's things growin' there, Corie."

Corinne laughed, hugged the child briefly, and then leaned back on her heels. "Well, why are you whisperin'?"

Kenny suddenly looked unhappy. "I think the other day I kilt somethin'."

Corinne looked suitably serious. "Did you tell Mr. Garrick about that?"

"He lets me call him Sean," she mumbled.

"Answer my question, Kenny. Did you tell him?"

When her sister shook her head, Corinne dared to glance over the top of Kenny's head at the man in question. He appeared at ease, thoughtfully smoking his pipe as he watched them. She wondered what sort of punishment he would enforce if Kenny had indeed *kilt* something. "I think you better tell him, Kenny. Maybe you didn't hurt anything important and it doesn't matter, but I've told you, you have to be honest with him. Men like little girls who are honest."

Kenny nodded. "Now?"

"I'll wait here for you, baby."

Sean was clearly perplexed by the manner in which Kenny approached him. The child seemed genuinely afraid, and he frowned at the young woman beyond, wondering what on earth she could have said that would make Kenny fear him. She had never done so before. He planted both feet on the ground, set his pipe aside, and leaned forward from the waist. "What is it, moppet?" he asked quietly, resting his elbows on his knees.

Kenny carefully set the treasured pot and spoon on the ground near his feet, and when she straightened, Sean took her small hands in his.

"Corie said I have to tell you," she muttered to her chest.

Corie. That was the name he had failed to remember all these weeks. "Did she?" he asked softly, his eyes momentarily darting to the elder sister. "And what do you have to tell me?"

"I kilt something."

Sean did not know whether to laugh or be alarmed. "*Kilt*," he echoed. "And what did you kill, Kenny?"

"Something in the garden."

"Really?" he murmured. If he had any luck at all, perhaps the girl had massacred Mrs. P.'s lilies. He'd been praying for the damned things to die for weeks. "Would you like to show me?"

Kenny nodded her head and looked at him hopefully—he hadn't even yelled at her.

When Sean stood, the girl easily took his hand and led the way to the corner of the garden she had claimed as her own play space. There she pointed to a yellow squash that had been severed from its host plant.

Thor nosed the thing and turned away, disinterested.

Sean squatted beside the girl and pretended to examine the situation. "Well, I think we're lucky, moppet. This fellow was about ready to pluck and send to the oven anyway."

Kenny brightened visibly when he turned his head and smiled at her. "Corie said maybe I didn't really hurt nothin'."

"*Anything*, Kenny. Is that what Corie said?"

"Right." She nodded vigorously. "She said for me to be honest and tell you."

Sean turned his head and looked over his shoulder at the young woman. He had to give the elder sister credit for trying to set the child in the right direction. Then he smiled at the tyke. "Corie's quite right, sweetheart. You must never be afraid to tell me anything."

"If you're not mad at me, can I ask you something?"

"You *may*."

"Is Corie going to live with us now?"

It was a question he had not anticipated, assuming Corie had been intelligent enough to explain the situation to the child before they had embarked upon their scheme. "No," he said firmly. "Corie has her own life, you know."

"Ah, she only steals stuff, and I don't think she even likes it anymore. She'd like it here with us better."

Sean got to his feet and rested the palm of his hand on the girl's head. "Corie will come to visit when she can, Kenny. But she can't live here."

Kenny craned her head up to look at him unhappily. "But she wants to live with us. She said if you weren't too smart, she'd come and live here, too."

Sean's smile wilted instantly. "Indeed. Perhaps you'd best ask *Corie* to explain the situation, moppet."

"Okay," she chirped and ran off to prop herself on her sister's thighs.

"Perhaps I'm *not* too smart," he muttered under his breath as he returned to his bench. "Perhaps the moppet's the brightest of us all."

"How come you're not goin' to live here, Corie?" Kenny asked, tipping her head back against her sister's breast. "Is he too smart for you?"

Corinne's complexion instantly flamed brilliant red as she looked across the short distance to the man who made a pretense of refilling his pipe. "Oh, Kenny," she moaned. "You didn't!"

"Didn't what?"

"What did you say to him?" Corinne asked, fighting her chagrin.

"I said you wanted to live here with us."

"No!" she whispered. "Oh, God . . . Kenny . . . what else?"

Kenny thought about that for a moment and smiled over at Sean before shrugging her shoulders. "Nothin'. I don't think. . . ."

"Kenny, you mustn't tell him things we talked about," she said impatiently. "You shouldn't tell him the things I've said."

Kenny was confused by her sister's sudden turn to anger. "But you said . . . yes, Corie," she finished meekly.

"If we're not careful, Kenny, he won't let me come here to see you. Don't tell him too much about me."

That was a heavy burden for a five-year-old. Kenny twisted out of Corie's hold and stood to face her. "But you're my sister, and Sean is always nice to me. He wouldn't stop you from comin'."

Corie suspected *Sean* could be not so nice if he ever considered she was being a bad influence. "You have to listen to what he says and not think too much about me, Kenny. He'll teach you how to grow up proper."

"I don't want to grow *proper*," she returned mutinously.

"Yes, you do, baby," Corie said, reaching for a small hand.

But Kenny was confused and unhappy, and she whirled away from these things she did not understand. "You don't like me! That's why! You don't want to come!"

The child turned and ran to Sean, and Corie felt the first painful loss of her young life: She had lost the one human being she loved dearly and in only a few short weeks. She scrambled to her feet and watched Sean Garrick lift Kenny to his lap and hold her close against his chest. Corie knew jealousy and hurt in that moment. Still, he could do so much more for Kenny, and a tiny part of her acknowledged the special relationship that had sprung easily between man and child.

Kenny would be all right.

It was Corie's heart that was breaking.

Chapter 7

Corie returned, via the backyard, day after day, and always, unless the weather was poor, Sean Garrick would bring Kenny to the garden and sit quietly by as the two sisters chatted and visited and frequently played with the faithful Thor. Kenny soon became more secure in the fact that Corie did care and would always come to see her, and her happy disposition was satisfying to both her new guardian and her older sister.

But Corie found these visits difficult and unsettling. For, although her loneliness would be assuaged for an hour or two, leaving Kenny in the afternoons only made the nights more empty. Also, Sean Garrick seemed to watch her so closely she wondered if he might be afraid she would steal the silverware right out from under his nose. One occasion she had caught him openly staring, and she wondered if those dark blue eyes were seeing something other than a thief. It was absurd, of course, but Corie actually began to think he might be taking her measure as a woman.

Silly thought, she knew, but it seemed that way particularly when he would continue to stare, frowning slightly, even when her eyes met his. Impossible! Still . . .

The autumn breezes persisted until leaves swirled about the streets and stately trees were left starkly naked. And though the days were mild, the evenings became chill with a cold dampness that seeped insidiously into a body's bones.

And despite good food and warm shelter, McKenna came down with the ague.

Sean was frantic as he stood by and helplessly watched the small child writhe about in her bed. He and Mrs. Pringle had piled one blanket after another over the girl, and a fire roared and crackled with a heat that seemed significant enough to melt the windows in their panes. Still McKenna shivered and moaned.

And she cried for Corie.

A boy was sent to fetch the doctor, and Jane was left to tend McKenna. Sean ran the half dozen blocks to Silver Street and down the steep incline to Natchez Under-the-Hill.

He had little trouble finding Tim's Place; McKenna had told him enough about the hovel where she had lived. But finding Corie could be another matter.

Entering the barroom, Sean was assaulted by a blast of noise and plumes of blue smoke that shook more than one of his senses. And this introduction spawned a first impression that was entirely correct: The place was a hellhole.

Eyelids drooping in an instinctively protective action, Sean made his way through the crowd of filthy, sour-smelling men to the bar.

"I'm looking for Tim," he said, leaning over the scarred surface.

A large man, heavily bearded, attended to dunking thick glasses into a tub of filthy water and did not raise his eyes as he asked, "Who's lookin'?"

"My name's Garrick. Sean Garrick. I've an urgent need to find Corie."

The man straightened and flashed a dark look at the younger man. "Corie, huh?"

"Are you Tim?" Sean asked hurriedly. They were wasting precious time.

"Might be," the man said blandly and applied a well-used towel to a glass.

"Don't hedge with me, mister," Sean returned heatedly. "I've got a sick child, and she's calling for her sister."

That got the man's attention. "Kenny's sick?" Tim's eyes immediately scanned the crowd, and he raised a hand, motioning to someone in the back of the room.

A young man of approximately eighteen years, with sandy hair and unkempt clothes, approached. "What can I do for ya', Tim?" he asked.

The large man pointed to the boy's right. "Says his name is Garrick and Kenny's sick. Take him to Corie."

Peter Kemper turned distrustful eyes in Sean's direction. "Garrick, huh?" he muttered resentfully as he inspected the swell.

Sean's impatience was growing by the second. "I've got to see Corie," he said.

"Maybe she don't want to see you," Peter returned, certain his stony glare would set the other man back a pace or two.

Instead, Sean took a step forward, saying harshly, "Are you prepared to answer to Corie when she learns her sister is ill?"

"For God's sake, take him to her," Tim ordered.

Peter shot a rebellious glare at the bearded man before muttering, as he turned away, "I'll tell her you're here."

"Got a bit of a thing for Corie, he has," Tim announced.

Sean watched the young man disappear down a dark hall. "Has he?"

"Oh, yeah. For years. She won't have nothin' to do with that, though."

Turning to face the other man again, Sean asked, "Why is that, do you think?"

"Wants to get herself out from Under-the-Hill," he said. "Smart girl, that Corie. She knows if she takes up with the likes of Peter, she'll never get out."

Sean nodded thoughtfully.

And then the bartender's eyes darted toward the darkened hall.

Sean turned to see Corie pressing cautiously close to the entrance. He pushed his way through the knot of men near the bar and was standing in front of her with no time lost.

"McKenna's ill," he said without preamble. "She's been crying for you."

Corie's hazel eyes darted to his. "Kenny? Not the fevers?" she questioned anxiously.

Sean nodded. "We can't get her warm. I've sent a boy to fetch the doctor, but I think you should come."

When he turned toward the doors of the saloon, Corie grasped his forearm. "Not that way. Come through the back."

Peter Kemper frowned as he watched them disappear into the darkness.

Corie proved to be quite a runner, but then Sean reasoned that she no doubt had to be quick. Living in a place like Tim's, self-preservation would surely require a number of talents.

By the time they reached the small house on Pearl Street, however, they were both breathless. Corie flung open the front door and charged inside.

"Top of the stairs on your left," Sean called as he followed close on her heels.

Corie was almost through the bedroom door before she had opened the thing.

Her arrival caused Mrs. Pringle to jump up from her chair. But there was little to say as the young woman raced to the bed and stared down at the quaking child.

"I'm here, baby," she said, but Kenny was beyond hearing. Corie turned hastily toward the housekeeper. "Is a doctor coming?"

"The boy said the doctor would be here as soon as he could."

An unladylike snort was Corie's response to that.

Sean stood directly behind her shoulder now. "There's a great deal of sickness about, Corie. The doctor will come."

"For the likes of us?" she asked disdainfully. "Not likely." And before Sean or his housekeeper could guess what she was about, Corie was stripping away her clothes.

"What are you doing?" Jane Pringle gasped, her hands suddenly gripping her apron.

"If you can't stand the sight of a little bare skin, ma'am," Corie mumbled, "you'd best leave. There's more than one way to get a body warm."

Sean understood her purpose immediately and politely turned his back as Jane Pringle fled the room.

Sean waited patiently, listening to the sounds behind him. "Has this helped in the past?" he asked for a want of something better to say.

"Not much," Corie said as she crawled under the blankets and pulled the girl's quaking body into her arms. "But it's all I know to do. You can turn around now," she added, giving a final tug on the blankets so that she and Kenny were wrapped in a warm cocoon. "At least you've got more blankets than we had," she said.

Feeling helpless again, Sean dropped into a chair beside the bed. He could see only the crown of McKenna's head and a small patch of white flesh where the blankets did not fully cover Corie's shoulder. "Is there anything I can do?" he asked after a time.

It was the first moment Corie'd had to pay him any concentrated attention. And as she looked up at him now, she could see fine lines of concern outlining his dark blue eyes. He had such a handsome face, but tonight he looked somehow older. "You're really worried, aren't you?" she asked needlessly.

He looked startled by the question. "Of course I'm worried."

Corie pressed her head into the pillow and closed her eyes. "This is why I wanted her to have a proper home. . . ." She sighed. "Why didn't it work?"

Stung, Sean straightened in his chair. "If you're insinuating I've not cared properly for McKenna . . ."

Corie's eyes snapped open and turned his way. "I know you've cared for her," she hastened to say. "Any fool can see that. I'd hoped she wouldn't get sick here, that's all." Her eyes dropped down to the small head resting on her shoulder then. "Get better, Kenny," she whispered, pressing her lips against the child's silky hair as she tried to pull Kenny closer. "Get better."

It was close to midnight before Dr. Thatcher could

attend the sick child, and by then Sean was nearly at his wit's end. "She's shaking so violently," he said as he ushered the doctor into the room.

Dr. Kevin Thatcher stopped dead in his tracks when he spied a young woman holding the ailing child. "Well," he muttered, approaching the bed. "Looks like someone's got some medical sense, at least. Who are you?" he asked as he dropped his bag on the nearby chair.

"I'm Corie," she said, looking more than relieved to see the man. "Kenny is my sister."

Thatcher's brows arched at that. "Sisters?" He turned to Sean. "You've taken in two girls?"

"Only Kenny," he returned hastily.

Thatcher continued to frown in confusion. "Really?" he muttered, bending over the bed.

But in order to get at Kenny, the good doctor had to reach over Corie.

He straightened and frowned. "I'll have to ask you to move out of the bed, young woman."

In spite of the seriousness of the situation, Corie could not prevent the wry smile that tugged at the corners of her mouth. "I think there might be a problem, sir."

Sean wondered what Thatcher might be thinking once the man realized that Corie was naked under those covers. But he didn't hesitate long enough to receive the dressing down he suspected he might receive from his friend. He moved quickly out of the room to return with a man's robe in hand. "Here," he said simply, draping the garment on the bed before retreating to a corner of the room.

"You've been through this with this child before?" Dr. Thatcher asked.

Corie nodded as she slipped into the robe, displaying as little of herself as possible. "I know enough to keep her warm, and in a few days the fever breaks," she said, moving out of the doctor's way. "But every time this happens, Kenny seems weaker, and the next fever always seems worse."

Thatcher fell silent as he went about examining the child.

Corie backed away from the bed, eventually standing in the center of the room, holding the large robe around her body. Each time this fever struck, it seemed more ominous, and Corie feared more and more for Kenny's life. And as the minutes ticked away, she became more desperate for an encouraging word. "She'll be all right, Doctor?" she asked.

Thatcher did not like the look of the child . . . she was frail. But he wasn't about to give up hope or allow anyone else to be defeated, either. "She's five, you say? You'll have to fatten her up once we see her through this."

He had not turned from the bed, nor so much as raised his head, but Corie took his words and clung to them. A radiant smile lit her face as her fingers gripped the folds of the robe.

Sean knew he had never seen a face quite so lovely. Despite her thinness, that smile changed Corie to the point that no one could dismiss the fact that she was beautiful. She turned to Sean briefly, and he found himself staring at her intently once again. He knew he did that often . . . whenever she was about. But he did not understand the significance of his attraction to her. There was something quietly purposeful and intent about this young woman, and she certainly had to be admired for her determination and pure gutsiness. Who else would dare scheme to use a man as she had used him? And who else would have the nerve to face him squarely with the truth? She had followed him and used him for McKenna's sake and had made no bones about discussing the situation with him. He should have been angry about being set up and targeted, but he found he could summon no anger against her.

Corie watched the doctor spoon-feed a cloudy mixture to her sister and gently massage her throat until Kenny was forced to swallow. And then he was closing his black bag, telling them to keep the child warm through the night. He would return in the morning. Before the two men had fully left the room, Corie had dropped the robe to the floor and joined Kenny in the bed.

"The doctor seems to think McKenna will be fine in a few days," Sean said as he returned to the bedside.

Corie looked up and smiled. "Thank you for bringing him here."

Slightly affronted, he asked, "Would you expect any less?"

"No. I wouldn't expect less, Sean Garrick," she said softly.

Frowning at her tone, he backed up until the backs of his legs hit the chair, and then he sat wearily.

And that is how Jane Pringle found them the following morning; Sean asleep in the chair. Corie and Kenny sleeping peacefully in the bed.

The child's fever had broken during the night.

Silently the older woman backed out of the room.

Corie awoke when Kenny stirred beside her. "You just go back to sleep," she said softly. Gazing over her shoulder, Corie was surprised to see Sean still asleep in the chair.

"Corie?" Kenny muttered against her sister's shoulder. "You slept here?"

"Yup. Mr. Garrick came to fetch me last night. We've been very worried, baby."

"I hurt all over."

"I know. But you'll feel better in a day or two."

"Perhaps a warm bath will help," Sean suggested as he stretched slowly to his feet.

"A bath!" Corie cried, clearly horrified. "She'll catch her death!"

Sean had heard that particular superstition before, of course. "I'll stoke the fire and warm the room, and we'll put warming pans in the bed so it's nice and toasty," he said as he smiled at the worried pair. "The hot water will help ease McKenna's aches."

"Bathin's not good for a body," Corie informed him. "Everybody knows that."

"Well, people are beginning to understand that's nonsense," he said and proceeded to build the fire to a hearty blaze. "Personally, I believe all that talk about baths causing the ague is nothing more than a ruse started by those who prefer to remain unclean."

Corie agreed that cleanliness was a good thing; however, she was not convinced a bath would not worsen Kenny's condition.

"Trust me," Sean said, seeing her frown. "I'll be back."

Several moments later an oval tub had been placed in front of the fire and filled with warm water. Mrs. Pringle fussed about, warming large, fluffy towels on a rack she had positioned close to the heat. She then filled two covered pans with live coals and hot ashes from the base of the fire and carried these toward the bed.

Corie had quickly donned her boys' clothes while

the room was vacant of all persons except Kenny and now stood watching these proceedings.

"I have to check my soup," Jane Pringle said as she placed a length of ribbon in Corie's hand. "You'd best tie McKenna's hair up out of the way," she added before leaving.

Corie moved to the bed and smiled as she bent over and began sweeping Kenny's glorious hair high on the child's head.

"See, Corie," Kenny whispered. "The only bad thing about bein' here is ya haveta take baths all the time."

"Well, maybe Sean's right. Maybe you will feel better."

"I don't think so, Corie," she said skeptically.

"Come on. Let's get this nightdress off," Corie said lightly.

And then Sean appeared, standing so close Corie could feel the heat of him. Her spontaneous reaction was to sidle away.

But if he noticed her skittish behavior, Sean gave no indication; his attention appeared concentrated upon Kenny. "Could I provide *my lady* a lift to her bath?" he asked, his smile growing as a small giggle escaped McKenna. "So, you're not so sick, are you, moppet? You can still laugh, at least."

"I'm all right, Sean," she said weakly, wrapping her arms around his neck as he lifted her.

He was glad and he told her so.

Corie felt an overwhelming warmth seep through as she watched them together. It was true, she felt a sense of loss, but how could she deny the relationship that had so quickly grown between Kenny and Sean Garrick. He was good for Kenny. And he was good *to* her. No matter how much she missed Kenny at times, she had done the right thing in giving her to this man. Sean Garrick had love in his heart.

Sean lowered his burden slowly into the warm water. "How does that feel?" he asked.

"Good," Kenny said softly.

He moved around the tub, supporting Kenny as he raised his eyes to Corie. "I'll support her head while you sponge her off."

Well, it wasn't a request, but he wasn't demanding, either, so Corie moved to the edge of the tub and dropped to her knees. She wanted to say something clever to the sick girl; something to make Kenny laugh. But her mind could wrap around nothing other than the strange feelings this moment was causing. There was a feeling of closeness she had never experienced before. A feeling of sharing an intimate moment with another human being as she remained aware of the man who loved Kenny and worried about Kenny, just as she loved and worried over Kenny. As she gently sponged warm water over the frail body of her sister, Corie was aware of the strong hands that supported Kenny's head and knew she would never have a greater sense of *family* than she had in this moment. It was a lie, of course. They were not a family. But the feeling was warm and special.

"You're very gentle," Sean said softly.

Corie smiled at Kenny, refusing to lift her eyes. "Of course," she said easily. "She's my Kenny."

Our Kenny, he thought.

"I've brought some broth," Jane Pringle said matter-of-factly as she entered the room some time later. Staring at Corie, she added, "I'll stay with the little one. Mr. Garrick wants to see you in his study."

"Me?" she asked, disbelieving.

"You. Don't be keeping him waiting."

Corie didn't take kindly to being ordered about, but she was curious enough about Sean's summons not to dally. Finger-combing her wild hair, she bounced down the steps and turned toward the back of the house.

Sean was there, staring thoughtfully out the window behind his desk.

"You wanted to see me?" she asked from the doorway.

Sean turned and stared across the room at the wild thing standing there. She could easily pass for a boy in that garb, for there was no evidence of a woman's softness beneath the loose-fitting shirt and pants. Only her long hair, brown shot with red, betrayed her gender.

He had dressed in a fresh white shirt that was open at the neck, and his hair had been neatly brushed, but Corie could see weary lines etched around his eyes.

"Come in," he said after an uncomfortable moment. "Have some coffee and rolls."

Corie crossed the room and sat before the desk as he poured steaming black brew into a delicate cup. "Thank you," she said, reaching for the cup and settling back in her chair. Waiting.

"I wanted to talk to you about Mrs. Pringle."

Corie lowered her cup and shot him a look of unconcealed surprise. "Mrs. Pringle?"

"She's not a young woman, you know, and is not used to children. It's occurred to me that I'm asking a bit much of her with the added burden of caring for McKenna when I'm not here."

Corie's stomach turned sour in an instant, and she cautiously returned her cup to the saucer. "You want me to take Kenny back?" she whispered brokenly.

"Good Lord, no!" he returned quickly. "Do you think I'd give her up now?"

Corie's stomach eased, and she frowned in confusion. "You're a strange man, Mr. Garrick," she said softly.

"Strange? Because I love McKenna?"

"You really do, don't you? And you make no bones about it. Most men would never confess to loving anyone."

It was Sean's turn to frown. "Really? Where did you gather that bit of information, Corinne?"

It was the first time he had used her full name. She had never cared for the name, preferring the shortened version, but somehow *Corinne* sounded nice the way he said it.

Sean watched Corie reach for her coffee and, after a silence that had stretched too long, prodded, "You haven't answered my question."

"I thought you wanted to talk about Mrs. Pringle," she said, raising the cup to her lips and refusing to look at him.

Sean smiled at her retreat to a safe subject and scrubbed a forefinger thoughtfully against his chin. "Yes, I suppose I did," he said softly. When Corie eventually raised her eyes, his face was a picture of sternness. "And I suppose, of necessity, the conversation should include you."

Her eyes wide, Corie sputtered, "Me?"

Sean took his time, rising from his chair and slowly pacing around the desk. "It has occurred to me that McKenna has needs other than those I can provide." He stopped in front of her and leaned his buttocks against the edge of the desk, his hands disappearing into his pockets. "I can feed and clothe her, and it's true I love her, but she was five years in your care, and I understand now how much she needs you. McKenna chatters excitedly, anticipating your visits, and she spends hours extolling your virtues after you've gone. The child loves you to distraction, and I don't believe she will do well without you.''

Corie did not fully understand all the terms he used so she grasped on to the one thing he said that needed to be clarified. ''You can see what my care has done for her,'' she scoffed, turning her head away. ''She still can't get through a winter without fevers.''

''Don't belittle all you've done, Corinne. And with few resources. If anyone should be condemned, I should think it would be your mother.'' He skirted the desk and returned to his chair, giving her time to think about that.

''Our mother couldn't . . .'' She hesitated, studying her cup and feeling his intense blue eyes upon her. ''She has problems of her own.''

It occurred to Sean that the woman's problems should have been those of caring for two daughters. ''You don't even resent her neglect, do you?'' he asked in wonder.

''You wouldn't understand. My mother wasn't always the way she is now. When I was a child, she spent time with me and taught me things,'' she said uncomfortably. ''I thought we were talkin' about Mrs. Pringle.''

With a sigh he let her have her way and settled back in his chair. ''I'm prepared to make you an offer of employment,'' he said carefully.

Corie dared to look him in the eye then. ''Employment? What can I do?''

''You were prepared to offer something when you first came here,'' he teased and then frowned as he acknowledged her sudden lack of confidence. ''I want you to do what you've done for the past five years.''

Her brows furrowing, Corie questioned, ''You want me to look after Kenny?''

"Precisely."

"You want to *pay* me to care for someone I love?"

Hearing a warning note in her tone, Sean sat forward, leaning his elbows on the desk. "I also expect you to help Mrs. P. whenever she needs help."

"You want me to come here every day?"

"I suggest it would be better if you lived here," he said matter-of-factly.

Corie's eyes narrowed suspiciously. "This is a small house, Mr. Garrick. I can't see that you need two women to keep it."

"And a very energetic child now lives here, Miss Alexander. I also entertain clients on occasion. I believe there is plenty of work for two."

So, she would be a servant, tending his house and serving meals. It wasn't exactly the manner in which Corie had dreamed of moving into a cozy home; but then, she supposed white knights were in short supply these days. No one was going to ride up, fall in love with her, and whisk her off to a married life of security and comfort. But she would be with Kenny every day, and she would not have to be scavenging for food or evading groping male hands at Tim's place. No matter Sean Garrick's reasoning, the offer was a difficult one to turn down.

"You've thought about this carefully?" she asked. "You haven't had much sleep."

"Actually, I've been thinking about it for some time now. Last night McKenna only confirmed her need. I'm prepared to offer a small wage and found, Miss Alexander. What do you think?"

"Something inside me says I should be saying no," she offered softly. "But I'll take the job, Mr. Garrick."

He smiled. "Good!"

Chapter 8

There were a number of major adjustments in Corie's life within a very short time frame. She had never resided with anyone but Kenny, and she had certainly never experienced another person's disapproval of her actions. Jane Pringle quickly rectified that particular lack of experience.

"It's not right you living here in the same house with Mr. Garrick," the woman said the instant they were alone.

"But I'm here to work," Corie said, justifying her presence. "I'm to help you and look after Kenny."

Stiffening her spine, Mrs. Pringle shot the younger woman a hurt look. "I've never needed help in the past."

Corie recognized hurt pride when she saw it. "But you never had a little girl here before, Mrs. Pringle," she said reasonably. "Mr. Garrick's afraid Kenny will whack you out."

"Indeed?" the woman asked stiffly and turned toward the stove.

"I'm sorry you're not happy with Mr. Garrick's plan. I think he meant well," Corie said quietly.

After a moment Jane turned toward the younger woman. As much as she respected her employer, she knew the *man*, and his decision had not been based on concern over a problem that did not exist; McKenna was not so much of an extra burden. And Jane could not believe that a woman of the streets, no matter her youth, could be as naive as this Corie pretended to be. Well, it was not her place to challenge what Sean Garrick did and with whom. And she could hardly fault a young woman for wanting to improve her lot in life. But the simple fact was, Jane could not approve. "You'd best get to work, then," she said grudgingly. "After you give McKenna a sponge bath, you can take one yourself before you touch anything in this house."

Corie's hands fisted at her sides. "I don't carry the plague, Mrs. Pringle," she rasped.

"No, but you could be carrying little creatures," the woman said unkindly. "On second thought, I'll tend to McKenna. You have a bath before anything else gets done in this house today."

"You're a very rude person!"

"Yes, I suppose I am," Jane said quietly. "And a plain-talking one. We'll fix you a bath, and I'll find you something of mine to wear. And it won't be boys pants," she added as she reached up for the large copper tub near the stove.

Moments later Corie had the kitchen to herself and was soaking in a tub of warm scented water. "Rude old biddy," she mumbled. "I should bring Tim in here. *Then* she'd see lice!"

After a few more muttered expletives, Corie leaned her head against the high back of the tub and closed her eyes, letting the warmth of the water wash away her anger. She supposed she should try to understand the older woman's position. Jane Pringle seemed to have a lot of pride, and Sean Garrick had managed to dent it good and proper. Corie hoped the woman would get over her hurt in a few days.

The bath was a luxury Corie had never before experienced, having grown used to sponging off with cold water in any corner she could find. Lying in hot water that smelled of roses must be the next best thing to heaven, she decided, and wondered if she would be allowed to indulge in this luxury often. Well, perhaps not with Mrs. Pringle's scent. And then the happy thought occurred—she would be paid a small wage and could buy her own scent!

Unbelievable!

Lulled almost into a stupor, Corie did not hear the kitchen door swing open a few moments later.

"Uh, sorry," Sean said softly. "I didn't realize . . ."

Corie's eyes opened, and she turned her head even as she sat up, shielding her small breasts with her arms. "That's all right. I should be gettin' out anyway."

Other than this one protective reaction, Sean was amazed that she seemed not at all embarrassed by the situation. But then he reasoned that appearing naked before men must be second nature to Corie.

"Were you lookin' for Mrs. Pringle?" Corie asked, rousing him from his thoughts.

"Yes. Ah, no. I was hoping to find another cup of coffee."

Corie's eyes slanted toward the stove. "Well, the pot is still warmin'. That's a good sign."

Sean smiled, feeling a bit ridiculous; why should he feel awkward when she quite obviously was not?

Skirting the end of the tub, he moved to the stove and reached into a cupboard above it for a cup. "Where is she, then? Mrs. Pringle, I mean."

"Probably outside burnin' my clothes."

Sean looked over his shoulder to see her eyes sparkling with laughter.

"I think she was afraid I would infest the linens. As well as everyone in the house," she added, smiling.

He frowned. "And would you?"

"Maybe."

"Really?" he drawled, preferring not to think about that too much. Having poured some coffee, he turned, cup in hand, and leaned back against the counter beside the stove. Corie was sponging water over her knee. "You don't seem to be objecting to that bath," he observed.

She laughed shortly. "Hardly! This is better than Mrs. Pringle's cakes."

He had already learned of her love of sweets. Now he was learning a bit more about her; and much of it intrigued him.

"I thought you'd be off to your warehouse by now," she said.

Sean raised his eyes from the study of her shoulder. "I won't go today, I think. Kenny seems to be sleeping well enough now, and I could use a bit of sleep. And I thought I might help you retrieve your belongings from your home, if you wish."

The sparkle immediately left her large hazel eyes. "There's nothin' to fetch," she said abruptly, looking away. "If you don't mind, Mr. Garrick, this water is gettin' cold."

Sean was instantly sorry he had spoken and firmly resolved never to introduce any word concerning her previous home in future. Perhaps she would forget that former life in time. Certainly he had the feeling she had not been fond of what she had done to survive, and she had made it clear that she had wanted a better life for McKenna. Even her friends had known of her determination to get out from Under-the-Hill. Well, she was out. Now he would see what she would make of it.

"Have Mrs. P. send round to the shops for some clothes for you," he said abruptly as he moved back across the kitchen.

"She's going to give me something of hers to wear."

He stopped in the action of pushing the door and stared at her. "I doubt that will be suitable."

"Well, you can't buy me clothes," Corie said firmly.

"Then we'll deduct their cost a bit each week from your wages," he said and left Corie staring at the swinging door.

In time Corie learned much about the keeping of a house and fine things. She almost drove Mrs. Pringle to distraction with her endless questions of how to care for this and that and what task she should tackle next. Somehow she managed to keep Kenny occupied and still lend a hand about the place. She turned everyday chores into an adventure in which she included her younger sister, and the small house on Pearl Street was often filled with giggles and laughter. Even Mrs. Pringle was forced to smile a time or two.

"I'm softening her up," Corie confessed to McKenna. "Did you see her smile?"

"You make everybody happy, Corie," the girl said, throwing her arms around her sister.

"There's one *fancy* I've yet to *tickle*, though, Kenny. And he's next."

In fact, Sean Garrick was a very happy man, regardless of the fact that he was not taken with frequent gales of laughter. Within weeks of Corie's arrival he found himself content to be surrounded by females. His table was now set for four, and he insisted they all eat suppers together. He would have none of Mrs. Pringle's ideas that children should eat in the kitchen at an early hour and that she should join McKenna there. McKenna was given a snack to tide her over until the seven o'clock supper.

And it was a lighter step that carried him home from his work each day because there was now someone there to greet him. Five years of loneliness seemed nonexistent each time he opened his front door and McKenna threw herself at him. He loved to hear her laugh, and the newest voice, added to that of the child's, also became a welcome sound.

In the evenings Mrs. Pringle would retire to her cottage, and Sean would read to McKenna in his study. With the evening's chill and damp, he would light a fire, settle in a comfortable chair before the hearth, and draw the girl up on his lap. One evening he spied Corie leaning against the doorframe listening, and he motioned her to the chair beside his own.

Corie soon came to love these evenings with the three of them warm and protected from winter's perils and Sean's deep voice making the stories come alive in her mind's eye. With her feet tucked beneath her, she would lean back, watching as he shared his attention between the book in his hands and the child in his lap. It was a scene that moved her like nothing else in her life had moved her. And it was Sean who had brought this about.

And the more she became attached to him, the more Corie feared him.

* * *

There was a Saturday evening in late November when Corie closed the door to Kenny's room, having settled her sister in bed for the night, as was her habit. Moving toward her own room down the hall, she was startled as Sean suddenly appeared at the door to the master bedroom.

"I'm sorry," he said, smiling as he watched her hand cover her heart. "I didn't mean to frighten you."

"I thought you were in your study."

He shook his head, drawing a set of white gloves across the palm of one hand. "On my way out," he said.

Corie's eyes quickly roamed the length of him. He was impeccably dressed in a black evening suit. "You look beautiful," she said in awe.

Sean laughed. "I'll take that as a compliment."

Corie nodded firmly. "It must be a special party you're goin' to tonight."

"A ball."

A ball. He said it so casually. "And with a special lady?" she asked.

"I'm escorting Faye."

Ah, Faye. Corie had heard that name too many times to be liking it. She had assumed for weeks now that he and Faye were lovers. And it made her stomach knot. "Well, have a nice time," she said as casually as she could and turned again toward her own room.

Sean clamped a hand onto her upper arm. "Would you care to go to a ball one evening, Corinne Alexander?" he asked softly.

"It's a cruel sense of humor you have there, Mr. Garrick," she said and roughly pulled away.

"I mean it," he said, following her down the hall. "I'd like to take you."

Corie turned on him angrily. "I wouldn't like bein'
the joke of the town, Sean Garrick."

"You would hardly be a joke, Corinne."

"And what would I wear? My shift?" she snapped.

"We'll buy you a gown," he said reasonably.

"I already owe you enough for the clothes on my
back."

"I would make it a gift."

"And I don't dance!" she said, fairly spitting with
anger.

"I'll teach you."

"You're making fun of me!" she said, close to
tears with this unexpected cruelty from him.

"I'm not, Corie," he whispered, stepping close. "I
think you would enjoy such an evening. And you
would meet a lot of people. You rarely leave this
house, and it's time you made some friends."

"I might even meet a man who could fall madly in
love with me," she said saucily.

"You might."

"You're a fool, Sean Garrick!" She whirled about,
closing her bedroom door firmly between them.

And the minute Sean left the house, Corie left, too,
racing toward the Hill.

It was cold and the dampness caused by the mighty
Mississippi River seeped into her bones as Corie sat
on the steps that led to her mother's door. She was
miserable of body and of soul as she waited, but she
had to talk with someone even if Constance proved
not to be in any condition to counsel her daughter. The
fact was, Corie had just plain outsmarted herself. She
had lived in a state of confusion for weeks and now
realized that she should never have picked a man like
Sean Garrick to become Kenny's guardian. If she had

really believed she would live with them, Corie would
have picked a homely man. One who did not cause her
heart and stomach to do strange things every time he
looked her way; and when he smiled . . . God help
her!

Yes, it was all very clear now. The plan had worked
well for Kenny's benefit, but it had gone wildly awry
from Corie's point of view.

Noises from the street echoed around her, and Corie
watched the small lights on the river as boats made
their way along. The sounds and sights were familiar,
but they did little to ease her mind. This was what she
knew best. This was a world in which she moved with
confidence; it was familiar and predictable. And as
hard as her existence Under-the-Hill had been, it had
not frightened her half as much as her new life. Kenny
was young, she could learn new ways and forget what
had gone before. But for Corie there was no easy
bridge to cross between the two worlds. And these
feelings for Sean that persisted in plaguing her would
come to nothing but hurt. She was certain he would
never take to a girl from Under-the-Hill, at least not on
a permanent basis, and that was what she wanted most
from a man. She would not repeat her mother's follies
of choosing a man and watching him leave. But every
day it was more and more difficult to act her normal
self when Sean was near her; she was becoming an
absolute ninny.

Hours passed as Corie sat there waiting for her
mother's door to open. She was lonely and wretched,
but when Sean joined her, Corie knew she would have
been better off waiting alone.

He just appeared quite suddenly, standing two steps
below where she sat.

"Have you been sitting here all night?" he asked.

Corie raised her eyes to his briefly and then renewed her study of the blackness of the river. "Not all night. Dawn is an hour or two away," she said.

Without ceremony he dropped his coat across her shoulders, sat beside her, and knit his fingers between his spread knees. "If you wanted to come here, Corinne, why didn't you ask me to bring you?"

Corie almost laughed at that. "I've been going up and down that hill on my own for years, Mr. Garrick. I hardly need an escort." And he'd been otherwise engaged—dancing with Faye.

"I don't like you sitting here alone all night. I would have waited with you."

Corie turned toward him, surprised. "Do you know why I'm sitting here?" she asked.

"Of course. You're waiting to see your mother," he said.

"And do you know why I have to *wait*?"

"I assume because your mother is . . . entertaining," he said simply.

Corie did laugh at that. "Well, that's nicely put."

Sean made no response, and a long silence fell between them.

"Why did you come?" she asked at last.

"Because I was worried when I returned and you were not in the house. I thought you might have come here," he said.

"You needn't worry," she said softly. "I'm quite safe here."

"Are you?" he asked, staring at her profile. "It's so safe and comfortable here that you devised a cockeyed scheme to find your sister a better life?"

"Not so cockeyed," she returned smugly. "It worked."

"Well, we won't rehash that part of our relationship."

"Is that what we have?" she asked cautiously. "A relationship?"

Sean smiled, confused by her tone. "We're friends. Don't you think that's a relationship?"

"You're my employer, Mr. Garrick. I don't think friendship is a good idea."

"What happened to *Sean*?"

"I've been doing some thinkin' while I've been sittin' here," she returned evasively.

"And you've decided against calling me by my given name?"

"That's right."

"Why?"

"*Mr. Garrick* is more proper."

"It certainly is." He sighed. "Why are you doing this? Have you been unhappy in my home?"

"Of course not. You've been . . ." She paused, searching for the word Jane Pringle had used to describe him. ". . . generous, allowin' . . . allowing me to live with Kenny. But you have a certain position in this town, and you have friends and clients who come to the house. And I must remember my position. I work for you, and it's easy to slip and forget what we are because you've been so good to Kenny and me. Calling you Sean is just not proper for a servant, and people could get the wrong idea. It could also be harmful to Kenny. So I've decided I should call you Mr. Garrick."

With an elbow on his knee, Sean had propped his chin on a fist as he watched her and listened. "That's an interesting idea you have there. And I have the distinct impression that this concept runs deeper than your theory about a name being too familiar. Am I correct?"

"Not at all," she said primly in a fine imitation of her mentor, Jane Pringle. "It's very . . . basic."

"Really?" he drawled, now truly curious about her thinking. "Would you care to explain then how Kenny could be harmed if you call me Sean?"

"It's not as simple as you make it sound," she snapped. She was growing uneasy with the conversation. And he stared so intently.

"You just said this is all very *basic*," he taunted.

"I mean, if someone heard me call you *Sean*, they might get the wrong idea!" Maybe she had given him too much credit for being smart! Maybe an evening with Faye turned his brain to mush!

"About our being friends?"

"Yes."

"And that would harm Kenny?" he asked in feigned amazement.

"Should *friends* be livin' in the same house?" she asked shortly.

"I see," he murmured thoughtfully. "You're talking about scandal."

"I don't care what you call it, Mr. Garrick. It adds up to trouble," she returned heatedly.

"Why didn't you just say so?" Inwardly he was smiling as he became convinced that she had been thinking beyond the bounds of *friendship*.

Corie shot him a dark look and returned her attention to the river. "I think you're tryin' . . . trying to get me mad."

"So, I'm a fool for reasons other than thinking you might enjoy a ball," he said quietly, ignoring her statement and following his own line of thinking; was he a fool for not seeing how she was feeling?

Corie's head snapped around. "I shouldn't have called you that. I'm sorry."

"No. No. I'm glad you did. It's provided me with food for thought." He continued to smile as he realized she had called him a fool only after he had agreed that she might meet a man who would fall in love with her. Did she want him to think that no man would fall in love with her? Or did she not *want* a man to fall in love with her? Interesting.

"I don't think I like you this way," she was saying.

Sean laughed shortly. "And I liked you better before you started thinking about things such as scandal."

"Do you want Kenny to be hurt? Or people to think bad of you? Do you want to lose Faye?" she went on foolishly.

"Faye?" Sean's brows arched severely, and then a slow smile spread across his lips. "Have you been thinking about Faye?"

"Not bloody likely!" she scoffed, pulling the coat around her as if that feeble cocoon would provide some sort of protection.

"I've been thinking about her," he confessed. "Quite a lot lately."

"Well, if you visited her more often, you wouldn't think so much about . . ." Corie closed her eyes, groaning as she realized what he might think of her words.

Sean laughed softly. Not only had she been thinking, Corie had obviously been observing his comings and goings as well. Much to his surprise, Sean found that he received some sort of perverse sense of pleasure in knowing that. He was also more pleased with his evening since he had left Faye and come to join Corie on the weathered old steps. He hadn't realized she had been so aware of him or their relationship; she tended to act quite reserved whenever she was near him. But Corie had revealed quite a bit tonight, if his instincts were correct, and he found that curious. He had, indeed, been thinking about Faye. Whenever he looked at Corie, he thought about Faye. Whenever he saw Corie and McKenna together, he thought about Faye—and not in a positive vein. He was finally beginning to acknowledge that his liaison with Faye was slowly changing. The relationship was crumbling, and he had yet to determine whether or not he wanted to shore it up. But as he looked at Corinne Alexander, he understood that Faye was losing ground and had been since that day he had introduced her to McKenna.

"Is Faye much like your wife was like?"

Startled, Sean laughed shortly. "Good Lord, no! What would make you ask such a thing?"

Corie shrugged and squinted into the darkness beyond them. "I don't know. Just tryin' . . . trying to fill the silence, I guess."

Sean stared at her a moment, although she refused to look his way. There was something insidious about this young woman. Something about her that was increasing his awareness of her in a manner that had nothing to do with his being her employer. And he was not at all certain that he minded. Whatever it was, it made answering her question about his past a necessity. "Marie was a shy, gentle woman. She was small and quiet and always very proper. I loved her very much."

"And Faye's not like that?"

"Faye is a strong woman. She's more . . . determined. She likes to have her own way, and she sees that she gets it."

"Is that how she got you?"

Sean laughed shortly; he hadn't thought about that in years. "I suppose so."

Corie looked at him then, questioning. "I don't think you hold a whole lot of love for this Faye."

For the first time since he'd joined her on the steps, they looked at each other; truly *saw* each other. "No. Love has little to do with my relationship with Faye."

"I saw her the day Kenny was sittin' . . . sitting on your stoop. She's a beautiful woman."

"Yes, she is."

"Kenny says she's not very friendly," she said bluntly.

So she'd been talking to Kenny about a few things? "I suppose she's not sometimes."

Curious. Why would a man choose a woman so opposite to the wife he had loved? "Well, she must have somethin', Sean Garrick."

A slow smile tugged at Sean's lips, and he actually felt a slight warmth of embarrassment. "I suppose she does."

With a sigh of frustration, Corie turned her eyes toward the river. "You're not giving me much to go on."

He laughed outright at that. "Use your imagination."

"I am, but I'm not coming up with much. Only one thing," she added frankly, "and I guess we shouldn't talk about that."

"No. I don't think we should."

"Men are funny," she muttered.

Sean thought it high time they changed the subject. "Do you miss your life here?" he asked quietly.

Corie turned her head briefly, eyeing him as if he'd come away and left his head at home. "Would you miss havin' to steal to keep food in your belly? Would you miss kickin' four-legged rats away in your sleep at night and swattin' the two-legged kind all day?"

"I suppose it was a foolish question," he admitted.

"You're right there, Mr. Garrick. I have a proper

job now and food every day.'' And she did not have to compete with the rats for a place to sleep.

"How do you feel about what your mother does? The way she lives?"

Corie stared him down then. "What kind of a thing is that to ask? There may not be many women like my mother above the Hill, but you must know some. How do you think I feel?"

"I'm inquiring about your relationship with your mother, Corinne. A friend asking politely how you *feel*," he added by way of reprimand. "There's no need to be defensive."

With a weary sigh Corie dropped her head forward. "When I was small, my mother loved me. She had schooling and came from a good family, and at first she taught me things. But too much has happened to her, and she can't seem to help herself anymore. Not for a lot of years now. We used to have a . . . relationship, as you call it. But not so much anymore. Mostly now I just feel sorry for her."

Sean thought he could feel the weight of the burden she carried and was instantly sorry he had asked about her previous life. "I'm sorry, Corinne," he said softly.

Corie's shoulders straightened then, and she planted both palms on her knees. "Don't feel sorry for me, Mr. Garrick. I'm doing all right."

"Yes, you are," he said quietly, getting to his feet. "Let me take you home now."

"I want to see my mother," she said. And she realized she did not want to give up this time alone with him.

"I'll bring you back another time," he said. "I'm cold and we both need some sleep. Come along."

Reluctantly Corie took his hand and walked by his side up the Hill.

Chapter 9

That night marked a turning point for Corie. While she had worked hard and been a willing student of the arts of caring for a home, she now became obsessed with learning all that Jane Pringle could teach. She worked endless hours, frantically ensuring that not so much as a dust mote marred any surface. The small house on Pearl Street became her greatest source of pride. And it became her prison. She set out to prove her worth to herself, to carve a nitch that could be recreated in any home in Natchez if she were forced to seek employment elsewhere; and the work helped her distance herself from Sean, thereby preserving her present situation so that she would never have need to do so.

Unwittingly, however, Corie only drew more attention to herself.

Kenny complained that the fun had gone out of the household tasks.

Jane Pringle noticed pale smudges under the older girl's eyes and warned her to slow down.

And Sean watched silently.

There were two welcome moments in Corie's day: when she fell, exhausted, into her bed and when she tucked Kenny in for the night.

"You never come for the stories anymore," Kenny complained one night as she crawled into her bed.

Corie sat on the edge of the bed. "I've got too many things to do," she said, smoothing the blankets in place as Kenny settled down.

"But you used to like Sean's stories."

"I did. But now I understand all the things that have to be done in the house, and I don't have time for stories."

"But—"

"Don't argue with me, baby," she said shortly. "I've told you, I don't have time for stories."

Kenny's lower lip jutted out, quivering, as her eyes darkened.

In the next moment the fall of booted feet on hardwood floor alerted Corie to the fact that they were no longer alone. She jumped to her feet and backed away as Sean approached.

He frowned at her nervous reaction but turned his attention to the child. "I've never seen such a face," he said lightly, easing down to take Corie's previous spot. "Why am I seeing this face?"

Kenny pouted, picked at the blanket covering her chest, and then raised her eyes to his. "Corie's mad."

"Is she?" he asked in feigned surprise. "Why do you suppose that is?"

And with reasoning only a child could provide, Kenny enlightened him. "I think it's because I tore my dress and Corie doesn't know how to fix it."

Sean's smile was genuine. "Well, I'm certain we can find a way to fix it, and then Corie won't be 'mad' anymore.'' He bent forward. "Come give me a hug and then off to sleep with you.''

There was no hesitation on Kenny's part as she threw her small arms around his neck.

Corie found herself turning from the sight of these two who so easily lavished love upon each other; it was something she envied, and yet witnessing it made her hurt.

"Good night, moppet,'' he said softly. As he stood and turned from the bed, Sean was not smiling. "I want to see you downstairs,'' he said as his eyes fell briefly on Corie before he turned toward the door.

Corie's initial reaction was to protest, but the brief look he had sent her way convinced her not to argue.

Once they had entered his study, and the door was closed behind them, Corie expected Sean to take the position of authority and sit behind his large desk. Instead, he motioned her toward one of the chairs in front of the fireplace.

"Sit down,'' he said with unconcealed authority.

Corie sat and smoothed her blue skirt of striped Hickory cloth.

Sean watched, realizing she must have practiced these motions, for she was more familiar with britches than skirts. And he hated the heavy, twilled garment she had chosen when she could have had finer materials. He had vowed recently to see her wear better.

Corie was very conscious of him as he stared at her, and then he turned away. From the corner of her eye she watched him take a glass and a bottle, returning to set them on the small table between the two chairs. He took his time pouring brandy and lighting a pipe, and all the while her nerves twitched under her skin as her fear grew over his possible reasons for wanting to see her here. But stoically she remained silent.

"I've been watching you," he said at last. "And I want to know what you think you are doing."

Clearly puzzled, Corie frowned. "I don't understand."

"You're driving yourself, Corinne. I've seen it, Mrs. Pringle has seen it, and Kenny is complaining about your lack of attention to her. You look tired and unhappy, and I think I've let this go on long enough. It's time for an explanation."

Corie's eyes dropped to her lap, and her fingers locked tightly together. "I'm here to work, Mr. Garrick, not to play. And I'm not unhappy."

And he didn't believe *that* for a moment. Reaching across the small space between them, Sean covered her small hands with his own. "I didn't hire you to become a drudge, Corinne," he said quietly. "I brought you here because McKenna needed you. Won't you tell me what's wrong?"

"There's nothing wrong," she said sharply, snatching her hands out from beneath his; his touching her made her stomach feel funny.

Sean sat back in his chair, taking a sip of brandy as his eyes studied her over the rim of his glass. When he had returned the snifter to the table, he said firmly, "You've been sadly remiss in your duties, Miss Alexander, and I want to know how you plan to correct that."

Corie's head snapped up, her concern more than evident. "I've been working hard, and I've learned so much. I thought you would be pleased."

"And what about McKenna?"

"Kenny?" she said, puzzled.

"I'm told she spends more time in the kitchen with Mrs. Pringle than she spends with you."

"That's because Mrs. Pringle gives her sweets," she said flatly.

"I suspect it's because Mrs. Pringle gives her some attention."

"Are you accusing me of ignoring my own sister?" she snapped.

"I am."

"I've spent the past five years raising her when no one else would."

"And now you've found another ambition?" he asked. "Is there something self-serving in what you're doing, Corinne?"

Corie opened her mouth to snap out a reply and then closed it again; she could hardly explain her actions when she wasn't totally certain she understood them herself. "I'm just trying to survive," she said quietly, her eyes focusing on the flames of the fire. "I just want to work."

"To the exclusion of all else? Don't you see you've gone to extremes, Corinne?" he reasoned. "We're all afraid to walk through the house for fear we might disturb something or leave a smudge or a telltale sign. You're holding three people hostage with your compulsion. And I want to know why."

Why was he so intent upon delving into her private affairs? "If I'm not working to your liking, Mr. Garrick, then I suppose you will have to let me go," she said loftily.

Frowning, Sean drew deeply on his pipe stem. "Is that what you want?"

"Of course not."

"Most people don't invite dismissal, Corinne," he said softly.

"Neither am I."

"You wouldn't miss McKenna?" he asked, as if she had not commented.

Suddenly her heart leapt to her throat. "You would let me see her," she said matter-of-factly.

"Would I, indeed?"

Corie's eyes raised quickly with his words.

"If you were to resume your previous life," Sean began, "I would have to reconsider your association with McKenna."

Stung by his cool and offensive tone, Corie turned smug. "I have learned a lot, Mr. Garrick. I don't think I will have to return to my *previous* life, as you put it."

"So, your future is secure?" he taunted.

"Yes."

"Not without references, Miss Alexander."

Corie merely glared at him.

"And what if some future employer should inquire about your previous experience? What do you reply then?" he asked. He hated what he was doing to her, but Sean knew of no other way to get her to talk about her reasons for wanting to leave. He was convinced that Corie had it in her mind that she would leave, and he would push until he got the answers he wanted.

"Why are you doing this?" she asked fearfully.

"Because I think we're skirting an issue, and I haven't quite figured out what it is. I only know that you've changed since that night we sat outside your mother's door."

"Can't you understand that I want to learn and I want to do well so that I don't ever have to go back?" she pleaded.

"Indeed," he said quietly. "I can understand that and admire you for it."

That comment caused Corie's heart to return to its rightful place. But it was a painful descent. "Then you can't blame me for wanting to better myself."

"True. But what I want to know is why you feel your future is in jeopardy," he said earnestly. "What has happened to you here that would cause you that kind of concern?"

That question caused her more anxiety than anything else he could have asked or said. Jumping to her feet, Corie looked down at him and said quietly, "I'm very tired. Excuse me . . ."

Sean set his pipe aside and stood before her. "You are *not* excused, Corinne. Look at yourself," he said softly, running the pad of his thumb lightly over the purple smudge under her eye. "What has happened?" he asked again.

Closing her eyes, Corie responded painfully. "I've never met a man like you before, Sean Garrick. You confuse me."

Smiling, when she opened her eyes, he said, "Would it help if I admit that you have caused me like feelings?"

Corie shook her head. "That only makes me afraid."

Leaving that thought suspended in the atmosphere, Corie turned and fled the room.

After a sleepless night of sorting through the enigma that Corinne Alexander had become to him, Sean put his plan into motion the very next morning. He'd known for weeks that he was drawn to her in a way that was totally foreign to anything else he had ever experienced. He had been wary and cautious, avoiding her until he could sort through his feelings and identify exactly what he wanted from her. And now he believed that Corie was engaging in a struggle similar to his own. Now he had a plan. He would see what stuff Miss Corinne Alexander was made of once and for all. It would take time, but he would know her and know her well.

That morning they were seated at the breakfast table. Sean waited until Corinne had poured seconds of coffee before he spoke.

"I want you to dress McKenna for an outing," he said, cutting a biscuit in half and reaching for the butter. "Yourself as well," he added, staring briefly at Corinne. "We're going out right after breakfast."

Corinne's eyes darted from him to Jane Pringle. "I have the cleaning up to do," she said in a voice that would hopefully hide her panic.

Mrs. Pringle frowned at the younger woman. "I'll do the cleaning up. You're to go with Mr. Garrick."

So he had discussed this with the housekeeper! "Where?"

"I have an appointment at my office that I must keep, but that should not take long." He smiled at Kenny and winked, causing the girl to giggle. "And then we're going shopping."

"Shopping?" Corie blurted. "For what?"

"The holidays will soon be upon us," he said, still grinning at the younger sister, "and we must be prepared."

"You mean Christmas?" Kenny breathed.

"I mean Christmas, moppet."

"Presents?" she asked in awe. "Will we buy presents for everybody?"

"Everybody, sweet."

"I don't think you need me for that," Corie put in. "I have a lot to do right here."

Sean did look at her then. "This is not a *request*,

Miss Alexander. If you have had sufficient to eat, please prepare to leave.''

It struck Corie how very much she had changed since coming here when she rose without further argument and did as he directed. She did not want to go, fearing she would somehow embarrass herself and him. After all, this would be her first foray into society in the company of a gentleman, and it was, to say the least, a little daunting. But she also understood he was leaving her little choice.

They left the townhouse before the hour had struck nine, walking south as the feeble winter sun etched the shadows of oak branches across their path. Sean stepped behind Corie, taking himself to her side on the outside of the street to protect her skirts, as any gentleman would. McKenna, eager with anticipation of the day's coming events, alternately skipped and hopped a few steps ahead of her guardians.

It took very little time to walk the few blocks from Sean's home to his cotton warehouse, but in that scant half hour Sean and Corie had directed their only conversations to McKenna; both felt that talking with the child was safe.

The plain two-story brick building was chock-full of cotton bales, but to the right of the entrance were two rooms designated as offices. Here was where Sean conducted his business and met with those who paid for his services of selling and shipping their cotton. He had access to the best markets in the world, and he demanded the highest prices. He was an astute businessman and was much sought after by many plantation owners.

But Corie knew all of that. She had known since the time she had first started to search out information about the man who would become her sister's guardian.

When they entered the outer office, a young man with thick spectacles peered up from a ledger. "Good morning," he called cheerfully, jumping to his feet.

Sean smiled and made the introductions. The young clerk was Daniel Harris, a relatively new member of Sean's staff. Daniel did not understand the relationship between Mr. Garrick and the Alexanders, but he was eager to make an impression, and delving into his employer's affairs was not at all the thing. He spoke politely to the young woman and then to the child and returned to his chair and his books.

"Would you like to see my office?" Sean asked, needing no second invitation to McKenna, who bounded through the door he held open.

Corie followed at a more sedate, almost suspicious, pace.

"It's not very big," Kenny complained.

Sean laughed. "It's financially astute to reserve the majority of the warehouse space for the cotton, moppet."

The girl turned from a place beside his desk and frowned her confusion.

"That means that the cotton is more important than I am," he explained.

"Nooo!" She giggled. "You're more important."

"Thank you, my dear," he said lightly, turning his attention to Corie. "Would you agree with those sentiments?"

Corie was not certain what was expected of her during this outing and decided to take the coward's approach. "Whatever Kenny says must be so."

Sean's dark blue eyes frowned into her hazel ones before he turned away.

But they were not to have time for sparring, or anything else, for that matter. Sean's client appeared, and Corie and Kenny were sent to wait out the meeting in the outer office.

And when Sean emerged several moments later, Daniel was in confrontation with a boy in worn-out, ill-fitting clothes.

Sean motioned Daniel into silence, escorted his client from the office, and turned an unhappy eye upon the two male occupants of the room. "Hardly businesslike behavior, Daniel," he said firmly. "What's this about?"

"This boy insists on seeing you," Daniel said smugly.

"That's fine."

"But he's certainly not a client," the clerk protested.

Sean detected a derisive note in the clerk's tone and walked across the room to place a hand on the visitor's shoulder. "You should learn not to burn your bridges, Daniel. This young man could be a future President."

Daniel thought that so absurd, he laughed. In the next instant, with one serious look from Sean, he mumbled something about coffee and left the office.

Not bothering to wait for the door to close, Sean turned to the boy and extended his hand. "My name is Garrick," he said, "I've seen you before."

"Yes, sir," the young man returned. "My name's Joshua. I do sweepin' up in some of the shops, and you always say hello."

Smiling, Sean recalled. "Of course! Sit," he said, pointing to Daniel's vacant chair while he raised one leg and rested on a corner of the desk. "What can I do for you?"

"Well, sir," the boy said, and then faltered, his eyes dropping away.

"Come now. You didn't come in here without a purpose," Sean coaxed.

"Well, you see, I have this chance to apprentice."

"Good for you! At what?"

"Barberin'."

Corie was astounded to learn that barbering required apprenticeship. And there were other things about this scene that had her fascinated.

"Barbering is a good profession."

Joshua bobbed his head in agreement, and then, after a cautious look at the other occupants of the room, blurted, "I need a suit of clothes, sir. I can't appear like this my first day."

Sean crossed his arms over his chest and smiled, understanding. "You're in need of a loan, then?"

"Yes, sir. I'd pay you back a bit at a time," Joshua said earnestly, staring directly into Sean's eyes. "I won't get much for a while, but I'll pay you back."

The older man stared at the younger man, taking his measure, until something in the boy's eyes provided Sean with the assurance he needed to make a decision. He stood, reaching into his coat pocket for his purse. "A suit of clothes and shoes, I should think," he said as he counted coins. "Extra shirts and socks," he muttered, before raising his head, hand extended. "Thirty dollars, should get you started. Would you agree?"

Joshua was clearly overwhelmed. "Sir, I won't be needin' all that."

"You will if you're to make an impression on your new employer," he said firmly, folding the coins into the boy's grimy palm. "And take a bath, Joshua. You can get one at . . ."

"I know, sir." He smiled. "At the barber's. That's where I'll be working."

"Good," Sean said, lightly clamping the boy on the shoulder. "Do well, young Joshua."

"I will, sir, and you'll see me regular once my wages start comin'."

"I know."

Corie and Kenny had silently witnessed the exchange, Kenny smiling madly and Corie flushing with embarrassment for Sean; he must surely be more of a fool than even she had realized.

"And thank you, sir!" Joshua called as he bounded out the door.

Sean turned to his young ladies and rubbed his palms together. "Well! Let's be off to the shops."

Kenny jumped to her feet, snatching a corner of Corie's cloak in with her own. "Sorry," she mumbled as Sean assisted her in getting free. "Let's go, Corie," she insisted when her sister failed to move.

Corie rose slowly, wrapping her cloak around her as she followed the others to the door. She was deeply troubled. Not only by what had transpired between Sean and Joshua, but by what it ultimately meant. Surely no one gave money to someone they did not know? But Sean had, and Corie did not suffer fools easily.

Sean turned back and closed the door once Corie stepped out onto the street. He was quick to halt her progress, however, when she turned right. "Where are you going?"

"To Franklin Street," she said, puzzled by his actions; it was his idea that they go. "To the shops," she added.

Sean firmly shook his head. "No. We'll go to Main Street, I think." Franklin Street was the center for wholesale merchandise and cheaper goods and the street life there was chaotic. Sidewalks were obstructed with all manner of humanity, and fishwives built fires in the gutters to cook their wares. He could do without the smell of frying catfish. No, he would not be taking McKenna and Corie there. ''If we do well with our shopping,'' he said, taking McKenna by the hand and turning Corie with a hand on her elbow, ''I'll treat my two favorite ladies to lunch at the City Hotel.''

''Really?'' Kenny breathed, although she had no idea what a City Hotel could be.

Corie was forced to smile at her sister's reactions to all of this. ''You certainly have one of us wrapped around your finger,'' she said lightly.

Sean's lips possessed a curious twitch when he turned her way. ''That is what Christmas excursions are all about, hadn't you heard? Entrancing children and young women.''

''I said *one* of us.''

''I know.''

Corie frowned as he grinned openly and turned his attention toward McKenna.

On Main Street they passed fruit stands, bootmakers, tailors, and bookstores. They browsed through the Patterson and Wiswall Merchandising Emporium, where Sean bought candles that were so small, Corie could only laugh at their uselessness. McKenna spied a bottle of scented bath oil that both Sean and Corie agreed was quite repugnant. But Kenny insisted it would make a wonderful gift for Mrs. Pringle. They bought it.

Farther along the street Sean led them toward the front door of a small, neat white cottage trimmed with black.

''But this is someone's home,'' Corie said, stating the obvious.

"It is. But it is also someone's place of business. Come along," he insisted as he juggled the parcels in his arms.

Of course, Kenny needed no coaxing and was, as always, close to his side.

And Corie had learned that if she hesitated, he would practically drag her along, so she followed. She had given up worrying about his intentions hours ago.

The door opened and they were met by a cheerful, portly woman who just had to be somebody's grandmother. "Mr. Garrick? Hello! I received your message. Come in. Come in, all of you."

Once inside a cozy, faded parlor, Sean made the introductions, his hands on Kenny's shoulders. "These are the two friends I mentioned in my note, Mrs. Steen. Do you think you can help before Christmas?"

Kenny did not understand what was happening, but her eyes were sparkling like crystals caught by candlelight.

"Of course I can help. You just leave this to me," the kind woman said, taking Corie's hand and prodding Kenny by the shoulder. "We'll just step back into my workroom while you make yourself comfortable here, Mr. Garrick. Don't you worry about a thing," the woman called back over her shoulder.

When they had disappeared, Sean settled himself in a worn but comfortable chair and looked about for something to read. "Gowns and hats," he muttered as he discarded one magazine after another.

Meanwhile, Corie had quickly realized what was happening. "There's been some mistake," she told the older woman. "We are not needing gowns."

"Oh, yes,"—she smiled—"very special Christmas attire."

"I don't think—"

"Perhaps you shouldn't think, dear," the woman said kindly. "I believe Mr. Garrick has his heart set on this. His message to me was quite clear. Now, let's find something very sweet for the wee one, shall we?"

An hour later the deed was done, and a glowing Kenny and a glowering Corie emerged from the back of the cottage.

"I'm getting a green gown!" Kenny crowed, diving for Sean's lap.

"Are you, darling?" he asked, smiling as the child positively made his Christmas complete. "Did you pick a pretty one?"

"It's bootiful!"

"Really?" Sean laughed. He noticed, however, that Corie was not laughing. "And is your gown *bootiful?*" he teased.

It didn't work.

"I believe we will have to discuss this, Mr. Garrick," she said, and everyone frowned at her tone.

Sean mumbled something appropriate to Mrs. Steen and ushered Kenny out the door behind her fuming sister.

"I can't afford a gown like that," Corie hurled at him the minute they were away from the cottage. "I'll be in my dotage by the time I pay you back for the things I've already purchased."

"The gown is a gift, Corinne," he said quietly.

Kenny's head rotated back and forth as she gazed up at them.

Corie was momentarily taken aback by his announcement, but she quickly recovered her senses. "And I cannot accept such a gift from you."

"From me or from any man?"

"From any man!" she snapped.

"Try," he said simply. "No one will know, and I want to give it."

Long moments passed as they visually confronted each other, right there on Main Street. Eventually Corie had to look away. "You're an impossible man," she said softly.

Sean smiled, the victor.

"Can we eat now?" Kenny asked, relieving the tension somewhat.

"Yes, moppet," he said, continuing to watch the older sister. "We can eat now."

The three-story City Hotel was another experience for Kenny.

"Would you like hot chocolate, McKenna?" Sean asked as they studied the menu.

Kenny frowned. "Mrs. Pringle says chocolate is bad for me."

Sean frowned thoughtfully. "It appears to me there are two occasions when chocolate is not only permissible but is advisable. One is while Christmas shopping. The second is when one is plodding through the forest looking for a tree."

"A tree?"

He laughed at the echo from his two companions. "A Christmas tree for the parlor."

Kenny clapped small hands and jumped about in her chair.

Corie frowned.

Chapter 10

It took forever to settle Kenny down to sleep that night; too much had transpired during the day and all of it totally new and wonderful for her.

Corie, too, had experienced several new things, but unlike her sister, she was looking at them through the jaundiced eye of an adult. An adult who understood her place in the scheme of things, and that was not as an equal participant in a *family* Christmas. Or a family anything, for that matter. Sean had gone too far in creating a happy haven for Kenny. Corie was grateful, for her sister's sake, that Sean was the way he was, but it had to come to an end. Both she and Kenny would suffer if a clearer head did not prevail. And the subject had to be broached before Corie lost her nerve.

With a prerehearsed speech rattling around in her head, she sought Sean in his study that night.

"Come!" he called in response to the light tap.

Corie poked her head around the partially open door. "Could I talk with you?"

Sean smiled readily. "Of course. Come in." He

stood and moved from behind his desk, motioning her toward the two comfortable chairs in front of the fire. "Would you care for something to drink? Wine, perhaps?"

"Wine?" she returned, her eyes reflecting her amazement. "I'm not a social caller."

"Does that mean I cannot offer you a glass of wine?"

"You're always turnin' things about on me," she muttered, sitting and carefully fanning her skirt.

Sean took one good, long look at the determination in her expression and made a decision. "Wine, it is," he said, moving to the cabinet. He smiled as he poured two glasses of wine because it had become evident recently that Corie clipped off letters of words only when she was rattled. It was becoming a distinct pleasure *turnin' things about* on her. "You wanted to speak with me?" he prodded as he walked toward her.

"I . . . want you not to include me in any further outings you may take with Kenny."

Sean stopped in the act of placing the two glasses on the small table. "Really? May I ask why?" He then lowered the glasses to the table.

Corie's eyes followed his hands as he tugged lightly on the legs of his trousers before sitting in the vacant chair. "Because I think it better if the two of you are alone."

"What you *think* isn't really an explanation, now, is it?"

"Well," she said, shifting uneasily, "I think Kenny should spend more time with you and less with me."

"Interesting," he murmured. "But I'm still only hearing what you *think*. *Why* are you thinking this way?"

The tension that had been building within her all

day finally snapped. "Because we aren't a *family*! Don't you see that? And we were doing *family* things today."

"That's right," he said quietly, reaching for his glass. "We were. And it was nice, Corinne. Even though you were miffed with me some of the time, I enjoyed the day. It was all very special. I don't remember a day like that since I was a boy."

"Well, it can't continue."

"Why? Because you're afraid?"

Corie's head snapped around and she glared defiantly. "You're playing games with the *girl* from Under-the-Hill!"

"I'm not playing," he said quietly and sipped more of his drink before continuing. "In fact, I'm very serious."

Corie laughed, but it was a sound of panic. "I don't understand what's happenin'," she said fiercely. "You watch me all the time and force me to do things you know I don't want to do. I just want you to leave me alone and let me do my work."

"I don't believe you truly want to be left alone," he said quietly. "And the simple fact is, I have more of an interest in you than having you care for my home."

Corie's mind raced for a safe way to end this fiasco. "Have you told your Faye about this?" she asked mockingly.

"Not yet. But I plan to. Very soon now."

Seeing no other alternative, Corie turned cruel in hopes he would believe she wanted no part of him. "Well, you'd best not shove her off yet, mate. I want no part of a fool, and you could be left without a woman. Men get cranky without a woman, you know."

But Sean had been studying her long enough to

recognize the ruse. "I assume you're about to explain why you think of me as a fool?"

"You can bet your last bale of cotton on that, Mr. Garrick," she said harshly, warming to her task. Getting quickly to her feet, Corie began to pace in front of him. "You continually allow people to make a fool of you."

"Do I?"

"You do. Remember today at your office? That boy is the second person I know of who made a fool of you. Do you think a woman wants a man who is a fool?"

Sean's eyes followed her progress, back and forth. "No, I suppose not. Would you care to tell me how I made a fool of myself today?"

"You were duped by that boy," she said with relish. "You'll never see that money again."

"You're wrong," he said quietly.

"And me. You let me dupe you into taking Kenny. Doesn't that make you feel foolish?"

"Was that your intent . . . to make me seem foolish?"

That gave Corie a moment's pause, but in the end she had to shake her head.

"People only make fools of us if we allow it to happen, Corinne," he said.

"Right!" she put in, seeing a way to make her point. "And now you've got Kenny!"

"That only makes me a very wise and a very fortunate man, my dear."

Stopping dead in front of him, Corie gradually realized all of her arguments had deflated. Piteously so. She felt humiliated by her own ineptitude. She had failed to intelligently convince him to leave her alone and that she had intelligently *chosen* to be left alone.

"Sit down, Corinne," Sean ordered softly and waited until she had done as requested. "I am a man who has always wanted children," he said, thoughtfully staring toward the fire. "I don't know if your little investigation of me turned up that fact or not. Regardless, had McKenna not been the child she is, I would not have taken her into my home. More important, I would not have allowed her into my life and close to my heart. Does that make any sense to you?" he asked, turning to look at her.

Corie nodded, agreeing because Kenny was one person she understood. "Kenny is a very special little girl."

"And how do you know that? You raised her," he said easily. "Is that the reason she is special?"

"No," she said hesitantly. "There is just something completely good and loving about her. I'm not nearly so open."

Sean did not have to be told *that* fact. "Can you believe that I sensed that good and loving nature in her?"

"I suppose," she said reluctantly.

"I felt the same thing today in young Joshua. He will do well, and he will return my loan."

Corie smiled haughtily, not ready to give up the battle. "Don't you ever make a mistake about people?"

"Yes, I have. But I'm willing to take my chances. Are you?"

Corie paused for a considerable length of time over that question, picking up her glass and sipping the wine as a hedge against answering.

Eventually Sean moved toward the fireplace and picked up the pieces of their conversation. "I suppose I should say I'm sorry for what I've done to you today,'' he said conversationally as he hunkered before the fire and poked about, adding a new log. "You did not want to be a part of something unfamiliar . . . our 'family' outing . . . and I forced you to come along. You wanted desperately to think the worst of me, to think me a fool, and I've tried to argue against your position because I want you to think otherwise.'' He stood then, turning and walking toward her. "But I won't apologize for these things, Corinne. I don't believe that deep in your heart you wanted to be left out today. You're just afraid of something unknown. It's very powerful, isn't it, my dear?'' he said softly, reaching out and gently pulling her to her feet. "And I don't believe you truly think I am a fool. I do believe, however, that I frighten you for other reasons, and I don't want that, either.''

"Don't do this,'' she pleaded as his arms slowly circled her.

"Tell me why you're frightened of me, Corinne?''

"Because I won't make the mistake of falling into something that cannot possibly last!'' she returned angrily. She pulled herself away from him then and put a half room's distance between them. "I will not love a man who will not stay with me forever. With me and *only* me! I will not be left to struggle and raise a child when I'm barely able to support myself. Is that clear?''

"Is that what you think I would do?'' he asked, managing to hide the hurt she had unerringly caused.

"That's what you all do,'' she said, choking back a sob as she turned away.

Now he understood why she had been driving herself; Corinne had been working and learning as a hedge against harder times she seemed certain would befall her. "Well, you're no longer incapable of supporting yourself. That's *that* neatly out of the way,'' he added thoughtfully as he approached. And then with sudden insight, he placed his hands lightly on her shoulders. There could be only one person in her life who could instill such ideas. ''Did she love him so very much?''

''Who?'' she asked irritably.

''Your mother?''

Nodding her head, she said bitterly, ''He not only abandoned her, he ruined her life.''

Sean wasn't certain whether or not she was crying, but he thought not. Still, he proceeded gently. ''Was the man your father, Corinne?''

''He made a fool out of her!'' she said heatedly. ''He and other men made her a pitiful woman.''

''Remember what I told you,'' he said softly. ''Others can only make fools of us if we permit it.''

Corie thought she felt the brush of his lips against her hair, but she was not certain. Turning angrily in his arms, she hissed, ''That's a high thought, that is. But how does someone prevent such a thing when your heart is so twisted with love you can't think straight? How do you prevent someone from hurting you when you can't see the blows coming because your eyes are closed to everything that could be bad about that person?'' Tears had risen in her eyes and now balanced precariously on her lashes.

Sean's heart wrenched in pain. ''Love isn't synonymous with these things, Corinne. You've had only one example upon which to base your concepts, don't you see? I would venture to say that few relationships are like your mother's.''

Corie brushed at a tear that had fallen to her cheek and stared up at him in wonder. ''Why are we talking this way?'' she said softly. ''Why?''

"I think we both understand that," he returned with a gentle smile.

"I came here to tell you . . ."

"Yes?" he prodded when she refused to complete her comment.

"I told you, you make me confused," she said, looking away.

Sean let her go when she twisted out of his arms and watched her cross the room to stand staring down at the fire. He was greatly encouraged that she had not run from the room. Returning to his chair, he picked up his pipe, tapped the used tobacco into a dish, and began to fill it again. "Do you know about Greek myths?" he asked conversationally.

Corie turned toward him, her hands locked nervously behind her back. "I knew a Greek sailor once. He said he wanted to *love* me. What do you suppose he meant by that?"

Sean's gaze slammed into hers. "I suspect you know."

A miserable smile twisted her lips. "I *suspect* you're right."

"Do you want to hear my story?" he prodded.

The smile altered to something more understanding, and Corie returned wearily to her chair. "You're a great storyteller, Sean."

"This story has a purpose."

"I wish I understood why I continually want your company," she muttered. "I know I shouldn't be here with you like this."

Sean smiled, inwardly pleased that she could put words to this side of her struggle. "The myth tells of a man named Pygmalion who carved a statue of a woman. He so loved his creation that he prayed to Aphrodite, the goddess of love, for a woman just like it. Aphrodite brought the statue to life, and Pygmalion married her.''

Corie thought it a ridiculous story. ''Statues don't come to life,'' she scoffed.

''Perhaps not. But dreams often do.''

''I don't see the point of this,'' she said, growing irritable with his games.

Sean drew deeply on the pipe, considering just how vulnerable he would be if he did not speak cautiously. ''I loved my wife very much, and after her passing, I thought I would never again seek such a relationship with a woman. But I was wrong in my thinking. And just when I became convinced that a second chance of finding someone special was all a dream, I met a young woman.'' He set his pipe aside and gave Corie the full benefit of his dark eyes. ''I met a young woman and thought I might want a woman just like her.''

With eyes growing larger by the second, Corie sputtered a bit before she could form an articulate sentence. ''Might? You're not certain?''

Shaking his head, Sean said quietly, ''I'm being honest with you, Corinne. I'm as confused as you seem to be.'' Perhaps *want* was not the word he should have used, he thought belatedly. He *knew* that he wanted her; he just could not seem to avoid the images of other men wanting her and, more important, having her. And *that* was where his confusion lay.

Corie pressed the fingers of one hand tightly against her lips and leaned heavily on the arm of her chair as she stared at the popping fire. ''And just what am I supposed to do? Why on earth would you tell me these things?''

''Because I don't want you shutting me out. I want

you to give us a chance to discover what this thing is between us.''

''There is nothing between us!'' she said heatedly, staring at him in horror. ''There can never be anything between us. What do you think you'll do, *Mr.* Garrick, the next time you have to attend a ball or a city function? Do you plan to drag me along as your lady?''

''I would hope I wouldn't have to *drag* you anywhere.''

''You're being unbelievably stupid!'' she cried. ''How would you explain me to your friends? Do you think they will accept a girl from Under-the-Hill into their ranks? Not bloody likely, *Mr.* Garrick. They'll throw me out and throw my past right back into your face.''

''You know so much about my friends, do you?'' he asked with deceptive calm.

Wilting with sudden perceived defeat, Corie said softly, ''It won't work, Sean. It can't happen.'' And she knew, if they tried to explore this thing between them, he would eventually be forced to succumb to the dictates of the world in which he had been born and raised and now existed. He would one day realize that she was not of his kind, that she was a detriment to his survival and success. And he would rid himself of her.

But Sean was on his feet, pulling her up from her chair and wrapping his arms loosely around her. ''Don't defame this thing between us, Corinne, until we fully discover what it is. Don't put obstacles in our path because of these things you perceive. Don't waste this opportunity we've been given. I admire you and I enjoy your company. Can you not at least say the same of me?''

"Is that all you want from me?" she asked warily. "Company?"

Sean's head slowly lowered toward her. "No. I don't think so," he murmured. And then his lips lightly touched hers, tasted, retreated, and lowered to taste again. "I don't think so."

Chapter 11

Over the course of the next few days Sean was relentless in his pursuit of Corie. She would suddenly find herself gently turned away from dusting or cleaning by strong hands that never hurt, only guided. And then he would kiss her. At times his kisses were quick, fleeting, as he passed her by on his way out the door to work of a morning. On other occasions, when he felt they were less likely to be discovered, he would sweep her into his arms and boldly deepen the kiss until they were both left breathless.

He turned up where she least expected and was never where she anticipated him to be.

Corie told herself that she was not encouraging his amorous attentions, that she did not care for his bold handling of her whenever he felt so inclined. But then, during the day when he was at work, she found herself constantly watching the clock, awaiting his return. And it was eager anticipation, not fear, that kept her watching.

He turned mysterious, driving Corie crazy as he

hinted about the coming holidays and then disappeared to the attic after reading McKenna her evening
story.

Friday evening, having tucked Kenny into bed for
the night, Corie decided to discover just what held his
attention in that dreary, dusty place every evening.

The door leading to the stairs creaked, and Sean
hastily snatched up an old tarp and concealed his
project. "Who's there?" he called, moving toward the
stairs. He smiled when he saw the auburn hair and pert
nose he knew so well. "McKenna's not with you?"

Frowning curiously, Corie made her way cautiously
up the last steps. "She's asleep. What do you do up
here every night?"

With his mischievous grin making him look very
boyish, Sean took her hand and guided her toward the
center of the attic where the ceiling was highest. "I'll
show you, but you must promise not to let McKenna
up here before Christmas."

Corie laughed briefly. "You really love this Christmas business, don't you?"

Sean looked momentarily shocked. "Don't you?"

"How would I know, Sean? I'm learning about
Christmas from you."

There was no remorse or resentment in her tone. It
was just a softly spoken statement, and it twisted his
heart that he had been so unfeeling. "I'm sorry,
sweetheart," he said.

"Sorry for what?"

"For all of the Christmases you've missed." And
then his eyes turned brighter. "But this will be a great
one, you'll see. Let me show you what I've got here."
He tugged until she fell to her knees beside him, and
then he was pulling at the tarp. "One of the best parts
of Christmas is the children," he said conversation-

ally. "I have friends with children, and I always enjoy visiting and getting caught up in their excitement Christmas Day. And this year we'll have McKenna. I'm making this for her."

The wood was fine and lightly golden and sawdust swirled about their knees as he swept the tarp aside.

"It's a cradle," he said.

Frowning, Corie nodded. "It's very small, Sean."

He laughed and reached for a bundle of brown paper resting on a trunk behind them. "It's for this," he said, unrolling the package to reveal a fair-haired doll with porcelain features. "Every baby needs a cradle, don't you think?"

The doll was beautifully gowned in pink with frills about the hem of the skirt. Corie reached for it, examining the fine detail of the painted face. Lifting the skirt, she smiled at the small pantaloons and black felt slippers. "This is beautiful, Sean. Kenny will love her."

Looking decidedly pleased, Sean's gaze turned on his creation. "I'm almost finished with this, and I've asked Mrs. P. to make a little blanket or whatever." Smiling at her, he suggested, "Perhaps you could help her?"

"Me?" Corie squeaked. "Sean, I still have trouble sewing on missing buttons." But looking at him, Corie knew it was important that she participate. Examining the cradle, she traced her fingers along a smooth edge. "Perhaps we could make a small pillow and quilt. That would be nice in this handsome cradle."

"I'm going to darken the wood," he said, "and then it's finished."

Corie glanced sideways at him as he examined his work. There was pride in his touch and in the way he gazed at the cradle. "You're a strange man," she whispered, finding herself in awe of him once again; she had been feeling this way quite frequently of late.

Smiling at her, Sean sat back on his heels. "Strange? In what way?"

"You take in stray children, you give money to ragamuffin boys, and you spend your precious time making cradles for a girl's first doll." She swallowed painfully, staring intently into the deep blue of his eyes. "And you dare to offer me affection."

Turning toward her, Sean pulled her up on her knees toward him. "That's my greatest satisfaction," he whispered, "offering you affection." His smile disappeared as his lips moved more closely to hers. "Would you care to experiment with a little satisfaction for yourself?"

She had no opportunity to respond, of course, and Corie had no intention of verbalizing with him at this moment in any event. Many things he had done in the past had moved her emotions in some small way, but tonight she felt overwhelmed by the goodness in him. He was a man unlike any other she had known. He did not force people to give up their life's blood in order to get what he wanted like other men. Instead he gave and gave of himself and reached out to others to give some more. Tonight she understood that only in the giving did he, too, receive. Tonight she understood that she would follow the lessons he had taught; she, too, would begin *giving*, in order that she might receive.

As Sean's kiss deepened, Corie knew that she would battle against her fears no longer. She was tired of waging emotional war. And she was tired of fending off something she wanted. She would partake of this relationship and follow where it led. If it was to survive for only one brief moment in her life, so be it. She would have memories at least. And they would have to be enough.

Sean pulled her tightly against his chest as his lips traced a path toward her ear. "God, you are sweet," he murmured.

Corie set her thoughts aside and concentrated only on what was happening between them. Her arms tightened about his neck, causing her breasts to raise up and caress the solid muscles of his chest. Her nipples tightened painfully as a flood of other foreign sensations robbed her of her ability to think. It was like a pleasant hell, this discovery of the unknown. The sensations that would normally be considered as discomfort produced warm, sweet, mellow feelings that completely overwhelmed.

Sean had not planned to take her. Not this early in their relationship. He was still unsettled about his own feelings; rationalizing the things she must have done in her previous life. But he had been without a woman, and he wanted this one more than any other. And, wonder of wonders, she seemed to have dropped the barrier between them.

"You make me ache," he whispered, his lips returning to capture hers as his hand slowly dragged across the material of her dress, moving slowly from her back to her ribs and upward. He gently captured one small breast and lightly rotated the palm of his hand until she groaned, making him smile. "Do you ache, also, darling?" he breathed, drawing her down on the floor until he was leaning over her. "Let me see if I can help," he said as his hands began to shakily attack the buttons of her gown.

Corie understood enough of what was happening. "There'll be no turning back, will there, Sean?" she whispered. When she felt her breasts bared to his gaze, and his warm lips on her flesh, she knew that they would never again be the same with each other. Surely, if these feelings were any measure of what was to happen, only good would come of it. But then, as her eyes closed and her breathing went awry, her greatest fear managed to make itself known. "Please don't leave me with a child, Sean," she whispered.

His hands stilled and his head came up. Frowning, he lightly stroked her cheek. "I understand," he said softly. "But surely you know how to prevent that, darling."

Eyes narrowed in arousal, Corie's restless movements stilled with his words. "How could I know?" she asked huskily.

Clearly confused, Sean said stupidly, "Well, how did you manage before?"

A space of several moments drew out as she searched his eyes for denial of what he might be suggesting. "Before what?" she snapped.

Dawning horror slowly etched across Sean's face as he realized he had inadvertently betrayed his assumptions.

Scrambling out from beneath him, Corie clutched the bodice of her gown as she backed away when he got to his feet. "Now I understand how it is!" she snapped again, and then she laughed without a trace of humor. "If I had made my way like *that*, don't you think I would have lived better than I did?" Saucily she placed a hand on her hip and imitated a stripper's bump and grind. "Don't you think I'm talented enough and pretty enough that I could have drawn the highest prices and Kenny and I would have lived well?"

"Don't do this," he whispered, walking slowly toward her. "Don't you see how I could have—?"

"No, I don't see!" she hissed. "I may have done many things in my life that would not be acceptable for a proper *lady* to do, Mr. Garrick, but *sellin'* myself is not one of them."

"Corie!" he called as she ran for the stairs. Sean caught her at the door to her room and spun her to face him. "I'm sorry," he said. "I can only say I'm sorry."

Tears rolled silently down her cheeks as Corie looked up at him. "I thought you cared for me," she whispered. "That you thought better of me than that."

Sean ran trembling fingers through his black hair. "I do, Corie. Don't you see, my own ignorance . . ."

"Pride kept me from going into the brothels, Mr. Garrick," she said, wiping the tears from her face with the palms of her hands. "Pride kept me from spreadin' my legs for a man's pleasure. *Any* man's." And with that she turned and firmly closed the door between them.

"Jesus, Mary, and Joseph!" he breathed, turning toward his own room. "Fool!"

Corie fell across her bed as tears of shame poured down her face. She did not know how she had said the things she had; shameless things she had heard from the mouths of the very type of women Sean Garrick assumed her to be. Prostitutes! Hussies! But it hurt so much that he could think that of her!

Lost in her world of misery, Corie failed to hear the door open or the soft footfalls that approached her bed.

"I can't leave it," he said softly, sitting next to her hip. "I can't leave it to fester overnight, Corie." He reached for her then, knowing she was crying, pulling her up against his chest and folding her securely within his arms. "I'm a sorry fool, my darling," he said. "I'm so sorry."

"How could . . . you?" she cried, gripping the front of his shirt.

"I have no excuses, sweetheart. Except perhaps that I'm conditioned by society more than I realized. It's generally believed that everyone Under-the-Hill must fit one of several categories. None of them flattering."

"But if you thought me bad, why did you let me live here?"

"I didn't think you bad."

Corie hiccuped and choked back a sob. "You thought I was one of those women, though."

Smiling sadly, Sean smoothed her hair back from her face. "I failed to delete one aspect of my conditioning."

"I hurt so much, Sean," she whispered through her tears, not understanding how another person's opinion of her could matter so much; it had never mattered before.

"I didn't mean to hurt you," he said quietly.

"I hate what my mother does," she said after a moment. Hiding her face against his neck, she whispered, "Men use her and I hate that."

"That's understandable."

"And that's why I could never do what she does."

"But had you . . . I would have wanted you anyway. Do you see that?"

Corie dared to look up at him then. "Does it make a difference . . . now that you know? I mean . . . did you want to do . . . did you want me because you thought I'd done it before?"

Smiling again, he stroked her cheek reassuringly as he nodded. "Wanting you has little to do with what has gone before, Corie. And the only difference is that being a virgin makes you very close to perfect,'' he said. ''I don't know if I can deal with *perfect*.''

A sound that was half laugh, half tear-strained sob, surfaced from deep within her. ''My mother is different from the others,'' she said. ''She's more to be pitied, Sean. That's why I can't stay away.''

''I've told you, I'll take you there whenever you wish to go.''

Corie quieted then, burrowing into his embrace as her tears ceased and her thoughts began to rumble around in her head. He felt so good, his hold secure and gentle. He was so different from anyone she had known, and that made him a little bit frightening. He demanded much of those around him. Just as he demanded much of himself. And she wasn't certain she was woman enough to satisfy all of his perfectionist's needs.

''Why do men want their wives to be virgins?'' she asked quietly.

Sean had thought she had fallen asleep and was startled by the fact that she spoke, let alone by the question itself. It took him a moment to collect his thoughts. ''When a man loves a woman, he wants to share special times with her. Physical loving is one of those times, and it's very special the first time, when he's introducing her to new and exciting feelings. And, if I were to be perfectly honest, most men are raised to cherish the fact that no man has gone before him.''

''Like he's staking a claim?'' she asked.

Laughing softly, he said, ''Not quite so unromantic, darling.''

''Was your wife a virgin when you married her, Sean?'' she asked softly.

"Yes."

"Would you have loved her less if she hadn't been?"

"No," he said easily.

Corie was satisfied with that.

Chapter 12

Jane Pringle arose and started working earlier than usual the following morning. It was Saturday, less than one week before Christmas, and Mr. Garrick had requested a substantial lunch be packed. Jane had declined his invitation to join in the search for a tree and a picnic lunch, although, as usual, she appreciated his consideration in trying to include her in his plans. He was like that; the man hated to see anyone left out. But Jane knew her place and refused to cross the boundary, unlike Corinne.

Jane had been thinking about Corie for weeks now, noticing the change that was taking place in her. In fairness, she could hardly blame the girl for being caught up in dreams of something better. Certainly Mr. Garrick could offer a young woman a good life, and he was a man of admirable character, but Jane had begun to fear what she sensed was happening between her employer and the younger woman. She had come to like Corie, actually. She was a young woman to be admired in many ways; she worked hard and tried to

137

learn, to improve herself. But the girl was striving too high and was bound to be hurt. After all, Mr. Garrick was a man of position. A man who had to be concerned about appearances for the sake of his business.

By the time Corie entered the kitchen, Mrs. Pringle had a double batch of biscuits baking and hot chocolate simmering and was slicing a chicken she had roasted the previous day.

"My, you're way ahead of yourself today," Corie said cheerfully as she gazed around the kitchen. "You must have been up for hours."

Mrs. Pringle gave the younger woman a morning nod and continued to carve the cold chicken. "Mr. Garrick requested a lunch packed early."

Corie turned from pouring a cup of coffee at the stove. "Today is *tree* day," she said, smiling. "Kenny's been counting the days, she's so excited. You'll be joining us?"

Shaking her head, Mrs. Pringle frowned as she lopped off a wing.

"Sea . . . Mr. Garrick will be disappointed. I know he—"

"Mr. Garrick understands that I know my place."

"Oh," Corie said softly, frowning as she realized the woman had not looked at her once since she had entered the room. "And I don't, Mrs. Pringle? Is that what you mean to say?"

Jane set the knife aside and wiped her hands on her apron. After what seemed a long interval, she looked at Corie and said quietly, "You must understand that I greatly admire Mr. Garrick. And I can understand how a young woman like yourself would be attracted to a man like him. You've done well since coming here, Corinne, and I don't want to see you hurt. But you *both* will suffer if you keep on, mark my words."

Corie's complexion turned several shades of red as her mind raced around the possibilities of what the woman had seen to make her say these things. "Mrs. Pringle, I—"

"I saw him kissing you in the dining room, if that's what you're wondering."

"I didn't want any of this to happen. I—"

"I know, dear," the older woman said kindly. "I just felt I had to . . . say . . . well, it won't be accepted. And before you find yourself too deeply in love with him . . ."

Corie smiled and eased onto a stool in front of the counter where Jane was working. "I think it's already too late, Mrs. P."

"Oh, dear."

"Yes. Oh, dear," Corie murmured.

Sean had rented a wagon and a pair of sturdy horses to take them out of town toward the road that led to many rich plantations. There were forests aplenty along the way, and McKenna scanned the trees looking for the perfect one.

"We'll get a big one!" she babbled happily. "Over there, Sean. There's a good one."

"Too big, sweetheart," he said. "Remember we have a ceiling to consider."

"How tall, Sean?" she asked. "How tall can it be?"

"About as tall as me. A bit more perhaps."

McKenna's eyes looked him up and down. "That's pretty tall," she said. Then she turned to her sister. "Mrs. Pringle says we'll put stuff on the tree, Corie."

"Decorations, darling," Corie said. "I heard all about it."

"Ribbons!" she cried happily. "Lots of ribbons!"

Sean took them around an area of deep woods and beyond to a hill that boasted smaller trees. "I think we should have some luck here," he said as he jumped down from the high wagon seat and assisted his two companions. Thor had jumped over the side of the wagon bed as soon as McKenna's feet hit the ground. "Now, don't you go off too far from me," he told McKenna. "I don't want you getting lost in the deep woods. Stay close."

Kenny nodded eagerly, although Sean wasn't certain she had actually taken heed.

Looking at Corie, he said, "Let's be certain we keep her in sight."

Corie nodded and grinned as the child darted up the hill with Thor on her heels. "Too late," she muttered and lifted her skirts to chase after her. "Kenny!"

"Here's a good one, Sean!"

Sean quickly secured the horses, snatched his ax from the wagon bed, and followed with long strides.

"Here's a good one!" McKenna called again.

The sisters stood by silently as Sean walked once around the tree. "A good size," he said, "but it's not even all around. Let's look for another."

Kenny ran circles around a dozen trees before she proclaimed. "The most *perfectist* tree, Sean! Right here!"

Thor caught his small companion's excitement and began to whirl in circles, barking for attention.

Sean proclaimed she was right about this tree. It stood over six feet, he calculated, but cutting would bring it to the perfect height. "Now, stand away," he said. "I don't want anyone hurt by flying wood chips."

Corie watched him heft the ax and swing, cutting a

deep groove into the bark. One cut angled down, the next angled up. The tree should fall in their direction. "Come on, Kenny. I think we'd better move over here."

McKenna was too excited to really take notice, however, and darted around the tree opposite Sean. He saw her and moved quickly to snatch her out of the way. "Now, go over there with Corie," he admonished. "And keep Thor with you!"

McKenna feigned a pout and moved to her sister's side.

"Do you want me to hold it, Sean?" Corie asked. "It looks about ready to go."

"Another few . . ." But the tree quivered and swayed, and Sean grinned at McKenna as he bellowed, "Timber!"

Only Corie realized what was happening and sprang toward him. Too late. "Sean!" He had disappeared beneath the branches of the fallen tree. Her heart in her throat, Corie danced around the tree, looking for a good handhold. "Sean. Oh, my God!"

Thor nosed around the tree, whining for his fallen master.

Corie was able to grasp hold of an upper branch and heave. Sean was lying on his side, unmoving. And when the tree was safely out of the way, Corie dropped to her knees, rolling him onto his back. "Damn you!" she sputtered when he looked up at her.

He was laughing!

And fending off his dog's zealous tongue.

"If I ever decide to change my line of work," he managed to say, "remind me not to take up lumberjacking."

"Sean Garrick, I thought you'd been hurt!" Corrie cried.

He sobered immediately, seeing her concern. "I'm sorry, darling," he said softly. "I'm fine."

McKenna flopped onto her knees in the mud beside him. "You're not hurt, are you, Sean?" she asked. "You got the tree down."

"Kenny, look at your dress," Corie ranted. "We'll never get the mud out."

McKenna frowned at this unfair treatment. "Yours, too," she muttered.

Corie looked down at her bent knees, and then at Sean lying in the dirt. "I think Mrs. P. will be very unhappy with us," she said and joined in as Sean laughed again.

Sean trimmed the lower branches of the tree and dragged it down the hill to the wagon while Corie tried to do something about McKenna's soggy condition. The child's dress and cloak were wet enough to be a hazard to her health in the chill air. Fortunately, Sean had planned the outing well and had included two blankets along with the basket of food and the ax.

"Look at this," Corie complained as she removed Kenny's dress and wrapped a blanket around the small shoulders. "Even your pantaloons are muddy."

"Bet yours are, too," Kenny mumbled.

Sean appeared with his arms full of wood and knelt nearby to start a fire. "We'll have the chocolate heated in a few minutes," he said. "That should warm us all."

Corie watched as he built the fire, then poured the chocolate into a tin, setting it near the edge of the flames. And when he turned his back on her, she grinned. "You should see yourself," she said lightly and reached out to touch his hair. "You've even got mud drying here."

Sean directed a lopsided grin her way and sat beside

her on the remaining blanket, pulling McKenna onto his lap. "Are you warm enough, moppet?" he asked, securing the blanket around her. "I'll catch it if you get so much as a sniffle out of this."

"Catch what?" she asked, frowning up at him.

"I mean your sister will be very angry with me," he explained.

"Naw," McKenna drawled. "Corie likes you. But if she gets mad at you, Sean, don't worry. She doesn't *stay* mad at people she likes."

"Is that so?" he asked, raising his eyes to the older sister, who had suddenly become preoccupied with studying the contents of the food basket. "You don't stay *mad*? And you *like* me?"

"Kenny talks too much," she mumbled, avoiding meeting his eyes by watching his fingers burrow into Thor's dark fur.

"I like a woman who doesn't stay *mad*," he teased. And then more seriously, he added, "And don't you think I knew that you *liked* me?"

Corie's complexion warmed and colored instantly. "Don't talk like that now."

"Now? You mean with McKenna listening?" He ducked his head and smiled at the girl. "Are you listening, moppet? How would you feel if I told you I like your sister, too?"

"I don't mind," she said quietly.

"There you go," he said, smiling triumphantly. "We have permission of the only one who matters."

Mrs. Pringle would have suffered apoplexy at the mere sight of the motley tree crew had she not been previously distracted. Mr. Garrick had planned such a nice day, but a sense of foreboding told Jane Pringle it was about to end in disaster.

Sean deposited the blanketed McKenna well inside as Jane backed away from the front door. "She got a little dirty," he said sheepishly and turned to go back outside for the tree.

"I'd say the child was not the only one rolling about in the mud," Jane said, frowning at the cakes of stuff on his navy pea jacket. When Sean turned back to her, grinning like a boy, she added, "You have a visitor, Mr. Garrick."

Without thinking, Sean reached up and scrubbed at his unkempt hair. "I can't see anyone today," he said.

Bending toward him, Jane whispered, "I don't think you're going to have much choice, sir."

Frowning at the woman, Sean turned reflexively toward the parlor doors as a movement there caught his eye.

"Hello, Sean, darling."

"Faye."

The woman's eyes took in his appearance and then settled on McKenna. Her smile disappeared instantly. After a brief scrutiny of the child, she returned her attention to Sean. "It appears you two have been . . . playing?"

"We've been out cutting a tree for the parlor," he explained, silently cursing himself for taking the trouble. "McKenna got her dress muddy."

"It seems to me, darling, she was in that condition when you found her."

"Sean, the basket is caught under a tree limb . . ." Corie stopped dead in her tracks when she realized why Sean had not returned outside. "Sorry," she muttered, blushing feverishly as she skirted Sean and reached for Kenny's hand. "We'll get changed now, I think."

"I remember that lady," Kenny said as she attempted to manage the steps despite the blanket falling about her feet. "She's not very friendly, Corie."

"Sssh!" Corie hissed, snatching the struggling girl up in her arms.

Faye watched their progress, examining the young woman closely as she took the child up the stairs. Only after they were out of sight and Jane Pringle had disappeared down the hall did Faye turn to Sean. "You were playing in the mud with *two* little girls, Sean? Really?" she drawled.

Sighing, Sean ran his fingers through his hair. "Obviously we're in a bit of a mess here, Faye. Perhaps I could call on you later? After I get the tree inside and I get cleaned up."

"Are you certain you remember the way to my home, Sean?" she said snidely. "I haven't seen much of you lately."

Frowning, Sean removed his gloves, studying the procedure as he asked quietly, "Have you come to fight, then, Faye? Is that why you're here?"

"I've been told you had lunch at the hotel with a child and a pretty young woman this week, darling, and it occurred to me you've been a bit distant. But really, Sean, I had no idea you were preoccupied with *two* children. Don't you have to be licensed or something to operate a home for wayward girls?"

"That's enough," he said softly.

"I don't think so, Sean," she returned evenly. "I have a great deal more to say, actually."

Sean didn't doubt that for a moment, and ignoring the mud he was leaving in his wake, he led the way down the hall to his study.

Once there, Sean ignored the proprieties, leaving Faye to close the door while he marched to the cabinet and poured a single snifter of brandy. "Very well," he said, turning with one hand in a pocket of his coat, "what did you wish to say?"

Faye began to think quickly of how she might diffuse the moment; after all, she had come here hoping her fears were unfounded. Hoping she could bring him back to her.

She smiled, moving gracefully across the room until she stood leaning on the high back of a chair near the fire. "I was being silly out there, darling. Forgive me. It's just that I've missed you, and I've begun to wonder if you've been angry with me."

Forcing himself to squelch his initial anger, Sean said, "I haven't been angry with you, Faye."

"Well, that is good news," she said. "You'll come this evening, then. We'll have a nice dinner and—"

"I can't come," he said.

"Well! Tomorrow, then . . ."

"Faye, I've been wanting to talk with you," he said. "Perhaps now is as good a time as any." Sean was not happy about this, although he knew the woman held no real love for him. Still, Faye did like having him about, and he suspected she would not take kindly to his decision to drop out of her life. Had *she* wanted him gone, however, it would have been different.

No, Sean had few illusions about the powerful Faye Doherty. He simply wished to avoid any real unpleasantness.

But Faye's intuition told her what was coming, and she wasn't going to like it one bit. "You're sleeping with that whore," she said, pointing in the direction of the stairs beyond the room.

Caught off guard, Sean took a threatening step forward. "That is not true, and she is not a *whore*."

"She must be quite a little slut. I know your

appetites, darling, and you haven't gone for weeks without it.''

With a weary sigh Sean set his glass aside and tried to reason with the woman. "Faye, you're lowering yourself, and there's no need.''

"It appears I *lowered* myself the day I allowed you to make love to me,'' she snapped.

"Allowed?'' he asked, almost laughing at the thought. "Allowed, Faye? Come on. As I recall, you couldn't wait for me to get out of my trousers. And why are you doing this? You don't care about me. You might like having me in your bed now and again, but you don't love me. What we had was mutually beneficial and it was good. But we've both known it wasn't love, and it wasn't permanent. Let's bow out gracefully.''

Faye turned from him, unwilling to allow him to think he could just walk away from her whenever the spirit moved him. He would walk away when she was ready to boot him out and not before. Turning back, she gripped the top of the wingback chair until her knuckles turned white. "I don't think you want to do this, Sean,'' she said.

Dark brows arching, Sean dared a curious smile. "That sounds suspiciously ominous, Faye. You wouldn't be threatening me? And with what? Remember, you're a leading citizen here in Natchez. You don't want to sling any mud that might soil your own skirts.''

"Now who's threatening?'' she snapped.

"Let it go, Faye.''

Clenching her fists, Faye decided that a verbal battle with him would not produce the results she wanted. "I suppose at your age a man needs to remind himself of his youth,'' she said.

"My age?" He laughed openly. "Faye, I'm four years your junior."

"But really, Sean," she said, as if he had not spoken. "The girl is so thin she could be easily mistaken for a boy. I didn't know you were that way inclined, darling," she added, turning toward the door. Pausing there, she turned back briefly. "I just hope the little tart doesn't give you anything nasty, Sean."

"Faye!" he bellowed.

Freshly washed and wearing dry clothes, Corie was trying to keep Kenny occupied while they waited for Sean to complete whatever business he was conducting with Faye. Corie had not needed to be told who the woman was, but Kenny eagerly relayed *her* first meeting with the woman. And, her relationship with Sean aside, *that* made Corie dislike Faye on the spot.

Even behind closed doors, raised voices could be heard in the kitchen, where Jane and Corie pretended nothing was amiss.

Kenny was more honest, however. "They're yelling at each other," she said. "I never heard Sean yell before."

"Quiet, Kenny," Corie said. "Maybe Sean has a need to yell. Finish your milk."

"I want to put the stuff on the tree," she whined.

"We can't very well do that until Sean brings the tree inside, now can we. Just be patient."

"It's hard being payshience."

Corie laughed and touched her sister's silky hair. "I know, baby. But I don't think it will be too long."

And then all three in the kitchen flinched as the rafters seemed to ring with "Faye!"

"Oh, dear," Jane said.

"Ohhh," said Corie.

Kenny looked as if she would cry. "Sean's really mad, Corie."

"But not at us, baby. You just finish your milk."

The house grew silent shortly after that, and Jane and Corie stared at each other, wondering who, if any of them, should approach the man in the study. But there was really no decision to make. Corie would be the one.

She hesitated outside the door of the study for only a moment and then peeked inside. He was sitting in one of the large chairs, tipping a snifter of brandy. "Do you want to be alone?" she ventured.

Sean lowered the glass and put it on the table. "Come here," he said.

Closing the door behind her, Corie walked close to his chair and did not protest when Sean grasped her wrist and pulled her down onto his lap.

"I just want to hold you," he said, wrapping his arms securely around her and leaning his head back, staring at her lovely face.

"Kenny reminded me that Faye isn't very friendly," she ventured.

Sean laughed at that. "She's a lot less friendly now."

Frowning, Corie dared to say, "She must love you very much, Sean."

"No, my darling. She loves me not at all."

"But—"

"I know. She made quite a fuss for a lady who doesn't love."

Puzzled, Corie toyed with the front of his shirt. "If she doesn't love you, why would she care about losing you?"

Sean had a ready answer for that, but he was sensitive enough not to make reference to what he and

Faye had done in the past. "Faye can be amazingly possessive when she wants to hold on to something . . . or someone. She liked my company and she liked to have me around when she needed an escort. If there is to be a parting of the ways, I think Faye wants to be the one to cry off."

Corie studied his eyes for a moment before asking, "Is that all?"

"What do you want me to say, Corie?" he asked softly.

She was the first to tear her eyes away, putting her arms about his neck and ducking her head.

"It doesn't matter now," he whispered as he felt her soft breath below his ear.

"I believe you," she said softly. Perhaps she was a fool, she thought, but she did believe him.

They sat there like that for long moments.

Corie reveled in the first real intimacy she had ever shared with another human being. He held her so easily, as if she had been born to sit on his lap and have his arms around her. And it felt good. It felt wonderful.

"I'm sorry Faye spoiled our day," Sean said eventually.

"We still have the tree to decorate."

"The tree!" he said with a laugh. "I've left the damned tree in the street. Not to mention the horses." He patted her hip playfully. "You'd best let me up, woman."

But Corie refused to budge or lessen her hold. "I want to ask you something first," she said quietly.

Curious, Sean relaxed in the chair again. "Ask away."

"Are you going to make love to me, Sean?"

There was a silence that made Corie fear she had been exceptionally stupid.

But then he whispered against her ear, "I want you, Corie. Very much. Is that what you're asking?" And when she failed to respond, he gently forced her head up so that he could see her eyes. "Is it?" he prodded.

"I just thought I should tell you . . . I mean, if you want me . . . I thought I should tell you it's all right."

"Does that mean you want me, too?" He smiled, his hand slowly running the length of her arm as he studied the flattering rose color of her cheeks. Of course, she may not know the answer to that. She may be confused about all of this. "Don't you realize I have trouble keeping my hands off you? I should not have started what we did yesterday," he said with a smile of deprecation. "Not that what we were doing was *wrong*, I just don't believe it is *right* for us at this time." Then, seeing Corie frown in confusion, Sean turned sympathetic. "You're so very young, my sweet. And in spite of your apparent worldliness I've come to suspect you are not so very worldly after all."

Thinking fleetingly of his decision to ask his mother to join him in Natchez for the holidays, Sean realized her presence would be a safety measure and that perhaps he should be asking Annie to stay on for a while after Christmas.

"Is that some nonsense Faye planted in your mind?" she asked.

Sean was obviously surprised by the question. "Faye has nothing to do with this."

"You say you want me, Sean, but now you're making excuses. I don't understand that. You're certain you're not making love with Faye?"

"Certain," he said, his frown deepening.

"Not for a while now?"

"No," he said firmly. "You're making this sound as if I'm on trial here."

"I just want to be certain Faye isn't draining you dry, Sean."

There was a bark of laughter, and tears formed in the corners of his eyes before he managed to say, "Perhaps you're more worldly than I realized."

Suspecting she had said something amiss in her attempts to convince him of her *worldliness*, Corie turned a brilliant shade of red.

Seeing her color rise, Sean wrapped both arms around her and held her close. "Forget about Faye, will you? She was a part of a different lifetime; my life before you," he whispered close to her ear.

But his statement only raised another concern in Corie's mind; Sean couldn't be expected to change his life, and yet how would *she* ever fit in it?

Chapter 13

That night, as they decorated the troublesome tree, Sean said he had two important announcements to make. Firstly, his friends Catherine and Stephen Fraser would be joining them for Monday dinner and staying until sometime on Tuesday.

The bottom dropped out of Corie's stomach.

McKenna jumped up and down, gripping the legs of Sean's trousers. "Will it be like a party, Sean?" she cried. "A Christmas party!" she said, excited by the prospect of *friends*. "Will Corie and me have dinner, too?"

Smiling, Sean bent and swept the girl up on one forearm. "Yes. You and Corie shall have dinner, too. It will be a small party. Would you like that?"

"Yes!"

"No!" Corie responded simultaneously.

Two sets of eyes turned Corie's way; McKenna's surprised and Sean's concerned.

"You should have told us sooner," Corie admonished as she feverishly wrapped a red velvet ribbon

153

around a large pine cone. ''How can Mrs. Pringle and I prepare a proper dinner on such short notice?''

Sean set McKenna on her feet and whispered, ''Help Mrs. Pringle with the eggnog, would you, moppet?''

McKenna was always eager to do as Sean asked, but in this instant, she was more eager for her first taste of eggnog. Nodding frantically, she whirled and raced toward the kitchen.

''Mrs. P. has been aware of this dinner tomorrow,'' Sean said as he joined Corie on the settee.

Corie shot him a quick, unhappy frown. ''But you chose not to tell me?'' she asked, setting the ribbon and cone aside in frustration; it looked so easy when Mrs. Pringle decorated.

''For obvious reasons.''

''But you expect me to—''

''I expect you to be yourself and to get to know my best friends. I think you will enjoy them.''

''I can't do that,'' she whispered and jumped to her feet, pacing away before turning to face him. ''You can't do this, Sean. You can't introduce me to your friends. Not if you want them to remain friends.''

''Now, just a minute,'' he said shortly, quickly stepping in front of her. ''What happened to the gutsy young woman who set out to find a better life for her sister? You didn't seem shy or frightened then. And you give my friends little credit.''

Because he actually sounded angry with her, Corie was uncertain how to explain. ''I can't do this,'' she whispered. ''Good Lord, Sean, I don't even know which fork to use!''

''That's not true,'' he said, softening his tone.

''I don't even talk like you!''

"Because your vocabulary isn't as extensive? Who gives a great goddamn?"

"I do!"

Taking a firm hold on her shoulders, he said, "Now, you listen to me . . . There is not a thing wrong with the way you speak. Your voice is sweet and you frequently say the most endearing things. . . ." Stymied, he took a deep breath. "I love the way you talk, Corie. Frankly, I'm not all that pleased that you've been trying to imitate Mrs. P.," he added.

Her frown slowly slipping, Corie could not avoid the light blush that colored her complexion. "You figured that out, did you?"

"I did. And it's not necessary. I like you the way you are, my love. I don't want you to change."

"I can't have supper with your friends," she said quietly. "It's not fair of you to ask me. I'm not ready." And she wasn't secure in his love. Not yet.

"We can't live in a cocoon, my darling," he said softly, taking her hand and leading her back to sit beside him on the settee. Sean took both of her hands in his as he angled his body toward her. "No one can live entirely alone, Corie. Other people are needed in one's life. And I think my friends could easily be your friends. I've told them about you, you see, and they are eager to meet you."

Horrified, Corie's troubled eyes darted to his. "What did you tell them?"

"How determined you are. How wonderful you are. What a caring, loving sister you are. Shall I go on?"

"That is not what I meant!" she snapped.

That *tone* told Sean just how truly frightened she was. "I've explained where you come from and how I became so lucky to have you and McKenna in my life. I've explained what a truly exceptional young woman you are and that you have become very important to me. Catherine and Stephen are very happy for me, Corie. They are genuine people. And I would not have invited them here had I not thought you would enjoy their company.'' Hesitating only briefly, he asked, ''Have you ever had a friend, Corinne? A true, female friend?''

''I can't do this,'' she whispered frantically.

''Then you are not the woman I thought you were.''

Her head snapping up, Corie carefully examined his expression. ''What kind of woman did you think I was?''

''Daring, strong, courageous,'' he said easily. ''One willing to take on the world.''

''But these are *your* friends, Sean.''

Understanding then that she worried more for him than herself, Sean pulled her hard against his chest. ''And I want them to have the joy of knowing you, Corie. I want them to know how very special you are. Just be yourself and Catherine and Stephen are bound to love you. I've waited to do this, you know? I've waited, hoping you would gain enough faith in me to realize that I would never subject you to a hurtful situation.''

What could she say to that?

Corie suddenly felt that running the streets of Natchez Under-the-Hill, scavenging and stealing , was a much less complicated, less frightening way of life.

''Do you think I would ask you to sit down to dinner with people who might make you feel uncomfortable, Corie? Do you think I'm insensitive to how difficult something like this might be the first time around? Catherine is a wonderful woman. She has a terrific sense of humor and is close to your age. You just might find something in Catherine and Stephen that you like. But above all else, just enjoy the evening.''

Corie just could not see herself enjoying the evening when she would be afraid of opening her mouth for fear of offending his best friends. She had watched Mrs. Pringle and tried to mimic her in many ways, but still Corie felt her manner was coarse in comparison to a woman raised in a proper home. In that moment Corinne Alexander lost sight of her strengths and failed to see that she possessed any redeeming qualities that could possibly make Sean proud; she was truly fearful for the first time in her life.

''What's your second announcement?'' she murmured against his shirtfront. She might as well face all the horrors and demons he could dish out in one night.

''My mother is coming from New Orleans to join us for the holidays.''

''Oh, God,'' she groaned.

Monday seemed to be a day of frantic movement for everyone residing in the small house on Pearl Street. Sean took McKenna out from under foot by taking her to his office for a few hours, and then they were to go by Mrs. Steen's home to pick up the two new gowns.

Meanwhile, Corie aided Mrs. Pringle in the dinner preparations. ''The table is set and the parlor is in order,'' she said, joining the older woman in the kitchen. Earlier they had shared the duty of preparing the guest room.

''I've made us a cup of tea,'' Jane said, taking the teapot and a plate of biscuits to the round wooden table in a corner of the room.

Corie retrieved two cups and saucers from the pantry shelf and joined her there. "Do people actually enjoy this?" she asked of her companion. "All this running around and fretting?"

Jane graced her with one of her rare smiles. "One gets used to it. And it is the expected thing . . . to entertain one's friends and associates."

Frowning, Corie confessed, "I'm frightened to death, Mrs. Pringle. Falling in love with Sean was easy, in fact, unexpected. *This* is not easy. If I had only thought what it would mean to care for someone like him . . ."

"He understands," she said, pushing the plate of biscuits toward Corie.

Corie shook her head. "I can't eat."

"Well, you had better," Jane said firmly. "And you had best get over this nonsense of being afraid of meeting people. You're going to embarrass Mr. Garrick if you don't."

It was the first time Jane had spoken in such a tone since the early days of their association, and Corie was taken aback. After a moment, however, she understood the woman's purpose and smiled. "Thank you."

"I'll help you with your hair later if you like," Mrs. P. said, smiling as she lifted her cup.

Jane Pringle displayed considerable skill in the dressing of Corie's hair. The front had a center part and was pulled into ringlets at the sides, while the back was pinned up into a mass of softer curls. The auburn hair glistened with highlights, adorned by a narrow white velvet ribbon.

Corie was then cinched into a corset, which narrowed her waist and accented her slim hips. The gown of winter white was then dropped into place. It was form-fitted and long-waisted, with a full floor-length skirt and elbow-length sleeves, fashionable for evening. But the V-cut, off-the-shoulder bodice caused Corie some concern.

"I'm almost showing my bosoms," she muttered, trying hopelessly to hike the bodice higher.

Jane Pringle forced the top of the gown back into place. "I may be old, but I know how much is decent for a young woman to display. Now, stop that," she said, slapping at Corie's hands.

"I'm not going down there like this," Corie said defiantly.

"Oh, yes, you are."

"I'll embarrass Sean for certain."

"You haven't seen yourself yet," Jane said, straightening the flowing skirt. "You'd rather wear boys' pants and shirts, I suppose?"

"Yes."

"Hmph. Turn around and look in that mirror." Jane physically helped the process, turning Corie by her shoulders. "Now tell me you'd rather wear trousers," she said.

Corie stood, speechless, her eyes roaming from her fashionable hairstyle down the length of the gown and back. Again and again she looked, disbelieving.

"And I'm going to tell you something," Jane Pringle said from behind her. "I used to help the former Mrs. Garrick prepare for evenings like this, God rest her soul, and I never thought I would see her replaced in this house. I might have disagreed with Mr. Garrick bringing you here," she said sternly, "but I've come to realize that you just might make him happy again. I've also discovered that you are a young woman of consequence. Just see that you do not prove me wrong." With that the woman turned and silently left the room.

Corie continued to stare at herself, trying to accept this outward change she was seeing, as Jane Pringle's words echoed through her mind. She didn't think her words had come easy, as the two women seldom displayed their feelings toward each other. It was a revelation to Corie that Jane thought anything of her at all, let alone a young woman of *consequence*. Still, as she looked at herself one last time, Corinne Alexander thought Sean and Jane might just as well ask a fish to walk on dry land as ask her to pretend to be something she was not for this evening.

Forcing herself to leave the haven of her room, Corie moved slowly toward the stairs and gripped the banister on her way down. The sound of Kenny's laughter and Sean's strong deep voice could be heard from the parlor as she walked in that direction, her hands gripped together in front of her.

Sean was seated on one of two settees that formed a conversation area before the fire and Kenny was chattering away, her small face close to his as she leaned on his knees.

It was the whisper of fabric that drew his attention. Sean looked over McKenna's head to stare at the vision standing in the open doorway.

"You must excuse me, sweetheart," he whispered to McKenna. "A gentleman must escort a lady to her chair."

Kenny's head turned toward the door. "Oooh, Corie!" she cried with obvious excitement.

When the child had stepped back, Sean got to his feet and walked slowly across the room, his eyes fixed on her. "Corinne Alexander" was all he said when he stood before her. He reached for her hand then and slowly brought her fingers to his lips as his gaze turned from one of awe to one of pleasure.

Corie was shaken by the intensity with which he studied her. But then all of her trepidation vanished because of him, and she began to take pleasure, for the first time that day, in having set out to please him. Sean was more than satisfied, and the look he sent her said as much. "Do I pass inspection?" she asked with a smile.

"You know damned well you do," he said. She passed inspection, all right, but he doubted she knew how truly beautiful she was. She had gained a few pounds since coming to his home, and her woman's curves were beginning to show a lot of promise. A year or two of maturing and Sean knew she would rival the most beautiful women in Natchez. Hell! In New Orleans as well!

"You look bootiful, Corie!" Kenny said, racing across the room to stand beside them.

Corie was torn, reluctantly, from those precious private moments she silently shared with Sean. The child's excitement over everything . . . Christmas and party gowns and this supper . . . was new for them both. And it was contagious. Corie turned, clapping her hands as she bent toward her sister. "Oh, Kenny. You look so grown-up and so pretty."

"I know," McKenna said with a hint of shyness.

Sean and Corie laughed as the girl's chest swelled with pride once she realized she had their full attention.

McKenna's full-skirted gown was of green velvet, a warm color that set off her natural blush and complemented the red highlights in her brown hair. The dress was trimmed with white lace where the short sleeves fell just below her elbows, and matching lace could be

seen aplenty on her snowy-white pantaloons. White
stockings and slippers matching the green of her gown
completed the girl's party attire.

There was no further time for shared admiration,
however, as Sean stepped around Corie and into the
hall. Corie experienced equal amounts of surprise, at
not having heard the arrival of Sean's friends, and
dismay, that they had actually *arrived* at all.

Sean had heard the distant murmur of voices and
pulled the door open just as Stephen assisted his wife
up the last step. "Hello, you two," Sean said, reaching out and taking Catherine's hand, snatching her
easily from her husband's grasp. "Come in and give
me a kiss, pretty lady," he teased, bending so that the
petite woman could brush his cheek. "And bring that
ugly man of yours along if you must," he added as he
extended his hand to Stephen. "Don't worry about
your horse and rig. I've arranged for a boy from a
neighbor's stables to take them for the night."

Corie and Kenny watched silently from the parlor
doorway as the flurry of greetings and teasing persisted amid the shrugging off of outer garments.

Stephen Fraser was a fraction taller than Sean's
six-foot height but of a slighter build. His hair was
light brown with a shock of white at the right temple,
and his brown eyes were full of laughter. As soon as
Sean had relieved them of their coats, Stephen
dropped down on one knee and assisted his wife in
removing her sturdy shoes.

"Such service," Sean teased, gripping Catherine's
arm to hold her steady.

Catherine grinned while handing a soft, kid slipper
to her husband. "This is why I got pregnant," she
said, her eyes sparkling. "I get all kinds of special
treatment."

Corie's eyes dropped to the woman's stomach, which rounded out her gown substantially.

"I know," Sean returned mockingly. "Otherwise he treats you abominably." He also subjected Catherine to a critical inspection. "Look at you," he said as his free hand lightly stroked her stomach and rested there long enough for him to ask, "You're well, Catherine? You look wonderful."

"I *am* wonderful," she teased. "And I suppose if I were a proper lady, I would blush madly at your handling of me. But I'm too proud."

"I thought the papa was supposed to be proud and boasting," Sean said, aiming his comment at Stephen as he stood up.

"It took so long to get her that way, we're both proud," Stephen said lightly. "Believe me."

Corie was quite surprised that these people would discuss such things openly; she had always assumed that people above the hill were too *stiff* and formal to discuss life's more base subjects.

Sean took Catherine's hand and drew her toward the parlor. "Come meet the newest members of my household," he said.

Stephen scooped up several gaily wrapped parcels he had deposited on a chair in the foyer and followed.

Corie could hear the happiness in Sean's voice, and his eyes, when they looked at her, reflected the same emotion. She steeled herself to make a good impression on these people he obviously cared so much about and smiled as they approached.

Sean made the introduction and Corie was surprised to see a warm and genuine smile light up the other woman's face as they shook hands.

"I'm so pleased to meet you," Catherine said.

"You're one of the reasons my friend here has been so much happier lately."

"And this is McKenna," Sean said with enough pride that one would think he was the child's natural father.

Catherine's eyes dropped to the child, and her eyes took on a magic kind of glow. "Oh, Sean. Little wonder you've changed." She bent and took Kenny's hand in much the same fashion as she had held Corie's. "Hello, McKenna. What a pretty little girl you are."

Kenny suddenly turned a bit shy and a forefinger went straight to her mouth as she leaned toward her sister's skirts.

Corie had never seen Kenny like this and placed a hand on her shoulder. "Say hello, Kenny," she ordered softly.

"You're pretty, too," the child blurted.

Catherine laughed lightly and straightened. "Thank you, darling."

But Kenny's concentration had already been diverted. "That man has a bunch of presents, Corie," she said.

"*That* man is Stephen," Sean said, taking the child's hand. "Say hello to Stephen."

Kenny nodded several times and smiled up at the man. And the presents.

Stephen took time to say a few words of greeting to Corie and then turned his attention to the youngest member of the group. "Do you have a Christmas tree, McKenna? Could you help me with these, do you think?"

"I'll show you!" she cried and darted into the parlor.

"The perfect excuse," Sean murmured, taking both

women by an elbow. "Let's make ourselves comfortable."

Kenny was on her knees, placing each parcel very carefully, as Sean led Catherine and Corie to a settee where they could watch the girl and enjoy her excitement.

"Sean explained that this is really McKenna's first Christmas," Catherine said easily.

Corie looked at the woman but sensed no hint of derision. It appeared Catherine Fraser was accepting Kenny and Corie as a part of Sean's life. "She's so excited about it all, it's not easy getting her to settle down at night."

Catherine reached across the small distance between them and briefly covered Corie's folded hands. "You're going to have such fun," she said. "Having a child in the house makes Christmas very special. Oh, hello, Mrs. Pringle," she added as the housekeeper entered and placed a tray on a table.

Jane Pringle greeted the two guests, inquired after their health, and then returned to the kitchen.

Watching the woman go, Corie felt a healthy twinge of guilt; she should be out there helping.

Sean ladled mulled wine into four china mugs before joining Stephen on the settee across from the women.

McKenna, looking a bit lost as to where she belonged, took a hesitant step toward him. Sean reached out a hand and, when she was near, pulled the girl onto his lap.

Separate conversations seemed to develop between the ladies and the men then, with Kenny content to lean back against Sean and listen to the words that seemed to rumble from deep within his chest.

Catherine's eyes continued to stray in the child's

direction frequently during the evening, and Corie
sensed that this woman would be a loving mother who
would give her child her full attention. That was
something Corie felt instinctively, for she had never
witnessed any real relationship between a mother and
her child. But then, she supposed she and Kenny had
developed a similar kind of relationship.

"Would you like a little girl?" she asked Catherine,
seeing the woman's eyes straying in Kenny's direction.

The men were seated at the dining room table,
enjoying after-dinner brandy and cigars and Kenny
was hovering near Sean's chair.

Catherine smiled and nodded. "To be truthful, I
would like several of each. McKenna truly loves Sean,
doesn't she?"

Corie's eyes turned briefly toward the dining room
before she spoke. "Yes, she does," she said quietly.

"Does that bother you?" Catherine asked. "She's
your sister and I understand you raised her on your
own. I would think it would be difficult . . . I
mean . . ." She stopped and laughed briefly at herself. "I don't know what I mean. Forgive me. The
question wasn't meant to be an intrusion."

"There is nothing to forgive," Corie returned with
a small shrug of the shoulders. "I'm happy Kenny has
Sean. I think she needed him."

Catherine took a sip of tea and returned the cup to
the table between the settees. "It's mutual, then," she
said. "Sean needed her, too." And then she eyed
Corie speculatively before she said hesitantly, "In
fact, I believe he needs you both."

Corie's body visibly started and a telltale blush
crept up from her neck. "I'm here only to help with
Kenny, " she blurted.

Catherine giggled and reached for Corie's hand. "Don't blush so. He's watching you."

Of course that made things worse; Corie's complexion was almost purple in hue by now.

"I think it's wonderful," Catherine chirped. "You look at him just the way I used to look at Stephen before we were married."

"I do?"

"Of course you do. Sean's a little more cautious in how he looks at you, but he's not fooling anyone."

Corie reached for her tea and then thought better of it, sitting back with obvious defeat. "Lord, if we're so . . . we aren't . . ." She closed her eyes then and said frantically, "My God, his mother is coming here."

Catherine really seemed to enjoy that bit of news. "Annie? That's wonderful!"

Corie's eyes snapped open. "Wonderful? But if *you* think there is something between Sean and me, she will—"

"Love it!" Catherine crowed softly. "Annie has been secretly praying Sean would find someone. She's very cautious in how she speaks to him about it, mind you. Annie's no fool. She doesn't believe in pushing her son. And Sean would retaliate in any case. He can be very contrary you know."

Corie was trying desperately to get her thoughts back in order; panic had set in over this conversation. "I believe you're making something out of nothing," she ventured.

"Pooh!" Catherine said. "Don't fence with me, Corie. We're going to be great friends, I think, and friends don't *fence*."

Corie seemed to wilt a bit, and her next words were very softly spoken. "You must know about my past,

Catherine," she said with resignation. "When his mother finds out how I lived, she won't be so happy about her son having anything to do with the likes of me."

"I don't care where you came from or how you lived and neither will Annie," Catherine said sternly. "I'm only concerned with the person you are and the way you are with Sean. Sean is important to Stephen and me, and he's been happier these past few months than he's been in years. Obviously that happiness is due to you and McKenna, and for that you earn our admiration and friendship. And Annie will feel the same, or I don't know her at all."

"But—"

"And if you hurt Sean, Annie and I will vie for the chance to scratch your eyes out."

There was a momentary strained silence as Corie stared at the woman, aghast. And then when Catherine laughed, she laughed. "I'll remember that."

Sean was watching the scene between the women from his vantage point in the dining room while he pretended to be engrossed in conversation with Stephen. He was pleased that the two women appeared to be hitting it off, for in his heart he wanted Corie to experience the many pleasures of friendship. And Catherine would make a sincere and devoted friend indeed.

"If you're so intent upon our beauties in there," Stephen said softly, "why don't we join them?"

"She is beautiful, isn't she?"

Stephen laughed lightly, his eyes following McKenna as she skipped toward the parlor. "I think you're caught, my friend."

Sean's eyes turned toward his friend. "I think I am, too."

"Well, what are you planning to do about it?"

"Nothing for a while. She's very different from Marie, you see. And . . . Corinne hasn't really found her niche as yet. I'm not convinced she's comfortable here, and I'm not about to declare myself and have her decide life would be too difficult or too complicated with me."

"In other words, you're afraid of scaring her off," Stephen said lightly. "I'm surprised at you, Sean. You're usually more surefooted than that."

Smiling ruefully, Sean picked up his drink and swirled the amber liquid around the base of the snifter. "It's been a long time since I've courted a woman, Stephen. You'll have to forgive my lapses."

After a thoughtful moment Stephen said, "I'll forgive you anything if you're shed of Faye."

Surprised by his friend's caustic tone, Sean frowned. "You understood my association with Faye."

"You could bed down with any woman of your choice, Sean. I never understood why Faye had to be the one."

"She's a beautiful woman," Sean answered cautiously.

"And hot? Is that it? She's also a shrew," Stephen added pointedly.

"Well, it's over. It matters little now," he said, draining the last bit of brandy from his glass.

"Just keep her away from Corinne."

"Why would you say such a thing?"

"I can't see Faye letting you go so easily," Stephen said with equal caution. And after a moment's painful thought, he added quietly, "There's some talk that you've moved a whore from Under-the-Hill into your home. Who might start such a vicious rumor?"

Angrily, Sean shot back, "She's a virgin, for chrissake! Tell them that!"

Three pairs of female eyes turned toward the dining room.

"Easy, man," Stephen said.

"I *hate* that," Sean said, scraping his chair back and walking toward the women.

Catherine cleared her throat and got to her feet. "Perhaps McKenna could open the small gift we brought before she goes to bed?" She looked first at Corie and then Sean, who nodded abruptly. "Wonderful! Would you like to open a present, darling?" she said, steering the child toward the tree. Anything to break the sudden tension in the room. "You bring that one out, McKenna. That's from Stephen and me."

Kenny needed no coaxing and was on her knees before Stephen could walk to his wife's side.

Sean dropped down beside Corie and stared angrily toward the three, seeing nothing.

"What's wrong?" Corie asked softly.

After several awkward seconds Sean turned his head and frowned at her.

"What is it?" she asked again.

"Come here," he whispered and placed an arm around her shoulders, easily drawing her close to his side.

"Sean. Not here," she whispered in return, her eyes darting toward his friends. But Catherine and Stephen seemed engrossed in watching Kenny.

"This is *my* house. Don't tell me *not here*."

"Sean, your friends . . ."

"Understand completely, Corie," he said, ducking his head close to her ear. "Do you?"

"I don't know what you're talking about," she

said, pushing against his chest. "Why are you so angry? Why are you behaving like this in front of them?"

He was forced to let her go or make a scene. And he didn't want that. "I'm sorry," he said, his head dropping back, his eyes closing. "I am angry but not at you. I think my noble intentions are getting the better of me."

Frowning, Corie asked, "What does that mean?"

Smiling ruefully, Sean lifted his head and leaned toward her. "It means I want you so badly, I'm becoming a frightful boar, my sweet."

Corie drew in a sharp breath before taking him to task. "How can you dare say such a thing here and now?" she rasped.

"Because I want you here and now," he teased.

"Sean!" she hissed softly.

"You don't really understand what it's all about, do you, Corinne? You guess what happens behind your mother's closed door, and that is all the knowledge you have."

"I think you've had too much to drink."

"Or not enough," he returned lightly and tore his attention away from her before he really did something boarish. "Let's see what you have there, McKenna!" he called.

Left in a puzzled semidaze, Corie wasn't certain whether she should be thankful for Kenny, in that moment, or curse her as the diversion responsible for her older sister being left in the dark.

Chapter 14

"Well, what do you think?" Catherine asked as her husband released the tiny buttons down the back of her gown.

"I think your shoulders should be declared a national shrine," he murmured, his lips grazing her soft skin.

Catherine laughed and turned to face him. "I mean about Corinne?"

"I think she's very pretty and scared to death of Sean," he said, dropping a quick kiss on the tip of her nose before he moved toward a corner of the guest room and the wardrobe there.

"No, I don't think it's Sean that's frightening her," Catherine said thoughtfully as she stepped out of her red velvet gown. "I think she's afraid of herself. I think she loves him and doesn't know what to do about it."

"Now, there's a hoot," Stephen proclaimed, discarding his shirt. "Show me a woman who doesn't

173

know what to do with a man, and I'll show you a babe in diapers.''

"You're jaded," Catherine huffed. "As I recall, I didn't know what to do with you.''

Grinning, Stephen dropped his trousers. "Aw, but you were a quick study, my love.''

"You are also a lecher," she said as she crawled naked beneath the quilts. "How are we going to help Corinne?''

It was Stephen's turn to frown. Seriously. "*We* are not going to do anything. You're planning some kind of interference between those two?''

"I never interfere!''

"Catherine," he warned.

"Well, Corinne needs a friend.''

"Then be her friend and let her find her own way,'' he said, settling down beside her in the wide bed.

"I'm cold," she said with a feigned pout.

Stephen laughed and pulled her close. "Then get over here.''

"Do you think they're lovers?" she whispered as she settled her head on his shoulder.

"No.''

"How can you be so certain?''

"Because Sean told me Corinne is a virgin.''

Catherine thought about that a moment and then giggled against her husband's chest. "*That's* why he was so bad-tempered tonight.''

The small house on Pearl Street was well constructed by any standards, but, still, Corie could hear the soft murmurings of the couple in the guest room through the adjoining wall. She lay in her solitary bed wondering what husband and wife talked about in the night and how it would feel to have a warm, strong body lying next to her own. She could barely hear Catherine's giggle, but the sound brought a smile to her own lips. It must be very special, whatever they were saying in there.

And then it occurred to her that they might be doing more than talking. Would *that* bring forth giggles? she wondered. It seemed to her that what men and women did in bed was quick and serious. Certainly she never heard her mother giggle in all the years she had waited on the outside of the closed door.

Somehow, Sean had known. He had known that she only guessed what went on in her mother's room. She had heard a few vulgar remarks about men from other prostitutes, but Corie had chosen to ignore such rudeness. And one's imagination could be a hindrance when there were no examples of loving couples about when a girl was growing up.

Strangely, Catherine's and Stephen's apparent acceptance of her in Sean's life had emboldened Corie. She understood clearly that she loved him. But she maintained some doubts about *his* love for her. She worried that the attraction between them might be a fleeting thing and not the one true love she hoped to find and hold on to until the end of her days. She believed that Sean wanted her, but Corie was wise enough and astute enough to understand that his desire might stem purely from the need of a woman; after all, as far as she could tell, he had been a long time without one. If there was one thing her mother had taught her, it was that men had *needs*. And if that were the case with Sean, then Corie could be on the verge of repeating her own mother's historical failure.

She heard the distant rumble of Stephen's voice, followed by another giggle from Catherine.

Bunching the quilt and pressing it into her stomach,

Corie wallowed in indecision before leaping silently
from her bed and crossing the room to the door. If she
was about to make a mistake, it was hers alone to
make. If this thing between herself and Sean did not
last, then she would have whatever he felt he could
offer and take that away in her heart. Her decision was
made.

Moving stealthily across the hall, she entered Kenny's room to be certain the girl was asleep. She was,
but with the quilts flung aside. Bending over the bed,
Corie smiled as she drew the blankets up over the
small form of her sister and the soft, stuffed lamb
Kenny clutched against her chest. The lamb was the
gift Catherine had brought, and Corie doubted that
Kenny would ever sleep again without it.

Straightening and continuing to stare, Corie hesitated only long enough to wonder if what she was
about to do could in any way harm this perfect world
in which Kenny now found herself. But in the next
breath she knew it could not; Sean loved McKenna so
much that nothing could happen that would make him
love the little girl less.

Creeping to the hallway, Corie eased the door to
Kenny's room closed and walked softly toward the
master bedroom near the front of the house. When
confronted with the closed door, she hesitated not one
second, but silently opened the thing and stepped
inside the room, sealing Sean and herself from the rest
of the household.

Sean had been in a state of semisleep but became
instantly alert when he heard the soft sounds of her
entrance. For a few seconds he felt he must be
dreaming. But then the tall, slim creature in white
moved toward his bed. "Corie?" he asked softly. "Is
something wrong?"

"You know there's nothing wrong," she said and took another step.

"I'm not certain it's wise for you to be here," he said, but there was little conviction in his tone.

"I'm certain," she said and stopped beside his bed. "You'll have to turn me away, Sean. If that's what you want."

Sean sat up and ran his fingers through his thick hair. "It's not a matter of what I want, my pet," he said, his eyes taking in the pristine white flannel nightdress. "It's a matter of—"

"I know," she interrupted, "of being noble." Her head tipped to the side, she asked curiously, "Will it change me so much, Sean?"

"No," he said, reaching for her hand but intending to touch only her hand. "But it will change things between us."

"For the better?"

Not certain how to answer, Sean's thumb raked across the knuckles of her hand in a nervous gesture that surprised her. "Usually it brings couples closer."

"But not always?"

Smiling ruefully, he said softly, "Not always, but most times I imagine."

"Then you should stop being noble, Sean, unless you don't want to be closer to me. And if that is the case, I would appreciate your telling me now, before I go completely crazy."

There was a soft, masculine chuckle before the bedside lamp was raised to a dim glow. "Sit," he ordered, patting the bed beside his hip and tugging on her hand. "Tell me what has you crazed."

Corie made herself comfortable and stared at him earnestly. "I think it's you. And maybe Catherine and Stephen," she added after a brief pause.

"Catherine and Stephen?" he asked in wonder. "What do they have to do with this?"

"Do people talk and giggle when they make love?"

Sean's eyes lit up with obvious delight; he did *love* her for the simple, forthright girl she was. "I suppose they do sometimes, darling."

"Catherine seems to be giggling quite a bit tonight."

Sean frowned thoughtfully. He did not want some outside influence driving her to him. If she had heard love sounds, it might have driven her to appease her natural curiosity. "Is that what brought you here, Corie?"

"No," she said, shaking her head as her eyes dropped to her hands in her lap. "I need to be with you. I think I've needed that for quite a while now."

Sean gently raised her head and stared into her eyes, searching. "Why do you think that, love?"

"Because you're on my mind all the time. Even when I should be thinking of other things. I keep watching you and wondering what it would be like to lie beside you at night and be warmed by you." And finally she admitted her most treasured thoughts. "I keep wondering what it would be like to have you touch me and make love to me. And every time you kiss me and move away you leave me feeling as if I've lost something precious. I know if you don't do something soon, I really will be crazy."

Drawing in a deep breath, Sean let it out slowly. He wanted her, of course. He'd wanted her forever, it seemed, and having her here beneath his own roof had become a kind of torture. Corie had come so far, yet there was a nagging doubt in his mind that she would be content to adopt his quiet lifestyle. That she could be happy as the wife of a middle-class businessman.

Still, there was hope in his heart that her feelings for him ran deeper than anything she had admitted and, if that were the case, then perhaps all she needed was to confirm to herself what was in her heart. "There'll be no turning back, Corie. Once it's done there's no turning back."

"I don't want to turn back, Sean."

Shifting in the bed, he held the blankets high. "You're shivering with cold. Climb in here."

"I don't think I'm cold," she said baldly.

He laughed lightly, turning on his side to face her. "I suppose there are other things that could make a body shiver."

Corie stared up at him, her expression deadly serious. "What?"

"Exhaustion. Fear. Anticipation. All of those." He touched her cheek and then ran his fingers toward her temple. "Are you exhausted? Do you fear?"

"Neither."

"Anticipation," he whispered, his lips moving slowly toward hers. "It will heighten the experience, Corie. Savor it."

Corie had tasted his lips before, of course, but never had he seemed to coax her into returning the gesture. His was normally the kiss of sampling and teasing, but it wasn't long before he kissed her in earnest. His tongue outlined her lips before gently parting them and daring to cautiously intrude. She was startled by this strange experience but soon found the merit in what he was doing to her and sought more.

And Sean was pleased that she seemed not to shy away but was desirous of being a willing participant. She needed only patience and teaching. But patience, for his own part, was going to be difficult to master. He had been long without a woman and long in wanting this one. The instant he had pressed against her side, his body had surged to life.

His fingers trailed across her shoulder until he felt the first swell of her breast. "I want to see you," he said, reaching down for the hem of her gown. "Let's be rid of this."

Corie raised her hips to aid him as he drew the gown upward. And then she frantically tugged at the ribbon to free the bodice of the gown. She felt the coolness of the night air against her skin in the next instant and opened her eyes to see Sean staring over every inch of her. Her nipples had puckered into tight peaks, causing her some embarrassment until Sean covered one breast with the palm of his hand.

"I've wondered, you know," he said. "I've wanted to touch you here."

"They're small," she said bluntly.

Grinning, he traced her breast with the tips of his fingers. "They're perfect. And beautiful."

"They are small," she said again as his head dipped toward her.

Sean took one peaked nipple between his lips and toyed with her until Corie could not suppress a soft moan. "Beautiful and sensitive," he said, moving to the other breast. "Perfect."

Corie quickly became lost in all the new sensations he was arousing within her. She felt her heart begin to race while her breathing become labored, and she wondered if she might die before she managed to give him all she hoped she could give. She wanted to please him, to give him whatever pleasure this loving would bring for him. She wanted, selflessly, to give him the world.

Sean moved quickly from the player in control to being controlled. He had bided his time and now time seemed to work against him as he sought to prolong this, their first encounter. But she was too precious, too soft and beautiful, and she fit too well against him. His hands frantically roamed her body, coaxing her into the same frenzy that eventually drove him to hover between her knees. He had wondered if he should warn her, if she understood that he might hurt her. And then there was no time for thought. He eased into her until he felt resistance, and then he stopped, stretching over her and cupping her face between loving hands. "I love you, Corie," he said, his lips lowering to her cheek as his lower body drew back and plunged forward quickly.

"Oh!" she cried softly as her head came up hard against his shoulder.

"I'm sorry, darling," he said. "That's all, I swear." But causing her pain had jolted his senses. Sean found a new reserve of strength because he did not want to hurt her further and because he wanted this to be the ultimate experience for her. "Just lie still for a moment," he whispered.

The pain had been fleeting, and Corie did not want his concern over her to ruin his ultimate pleasure. Shaking her head to deny his last words, she said, "It doesn't matter."

"It does," he breathed. "Just wait a moment and you'll be used to me. And then we begin again."

Again?

Soon she understood what he meant as Sean moved tentatively within her, watching her face closely for any sign that he was hurting. But pain was the farthest thing from Corie's mind as his movements built a growing tension in her body. And then she was rocked by something so totally unexpected, her body stiffened before a series of tremors had her calling his name and clasping him to her.

"Corie," he cried softly before burying himself and withdrawing, only to return quickly, pressing against her as his body began to shudder and rock.

Corie felt him draining into her. She wondered briefly what it all meant before a glowing warmth washed over her body and she drifted back heavily onto the pillow even while her fingers and palms pressed firmly against his back.

Sean's cheek was pressed against hers while he breathed deeply, waiting for enough strength to move away from her. He raised his head and smiled at the peaceful look of his angel before he kissed one closed eye and then the tip of her nose. "You're all right, Corie?" he questioned softly.

The corners of Corie's mouth tipped upward as her chin slowly dipped down in what he had to interpret as a nod.

Sean felt more pleasure in that moment, knowing she was languorously content, than with anything he had experienced for years. He kissed her briefly as he slipped from her and then stiffened his arms in an attempt to move to her side.

Corie knew instinctively that he was about to move away and tightened her hold. "Don't go," she said, her eyes popping open.

The palm of Sean's hand touched her cheek as he smiled. "I'm heavy for you, Corie. It's time for me to move."

"But I like the feel of you."

"You'll like me better if you can snuggle close, my sweet," he said and tipped onto his side, holding her against him. "How's that?" he asked, wrapping his arms securely around her.

Corie buried her face against his shoulder and smiled. "The exercise has made your heart race," she said softly.

"The exercise?" He chuckled. "I hadn't thought of it as *exercise*."

There was a momentary silence before Corie asked, "What happened to me, Sean?"

Sean's lips pressed against her temple before he spoke. "It's called by many names. Climax is the most usual, I suppose."

"Can we do it again?"

With a grin of delight Sean's head pressed back into the pillow. "We *can*. In time."

Corie raised her head then, moving up over his chest as she stared into his eyes. "How long is that?"

"With you," he said lightly, his palm playfully slapping her buttock, "probably not long."

But Corie's thoughts had already been distracted as her eyes followed the movement of her hand across his chest. "Your body is different from mine," she murmured.

He laughed. "Thank God for that."

"I mean here," she said as her skin color heightened at his suggestive tone. His chest was firm, where hers was soft, and he was covered by a mat of dark hair that was somehow exciting as she looked at him and touched him.

Sean cradled the back of his head with one hand while the fingertips of his other hand lightly roamed the length of her back. He lay quietly, his eyes following hers as she discovered the many differences between them. She was boldly curious, showing none of the feigned embarrassment or coy shyness he had seen in other women, and he liked that in her. In some ways she was like a wondering child when she discovered something new; to Corie it was all a part of learning. The difficulty was that her voyage of discovery, with her unschooled, innocent caresses, was making it very difficult for Sean to lie still as his body took over from his mind's good intentions.

Corie loved the look and feel of him, and she suddenly felt she would never get enough of being close with him like this. There was something magnetizing about him that made her want to be closer to him than holding him would satisfy. She had never been so close to another living being, and she felt she had already formed an addiction for this particular human.

Her hands roamed freely as she learned every muscular part of him. Her lips and tongue toyed briefly with his nipple, much in the same fashion as he had toyed with hers, just to gauge his reaction and for the experience of teasing him. Playing with him, Corie soon felt an urgency beginning to grow within her. But when she would have touched that most male part of him, Sean's hand captured her wrist just short of her mark.

"Are you hurting, Corie?" he rasped when her eyes moved to his.

Slowly she shook her head.

"Do you realize what you have done, sweet one?" he asked, marveling at how easily she had brought him to arousal.

Corie suddenly found herself on her back, her heartbeat quickening.

"Oh, God," he breathed against her neck. "I need you, Corie."

Corie briefly closed her eyes and took those words deep within to forever hold them there. No one, no one in her entire lifetime, had ever said he *needed* her. And while she rejoiced in feeling needed, she discovered needs of her own. "I don't think I'll ever get enough of loving you," she said. And when he raised his head, she ran her fingers through his thick, black hair. "I want to see it happen to you," she whispered, as if unsure of whether she should suggest such a thing.

Every muscle in Sean's body instantly tensed as he moved over her. Her innocent expression of *giving* swelled within his chest. He took her hand and cautiously schooled her. "Guide me," he said, his voice a husky whisper.

Corie followed his instructions and then pressed her head deeply into her pillow, closing her eyes as she savored his slow possession of her. So slowly. And then he rested deep within her. She waited only a moment before realizing something was different; he wasn't moving as he had before. When she opened her eyes, he was smiling.

"I want you to move your hips," he said, his breathing strained as his hands began to guide her into gentle circular motions.

Confused, Corie frowned, her brows arching together as she tried to find the meaning behind this strange behavior. But his purpose quickly became clear. She had once seen a tiny spark erupt into a dancing flame that quickly consumed an entire block of buildings. A similar tiny spark was quickly born where his body joined hers.

Feeling her tighten around him, Sean buried his face against her hair and pressed his lower body high against her. "Now!" he breathed and held her as her body convulsed against him.

After a moment Corie sighed wearily and pressed her lips against his ear. "I wanted that for you," she said and felt his arms tighten momentarily.

"Never fear, you're giving it," he said with difficulty as he began to move within her again.

Corie could actually feel the heightening tension in
his shoulders as his strokes become short and quick,
and then his body was stiffening beneath her hands as
his head arched back. It was the most beautiful sight
she thought she had ever witnessed.

When he was able to move, Sean reluctantly rolled
to his side and tucked her under his arm as he stared
up at the ceiling. "I think I should have chosen an
older woman," he muttered. "One who has an energy
level more equivalent to mine."

Corie's head popped up from his shoulder, and she
frowned down at him. "Exactly what does that
mean?"

"It means, *exactly*, that I don't think I can keep up
with you."

Her frown turning to a slow, mischievous smile,
Corie settled her head on him again. "I'll help you.
Keep up, I mean."

Sean laughed lightly. "You've done a fine job so
far."

Corie giggled and buried her fingers into the hair on
his chest.

After a moment she asked, "Sean, do you think I'm
like my mother?"

Taken aback by the question, Sean's eyes dropped
to the top of her head. "I do not," he said adamantly.
"What would make you ask such a thing?"

Corie tipped her head back then, and her troubled
eyes connected with his. "Because I like this."

"Loving?" he asked and, when she nodded, posed
a question of his own. "Do you think what your
mother does is *loving*? Do you think you would feel
the same with many men as you feel with me?"

Corie did not even have to think about that. "No."

"It's not wrong for you to enjoy what we've done tonight, Corie. This is very special between us, and don't you ever doubt it."

Hearing a hint of harshness in his tone, Corie said, "I didn't mean to anger you, Sean. I didn't know if I should . . ." Not certain how to continue, Corie chose not to look at him and dropped her head down to his shoulder again.

"Should what?" he prompted.

"Well, would a real *lady* like to do what we've done?"

Forced to study the crown of her head once more, Sean smiled in sympathy with her thoughtful struggle. "You're a real *woman*, my pet. And real women are comfortable with liking what we've done."

"Truly?"

"Truly."

"That doesn't make me a lady," she said thoughtfully.

"There are varying definitions for the term *lady*, Corie, and not all of them flattering nor desirable to a man. You're a gracious lady by *my* definition and a good person and a good woman. I want you to be confident in that."

"Is that what you love about me?" she ventured boldly.

Sean laughed. "Am I so easily read?" he asked, grasping a handful of her hair and gently forcing her head up.

Happy that he had not denied loving her, Corie said lightly, "You're not easily read at all. I was fishing."

"Well, I'm caught," he teased, pulling her up on his chest. "And how am I to get a confession from you?"

"I haven't heard your confession yet."

"You're a cheeky little thing," he muttered, his forefinger tracing her lips as he said thoughtfully, "But it's true. I do love you."

His softly spoken words seemed so sincere they brought tears to Corie's eyes.

"What's this?" he asked, frowning when he saw a fat drop of moisture poise on her lash. "My loving you is supposed to make you happy," he added with obvious concern.

"It does," she cried, her tears flowing freely. "No one has ever said that to me before."

"Oh, Corie," he breathed, his arms wrapping tightly around her as a painful knot rose up from his chest to his throat. "I promise to tell you I love you every minute of every day."

Embarrassed by her own weakness, Corie tried to laugh at that, but all she managed was something between a hiccup and a croak. "Don't you think you'll grow tired of saying it?"

"Will you grow tired of hearing it, my darling?"

"No."

"Are you done with your happy tears?" he asked after a moment. "Are you feeling better?"

Corie nodded and wiped at her cheeks with her fingertips.

"Then I think you should sleep. But sleep knowing that I love you, Corie," he said softly.

He thought she might have been asleep before he had even wrapped the quilts securely around her shoulders, so still was she. But sleep did not come quickly to Sean. He was warm of spirit and content of thought as he simply relaxed and enjoyed this new experience of holding her and having her in his bed. It was true: He loved her and had known he loved her long before he had found the courage to say the words. He was indeed a happy man as he realized he would marry her and grow old with her. And, acknowledging that he had spilled his seed within her twice this night, he would marry her with little time lost. Besides, now that he had her in his bed, he wanted her there with him every night and with no thoughts or fears about discovery. He did not want to have to return her to her room before the rest of the household arose of a morning, as he would have to do before dawn of this new day. Nothing, nor no one, would tarnish his Corie's reputation before the eyes of the world; at least no more than had already been achieved by some dim-witted gossips. He would see to that.

Before he drifted into sleep, Sean determined that he would ask Corie to marry him the very next evening, when they could be alone.

Chapter 15

Corie was genuinely sorry when Catherine and Stephen said goodbye before noon of the following day. She understood that Catherine's parents would be arriving from the East any day, and the young couple had much to do by way of preparation for extended family visits, but she also greatly enjoyed their company.

It was not until after the house had quieted and Sean had departed to his office for a few hours that Corie began to think over her new role in Sean's life. She was his lover now. Not his whore, but his lover; she firmly believed that. And he had been right when he said it would alter things between them. She'd been shy upon greeting him in the dining room for breakfast. Particularly with others present. And this shyness puzzled her when she had not been shy with him at all while they had played in his bed.

She had also been puzzled about waking in her own bed and how he had managed to get her there without disturbing her sleep. But that question would have to wait until they had a private moment.

She had been shy about facing the Frasers, and even Kenny, fearing she must look different this morning; she certainly *felt* different. A wonderful difference. She felt loved and warm and protected, and her complexion must surely have given their game away when she had bent to pour Sean a second cup of coffee at the breakfast table and he had whispered, "I love you."

The fleeting look she had shared with Catherine told Corie the other woman understood what was happening between them. Catherine had smiled happily.

There was much Corie understood now about relationships between men and women and, in fleeting moments of doubt, much she did not. She understood that no matter what happened between Sean and herself, she had been right to go to him last night. It had been right for her and right for him. What had happened between them would be burned into her memory, and the emotions he had stirred would move within her forever. If ever there came a time that she had to be without him, she would remember what he had given her.

Throughout the afternoon, as Corie's mind mulled over everything except the tasks she completed one by one, she came to understand that she was not at all like her mother. She would never take what she had shared with Sean and try to share that with another man or, worse, turn it into something sordid for money. She thought that Constance could not have possibly loved her father, or held any of their personal memories dear, and do what she had done for so many years.

That mode of thinking only served to pose other

questions that plagued Corie while she worked until, eventually, she set aside her polishing cloth and tipped her head around the kitchen door.

Kenny was busy helping Jane Pringle make Christmas cookies, although, from the rim of chocolate around the child's mouth, it appeared that more were disappearing than were being placed inside the cookie tins.

"I'm going out for just a few minutes," she said to the woman before admonishing her sister. "Don't you ruin your supper by eating too many of those."

"Can I come, too?" Kenny asked, scrambling down from her chair.

"Not this time, baby. But I won't be long."

"Where are you going?" the girl asked, following Corie toward the front door.

"None of your business."

"Why not?"

"Why? Where? Can I?" Corie sighed. "You ask too many questions. Go back to your cookies."

"You're mean." She pouted.

Smiling, Corie bent and kissed the velvety cheek. "I know. Sean will be home soon. You can ask some questions of him."

"He'll ask me where you are," Kenny said sagely.

"No, he won't."

"Yep. He always does."

For some reason those simple words made Corie feel warm inside. "Does he, Kenny?"

"Yep. I think he likes you, Corie."

"Do you really think so?"

She giggled. "*You* ask a lot of questions."

Corie stared thoughtfully at the small girl for several moments, and then she asked, "How would you feel if I liked Sean, Kenny?"

"Well, I like him, too."

"I know, baby," she said, squatting down and taking one small hand into hers. "But I mean if I had a grown-up liking for him."

Kenny's small nose wrinkled in thought. Not having a lot of experience with *grown-up liking*, she could only come to one conclusion. "You mean like mama, Corie?"

"No," she said quickly, her eyes darting toward the closed kitchen door. "Different from that. I mean if I loved Sean."

Kenny began to look truly worried then. "Does that mean I have to find someplace else to live?"

"No, Kenny," Corie said with concern. "Why would you think that?"

"Because we had to go someplace else when mama—"

"No!" she whispered frantically. Not you, too, she thought. "There is a *big* difference, Kenny. I've learned that and so must you. You and Sean and I can all love each other and all live together and be happy here. It's different, Kenny, I promise you."

"Are you sure?" she asked in a small voice.

Corie pulled her sister into her arms. "I'm sure, baby. I'll love you just like I always have, but I've learned that I love Sean, too."

"Will Sean still love me?"

"Yes. Yes, baby."

There was a prolonged silence in which Corie held her breath, wondering if such a little girl could possibly understand such big things.

"All right," Kenny whispered at last. "I guess you can love him, too."

As Corie walked quickly along Broadway toward Silver Street and the hill that led down to the Mississippi River, she worried that perhaps she should not have spoken to Kenny. But Kenny was a perceptive little girl, and Corie was afraid her sister would sense something different between Sean and herself. It was better that Kenny understand that the change would not affect her own existence. Now Corie worried, however, that she had not explained the situation clearly enough for a five-year-old child to comprehend. The girl must be made to understand that there was a big difference between what her mother did and what her sister was doing. Corie wondered if Sean might be better at explaining.

It had been two weeks since Corie had hurried along the streets of Natchez Under-the-Hill. Sometimes Sean made it difficult for her to slip away without him knowing where she was going. Not that her mother appreciated the visits, but Corie found she had been unable to stay away. She would bring an offering of food: bread and fruit and sometimes a treat of something sweet. The food went untouched, she suspected, but it was something she had to do.

As she climbed the stairs to the room above Tim's Place, Corie braced herself for the world beyond that wooden door at the top of the landing. It was somehow more and more difficult to come back here and see how her mother lived. And it made her feel guilty each time she stepped into Constance's room because she understood she was growing away from this place more day by day and because she and Kenny were now living so well. Realistic to a fault, however, she knew that nothing could be done for her mother, and in fact, she had begun to wonder lately if Constance would actually live much longer. The woman's abuse of body and soul had just gone on for too long. It was a fact that Constance did not even leave her room anymore; there was little use in walking the streets when new customers showed no interest. Only old and regular customers still came. Old and regular drunks. Constance's counterparts.

Corie opened the door, took a single step into the room, and immediately stepped back. She wondered that the odors in this room had never seemed to bother her until she had lived in the small clean house on Pearl Street. The room was dark, as usual, so she left the door ajar as she picked her way across to the rumpled bed.

"Mama?" she said softly. "Mama," she called again when there was no response from the folded lump on the bed.

"What?" the lump croaked, startled at the intrusion once Corie's voice had penetrated her rum-soaked senses. "What do you want?"

Corie watched her mother laboriously stretch and turn toward the open door and the light there. "It's me. Corie."

"I know who you are," Constance rasped, her voice sounding as if she had swallowed sand. "Only a brat would wake me at this hour."

This hour? Corie knew her mother did not know the hour, nor would she care. She'd care only that she had managed to sleep for a time and that sleep had been interrupted.

"I've brought you some food," Corie said quietly as her mother struggled to sit on the side of the bed.

"Make me some tea," Constance ordered and then waved away the apple that Corie held out to her. "Take that damned thing away and make me some tea."

There was no tea, of course. *Tea* meant rum in a cup and had for years.

Corie found the cup on a scarred table near the bed. The bottle of rum was more elusive, however, and it was several moments before she had located the thing.

"Hurry up," Constance squawked. "I don't know why I bother with you, Corie," she said, moving slowly toward the only chair in the room. "You're no help to me."

Corie was stung by the words, but she had heard them before. She merely looked at her mother's disheveled appearance, frowned deeply, and "made the tea." As she offered the cup into her mother's shaking hands, Corie stared at the matted, faded red hair and wondered if Constance could be infested. It was highly likely, she knew, having been infested herself on more than one occasion despite the efforts she had made toward cleanliness. Taking a last look, she shuddered and moved a few safe paces away to lean against the wardrobe with the broken door.

Constance drank, and drank deeply a second time before raising her head and squinting at her daughter. "What do you want?"

"I came to see you. That's all."

Constance made a disbelieving face and raised the cup to her lips again before speaking. "You know I'm busy, Corie. You shouldn't keep bothering me."

"Do you remember where Kenny and I are living, Mama?" Corie asked and earned a snarled reaction.

"Don't you talk to me as if I'm in my dotage, brat! I know you're living with some swell above the Hill."

Corie hated the fact that this woman, this broken, sodden excuse for a woman, still had the ability to hurt her so severely. Once again she was sorry she had come.

"He's probably doin' you every night and all day Sundays," Constance mumbled into her cup before squinting toward her daughter. "I bet you're caught, ain'tcha? You needn't come to me for help, Corie."

"I ain—I'm not caught, Mama," she said unhappily.

"Not yet!" Constance cackled. "You keep letting him put his thing in you, Corie, and you're goin' to get a babe. I told you about that." And then her brow furrowed deeply. "I did tell you about that, didn't I? But then you could get it fixed, I guess," she added, more to herself than to her daughter. "If he coughs up the money."

Corie had some inkling of what her mother was referring to and wanted no part of back-alley abortions. If she came with child from Sean, she would keep it. And she would *love* it. No matter what her future might hold, she would not deny her child the way *she* had been denied a mother's love.

Constance refilled her cup and angrily swept a mass of hair off her forehead. "You've got to go now, Corie," she said gruffly. "You'll scare my gentlemen callers away."

"Did you love my father, Mama?"

Constance stiffened in her chair and glared at the fashionably dressed young woman she barely recognized. "Don't you speak of that man!" she ordered.

"Did you? You must have loved him to leave your family for him."

Constance hated those memories that could come flooding back with just a single mention of Jason. She hated them and she fought them, every day of her life. "You see what loving a man does for you!" she cried, swiveling on the chair to face her daughter. "You're going to end up the same, Corie!"

"I'm not," Corie said firmly.

"You will!" Constance cried. "You and your fancy clothes and your fancy house I bet, too. You're letting that swell diddle you, aren't you?'' she whined. ''I warned you about that. But it doesn't matter. You never listen. You're just like your father, thinkin' you're so smart and everybody else is dumb. That's the way you always acted, Corie,'' she accused, managing to get to her feet, taking a few steps toward the younger woman. ''He was nothin', but he thought he was *everything*. Just like you,'' she raved. ''He treated me like I was dirt. Me—from a good family!'' Constance pressed a forefinger into her chest, and her face became distorted as she advanced on Corie.

''But you came here with him,'' Corie said quietly.

Constance laughed bitterly. ''You fool! Of course I did. He ruined me. Just like your swell has probably ruined you.''

''It isn't like that.''

''Hah! That's the only way it can be, you stupid girl. Just don't you be bringin' any brats down here to me. I'm not supportin' any more kids.''

Corie thought that would have been funny had it not been so tragic; Constance could hardly claim she had supported her two daughters.

She should not have come. None of the answers she needed would be found here, and her mother's uncaring, unloving attitude seemed to sting more today. Obviously she had come looking for the wrong thing in the wrong place.

''You just make sure you get everything you can from that man,'' Constance raved on. ''You make him pay, Corie, and you save it all up. You can live like the damned queen you always thought you were, but when he leaves you, you'll be glad for listenin' to me. You just take every penny for the day he kicks you out his front door. They love you only until your belly swells up and gets in the way,'' she whined. ''And then they . . .''

A long shadow stretched across the wooden floor from the door, drawing the woman's attention and causing her to halt.

It caught Corie's attention as well, and she turned to find Sean standing on the threshold, frowning.

''I think you've heard quite enough, Corie. Let's go home.''

''I told you, Corie,'' Constance said roughly, flinging her mass of hair back over her shoulder. ''I told you you'd scare my gentlemen callers away. Scoot now,'' she said, taking a step toward Sean. ''Hello, darlin'. My friend here was just leavin'. You're right on time.''

Corie's expression began to crumble as she realized her mother could not understand why Sean was there.

For his part, Sean tried not to show the distaste he felt as the thin, filthy woman, who tried to walk seductively and could barely walk at all, moved his way. ''I've come for Corie, Constance,'' he said quietly. ''I'm Sean Garrick.''

Constance, seeing a trick lost before she had a chance to win him away, exploded into anger. ''Well, take the slut!'' she screamed. ''And when you're done, don't be sending her back to me!'' She tried to turn on Corie then, stumbled and went down on one knee. Both Corie and Sean reached for her, but she shrugged off their help and grabbed the seat of the chair, pulling herself up to sit. ''Get away from me,'' she said brokenly. ''Get out!''

Corie stood in momentary indecision, shocked by the fact that her mother was so unstable of mind and weak of body. A single step, hastily taken, had been more than she could manage. And as for her ability to reason . . .

It was Sean who brought her back to reality.

Gently gripping her elbow, Sean coaxed her toward the door. "Come, love," he said. "It's time to go."

Corie looked back over her shoulder one last time and then stepped out onto the landing. They did not bother to close the door and could hear Constance mumbling angrily as they made their way down the steps.

"I'm sorry you saw that," Corie said quietly.

Sean's hand tightened on her elbow. Having heard much of what had been said, he was angry for Corie's sake. "Why did you come down here when I expressly requested that you not?"

Looking up and seeing his anger, Corie frowned. "You asked me not to come *alone*, Sean," she said defensively. "But I didn't want you to see her like that."

"Do you really think it matters?" he asked.

It might, she thought. Now that he had seen her beginnings.

When they reached the bottom of the steps, Sean turned her to face him. "I heard enough to know I don't want you to come back, Corie."

"I can't seem to help myself," she said quietly. "She's my mother, Sean."

With a weary sigh Sean combed his fingers through his hair in frustration. "What kind of a mother would treat a daughter as Constance treats you?"

"A pitiful one. But she's all I've got."

Sean's eyes took in the people on the street and quickly pulled Corie with him toward the back of the building, under the stairs. Placing her back against the wall with both hands on her shoulders, he said,

"That's not true, Corie. You have Kenny and you have me. I love you," he said quietly. "I don't want you to be hurt. And the things your mother says . . . the way she treats you must hurt."

There was no denial for that.

"She's a bitter and twisted woman, darling. I'm sorry, but it's true. Are you bringing her food, Corie?" he asked quietly and with sudden insight. "Are you trying to look after her?"

"I don't think she eats much of it anyway," she said.

"If I promise to see that she gets food regularly, will you stay away?"

Corie searched his eyes, wondering at his true purpose. But she knew that he was giving again . . . just as he always gave. And this time he was doing it because he thought he was protecting her. "Aren't you a little bit afraid that I'm just like her?" she asked softly.

"From what I've seen of your mother and what I know of you, I have no fears whatsoever," he said firmly.

"But I've slept with you," she said.

Sean's fingers bit into her shoulders. "And you think that makes you my whore? Dammit, Corie!"

"I know it's different," she said softly as tears came to her eyes. "But bad breeds bad, Sean."

Sean dropped his hands and stepped away, then turned back quickly, his control over his anger slipping. "I don't know whether to shake you or spank you," he rasped, his eyes searching her face, the sight dulling his anger as sadness took over. Taking her hand in his, he said, "I wish I knew what was going on in that pretty head. You are not your mother, sweet one. I'm not your father, for that matter. This is about you and me and not some historic tragedy. I love you, Corie, and that is all that matters.''

There were other things that mattered, she thought, but perhaps not here and now. Perhaps in the future, but not here and now.

''I want to talk with you,'' Sean was saying. ''But not here. As soon as we settle McKenna in her bed tonight, I want you to come to my study where we can talk alone.'' His fingertips lightly stroked her cheek, and he smiled wearily. ''I'll never believe you're bad, love. I'll never believe you're like *her*.''

Then why did she feel frightened half out of her wits?

Chapter 16

It seemed to take forever to get through supper, a meal that Corie could barely touch, and get Kenny settled into bed. Sean's nighttime story was longer than usual, Corie was sure, and then Kenny had to relate the entire thing while she was dressing for bed. But finally the child wore herself out and snuggled down beneath her quilts.

Corie then wavered between going to Sean, as he had requested, and hiding beneath the quilts of her own bed. Never before had she felt so wary and indecisive. But then, never before had she placed her fate in someone else's hands. Her life had revolved around making decisions for her own survival, and when Kenny had come along, she had made decisions for them *both*. Now she had given herself to a man, and regardless of the love she had for him, she supposed she was expected to defer to him on occasion. In the past she had frequently thought it would be wonderful to have someone stronger than she to make difficult choices for her; someone strong to lean on now and again. Now, she suspected, Sean was about to offer just that. She had little doubt that he wished to discuss the terms of their relationship and how they would conduct their affair from this point onward. And as much as she loved him, Corie had some obvious concerns about what his proposal could mean.

Sean had left the study door open, and she could hear the sound of thumping logs and knew that he was stoking the fire. The room would be toasty warm even before he hunkered down and started playing the logs about with the poker. She had seen him perform this simple task so often. He made it seem very much a man's task, and she loved to watch him. For that matter, she loved to watch Sean perform all manner of tasks about the place.

Thor was there, curled up on his rug off to one side of the fire. The great beast raised his head as he sensed Corie's presence and then lowered his muzzle to his paws.

As soon as she stepped to the open door, Sean's head turned and he straightened to his full height. He smiled, returning the iron poker to the stand before he walked toward her. "Did you have a hard time getting her down?" he asked.

"You know I have to hear the nighttime story one way or another," she said.

"You should join us and hear it the first time around."

"I would hear it twice then," she said with a small laugh. "Your version and Kenny's."

His smile broadened as he stepped in front of her and took her into his arms. "Hello," he said. "I've been waiting to be alone with you the whole day."

"Me, too," she managed before his lips captured hers.

It was a kiss that said I've been waiting, I've missed you. It was a kiss without passion but with a gentle love that filled Corie's being with wonder that this could be happening to her.

Sean raised his head, his eyes briefly searching her face, adoring the sweet innocent look of a young woman who, by all the laws of this world, should not have remained innocent. But she had and he was learning daily just how incredibly naive she was about many things. "I have wine for us," he said, taking her hand and leading her to a chair before the fire.

Corie smiled at the crystal decanter and glasses he had placed on the small table between the chairs. She wondered only briefly if the wine was for celebrating or drowning her sorrows; and then she hastily put that thought aside. Sean loved her. There would be no sorrow.

Sean seemed quietly thoughtful as he poured wine into the glasses, settled into his chair, and reached for his pipe. He was carefully tamping tobacco into the bowl when he spoke. "I've been wondering why you would go down the Hill today of all days," he said, lighting a taper from the lamp on the table. "It seemed odd to me that you would choose today to see your mother when I know you haven't been there for weeks."

"You know that I've been going there?" she asked, clearly surprised.

"McKenna's fairly perceptive, Corie. She's made assumptions about where you go, and it worries her. When she's worried, she always tells me." He grinned around the pipe stem before drawing in to bring the tobacco to life. "You must remember that, darling," he teased as smoke billowed around his head. "I've had this idea that your visit today had something to do with what happened between us last night. Would that be a fair assumption?"

Corie frowned, nodded reluctantly, and then chose to stare at the fire.

"So I've been asking myself what there could be about our making love that would make you feel you would want to see your mother today. And I think you answered the question quite adequately this afternoon when I went there to get you. You asked me if I might be afraid that you are like your mother. I assume that comes from the fact that you gave yourself to me. Am I still on the right track?"

"I guess so," she said softly.

"You *guess*?" he returned gently. "Are you *guessing* because you're confused, Corie?" he asked, setting his pipe aside and leaning toward her.

She faced him then, her perplexity mirrored by her frown. "It seemed clear to me last night and for days before that. All I wanted was to be close to you. I love you and I didn't know how else to show it."

"A whore doesn't love and concern herself with how to show it, Corie, so get *that* idea out of your mind. I told you that things would change between us, and perhaps that is a little bit frightening. Would you agree? Is that why you went to your mother today? Because you needed someone to talk with?"

"It was a stupid idea," she said.

"It was," he agreed, pulling her across the short distance between them and onto his lap. "You should have come to me. I may be part of the problem, but I could also be part of the solution." He braced her shoulders against his arm and tipped her back so that he could see her face. "Tell me what your fondest wish might be."

Her brows knitting together, Corie wondered at this change of tactic and how much she should trust him with her deepest desires. "To love you," she said cautiously.

"Beyond that," he prodded.

"To have *you* love *me*."

"You have it," he said boldly. "What else?"

Hesitating, Corie's eyes darted around the planes of his face as she searched for some sign that he would not laugh at her. But if she could not have this with Sean, she knew instinctively, she would have it with no one. "To have you want no other woman."

"That wish shall also be granted," he said easily. "In what capacity?"

"Pardon?" she asked, frowning again.

"How do you want me?"

"What are you asking?"

"Do you want me faithful to you and only you for a short time or a long time?"

"Forever," she whispered.

"Done!" he said, laughing. "As soon as we can find a preacher."

It took a moment for Corie to absorb what he was saying. "You want to marry me?"

"Of course. Do you think I'm about to leave you free for some other fellow to step in and steal you away? Not bloody likely."

"You don't have to marry me, Sean."

His smile disappeared instantly. "Does that mean you don't want to marry?"

"No, it's just—"

"Then say, 'Yes, Sean, I would love to marry you.'"

"Yes, Sean, I would love to marry you."

"You don't sound too certain," he prodded, giving her a playful shake.

"I am," she breathed. "I just don't believe it."

"Believe it, Miss Corinne Alexander soon-to-be-Garrick. Because I'm not letting you go."

Something within her seemed to understand all of a sudden, and Corie threw her arms about his neck.

"And if I ever catch you with your self-respect down about your ankles again," he threatened, "I'll paddle your backside."

She tipped her head back then, trying to read the meaning behind his words.

Sean's hand stroked her cheek, and his fingers lightly combed a wisp of hair away from her temple. "You and Kenny have filled a void in my life. I've found I enjoy my small family, and I don't want to ever let that go. I've long admired you for your independence and your determination not to go back down the Hill. Don't slide back down there, Corie, because what we have between us might seem frightening for the moment. I'm a little bit frightened, too."

"You're scared?" she asked, disbelieving.

His shoulders shrugged casually. "It's pretty powerful, this thing between us. But it's a good thing, and I know it's right for us to let it develop to its full potential. I think we're bound to grow old together, love."

That sounded unbelievable, too; her only dream in life had been to find someone who would be with her always, to love her and her alone. Always. And Sean was offering her dream up to her as if it were as easy as crossing the street. It couldn't possibly be that easy to achieve something so long wished for as this. And in order not to destroy the potential of her wish coming true, Corie determined in that moment not to ever let Sean see her doubts. "Let's," she said, flashing a confident smile. "Let's grow old together."

"Done!" he said and gathered her against his chest.

Hours later as they lay basking in the warmth of their love-spent bodies, Corie curled more securely against Sean's side and asked softly, "How long will your mother be here?"

"Originally she had planned to stay only a few days. She apparently has plans to celebrate the New Year with friends," he said. "But I'm certain she will want to stay for the wedding."

The wedding. *Their* wedding. Corie kept the thought rolling around in her mind. It made her very happy to think about that event and about being in love. It all seemed a bit unreal, but she forced herself to believe because she wanted so much for it all to be true. Still, when she spoke, there was unmistakable sadness in her voice. "Then we can't be together like this again for weeks."

"Oh, yes, we will," Sean said firmly, rolling onto his side to face her. "I don't care who comes to stay in this house, I'm not giving you up. You're mine, my pet, and if I can't openly have you in my bed every night, I'm not above a little midnight skulking."

"I can see it now." She giggled. "A little gray-haired elderly lady lacing into you when she catches you sneaking into my room."

Sean smiled at the thought and nudged her ribs with his fingertips. "And she would do it, too. Therefore, *you* shall come to *my* room. But be prepared, my darling, I warn you. Do not get caught," he teased.

Chapter 17

"They're coming!" Kenny cried, causing Thor to echo her excitement with loud barking as the dog raced on the child's heels toward the kitchen. "They're here!" she cried again as she burst through the door.

"All right, McKenna," Jane Pringle admonished. "Quiet your voice now," she added, then turned to Corinne. "You leave those apples for me to finish peeling. I think Mr. Garrick would want you and McKenna to greet his mother properly in the parlor."

Corie nodded, knowing the woman was right; Sean had specifically told her that she was not to act as an employee in his home. She was soon to be his bride, and he would tell his mother so at the first opportune moment.

She rose, straightened her skirt, and patted her hair at the temples nervously.

Jane Pringle smiled knowingly and smoothed a wisp of Kenny's hair back from her face. "You both will do Mr. Garrick proud. Now, get out there."

Corie took Kenny's hand and led her through the dining room to the parlor, where they stood stiffly in the center of the room.

Thor took a sentinel's position, sitting on his haunches on Kenny's free side.

"What do I call her?" Kenny whispered.

Corie could hear Sean's voice from the foyer and a woman's reply. "Mrs. Garrick," she said quietly. "I told you."

"But she's not married to Sean," Kenny said reasonably.

Corie bent at the waist and said frantically, "Mr. and Mrs. Garrick had a son named Sean Garrick, Kenny. I told you how that works, too."

But Kenny was confused by all of this, not having known family relationships in the past. She had just never thought of a man of Sean's years as having a mother. "If I'm Sean's daughter, is Mrs. Garrick *my* mother, too?"

"No. You aren't really his daughter."

"But he says I'm his daughter," she returned, unhappy with Corie's shortness.

There was no time for further explanation, however, as Corie caught a movement from the corner of her eye. Straightening to her full height, she held tight to Kenny's hand as Sean escorted a gray-haired woman of stature into the room.

He flashed Corie a confident smile as he walked toward her. "Here they are," he said proudly. "Mother, I'd like you to meet Miss Corinne Alexander."

Annie Garrick nodded as Corie dipped a curtsy while trying desperately to remember all Jane had taught.

"And this is McKenna," Sean added, smiling as

Kenny executed a curtsy that was closer to an awkward bow.

Annie studied the child who was staring up at her with unabashed curiosity. She was a pretty little thing, one had to admit. "So you're livin' with me Sean, are you?" she asked.

Kenny's eyes rounded in wonder at the sound of the woman's voice. "You talk different," she said baldly.

"Kenny!" Corie said softly, feeling warmth creep over her complexion. But to her surprise, Annie Garrick laughed.

"So you'd not be knowin' the Irish," the woman said. "Why don't ye come and sit by me?" she added, reaching for Kenny's hand and casting a baleful eye at Thor as she walked around Sean. "I see ye've still got that beast," she muttered.

Sean grinned at Corie before directing her to a chair opposite his mother. "Thor is McKenna's guardian, Mother. I can hardly let him go now."

Sure enough, Thor ambled over to the settee and flopped beneath Kenny's feet, which hung in the air as the child sat back.

Annie watched as Sean waited until Corie had settled herself before he sat in the chair beside the young woman's. "So ye contrived to have my son take in this girl," Annie said forthrightly.

Caught off guard, Corie's eyes flashed to Sean.

He shrugged lamely and grinned. "I told her the whole story." And then he directed his attention to his mother. "She's got the Irish curiosity, you see, and would have ferreted out the truth of it anyway."

Annie cast him a warning glance before returning her attention to Corie. "And ye've got yerself living here, too?"

Corie wasn't certain whether or not she liked this

line of questioning and suddenly sat up straighter in her chair. "That wasn't part of my plan," she said. "At least not initially."

Annie was clearly taken aback by that and stared at the girl before laughing. "Faith! And how did you manage that, then?"

Still uncertain of the woman, Corie answered simply, "Kenny got sick."

"Oh," Annie said quietly as her eyes darted from Corie to Sean to the child. "She doesn't look sick now."

"Mother," Sean warned.

"Well, I'm just tryin' to determine the young woman's status, since ye've not been so forthright about that. What do you do here?" she asked as her attention returned to the one under discussion.

"I look after Kenny and I help Mrs. Pringle," Corie said easily while she silently added . . . and I sleep with your son.

"Ah. So you cook and clean?"

"I don't cook."

"Sewing, then? Did you sew that gown you're wearing?"

Corie was getting a little tired of these pointed questions but supposed it must be natural for a caring mother to have some concern about what was happening in her son's home. "I don't sew."

"Thank God for that," Annie said. "And don't buy another thing from whoever made that," she said, eyeing Corie's gown. "And you're far too pretty to wear gray."

"Mother!" Sean said again, but to no avail.

Corie sat stunned and then covered her slow smile with her fingertips; she'd never met anyone quite like Annie Garrick before.

"Well, ye should see the girl decently gowned, at least," Annie told her son.

Jane Pringle saved the day by entering with a heavily ladened tray of tea service and cakes.

Corie had an opportunity to study Sean's mother without the woman being aware as the two older women greeted each other. Annie Garrick was tall for a woman and slim still, except for a slight thickening about her middle. She had dark hair that was graying prettily, and her eyes were the same dark blue that her son possessed. She was a woman of presence and, Corie was learning, a woman to be reckoned with.

Annie Garrick busied herself by pouring the tea as she surreptitiously made note of the glances taking place between her son and the young Miss Alexander; there was more afoot here than guardianship of a five-year-old girl.

While Kenny chattered on about their plans for Christmas—only two sleeps away—the adults sipped tea, and Annie silently appraised the possibilities of her son's new situation.

Mother and son shared some private time in Sean's study shortly after supper that night while Corie took Kenny up to bed.

Annie sighed, holding up an empty wineglass. "Jane Pringle is still an excellent cook."

"Yes, she is," Sean agreed, picking up on the silent cue and refilling his mother's glass.

"I like McKenna," Annie said, smiling up at him when Sean presented her with the wine. "It's amazing she's as sweet as she is, knowin' her beginnin's."

"Some days I can't wait for her to get up in the mornings," Sean said as he stoked the logs in the fire. He returned to his favorite chair and reached for his pipe. "And most days I hate to see her have to go to bed."

"She puts the sunshine in your days, does she?" Annie asked wisely. "So, you'd not be mindin' raising another man's child?"

"Too late for that, Mother," he said. "I love her too much for a minor detail such as that to interfere."

"But it's not like she's yere own, Sean."

"Yes, it is. It's exactly like that."

"But ye'd not be givin' up hopes of a son?" she asked bluntly.

Sean laughed before blowing smoke rings about his head. "A son would be nice, too."

"With Corie?"

Grinning, Sean reached for his own wineglass. "So you think you've got that all worked out, do you?"

"I'm not so simple as ye might think. I got eyes in me head."

"And how would you feel about that, darling?" he asked. "Knowing Corinne's beginnings match McKenna's?"

"Me own beginnin's weren't so auspicious," she said shortly. "And don't ye be lettin' on that I'd judge the girl by that. Neither one o' them. The older one must have a few good licks o' sense for the little one to be the way she is. Are ya' thinkin' serious then, Sean?"

Sean could not mistake the hopeful note in her voice and set his pipe aside, reaching out for her hand. "I'm thinking very seriously, sweetheart. What do you think about that?"

"I'm thinkin' if you love her and she loves you, that's all that'll be matterin'."

"That's all that'll be matterin', love," he said in earnest imitation of her brogue.

*   *   *

The following morning at breakfast Annie Garrick took one look at her son, a second look at Corinne, and asked Sean for a private word.

Entering his study, Annie asked him to close the door and immediately said softly, "I'll be about askin' Jane Pringle to help me arrange a small weddin' dinner," she said. "Are ya' plannin' on invitin' the Frasers?"

"What's this all about?" he asked lightly.

"Ye'd best be marryin' that girl and right away, to my way o' thinkin', Sean Garrick. I'll not be havin' me own grandson branded a bastard."

For the first time since he was a virgin boy, Sean blushed heatedly.

Annie Garrick merely laughed.

Chapter 18

The following three days were the most magical Corie had ever known; the bustle of Christmas preparations alone would have kept her breathless, and preparing for a wedding made the days even more frantic.

Upon learning that her future mother-in-law had stepped up their plans, and why, Corie had blushed madly the first moment she set eyes on the woman.

Annie's laughter at first sight of the girl had filled the parlor. Hugging Corie fiercely, she whispered, "Ah, I'd not be blamin' ye," she whispered for Corie's ears alone. "Sean's father, rest his soul, had the same effect on me."

Corie had kissed the older woman's still-smooth cheek and whispered in return, "Thank you."

"Ye just be givin' my Sean the happiness he deserves. And a fine son or two to boot," Annie had said.

All the excitement and activity were too much for a five-year-old to deal with, however. Kenny ate little and became defiant about bedtimes, displaying the first signs of stubborn temper that Sean had ever witnessed in the child. Corie usually managed to talk with her sister and calm her into a reasonable mood, but Christmas night the lack of sleep and the sheer stimulus of gifts and more attention than the girl had ever experienced in her life took their toll; Kenny ended the evening in tears.

Sean picked the child up and held her against his chest as he walked up the stairs. "Too much, too soon, I think, moppet," he said softly.

"I want to play with my dolls," Kenny whined.

"They'll be there tomorrow, sweetheart. Right now I think it's time you curled up with your lamb and went to sleep."

"No!"

"McKenna!" he said sternly.

Corie had run ahead to Kenny's room and turned the quilts down on the bed. "Come on, baby," she said as Sean set the child on her feet. "I'll help you get undressed."

"I don't want to go to bed," Kenny said defiantly.

"Don't start that again, Kenny," Corie said firmly. "You're not going to bed."

"I'm older," Corie said reasonably as she pulled the green dress over Kenny's head. "And I'm not nearly so cranky."

When Kenny's head emerged, she accused, "And you didn't go to bed last night."

Corie's eyes rounded in dismay as she stared at the girl. "What do you mean?"

"I woke up and I looked for you, but you weren't in bed."

"What did you do then?" Corie ventured uneasily.

"I heard you talking to Sean in his room, and I

thought you must be waiting up for Santa. But if he catches you awake, Corie, he doesn't leave any presents.''

Corie flashed Sean a look that positively screamed *help*! as she dropped a white flannel nightdress over Kenny's head.

"I'll try and explain to her tomorrow," Sean said quietly.

"'Splain what?" Kenny blurted.

"Nothing, moppet," Sean said, snatching the girl up and dropping her on the bed playfully. "Now, go to sleep."

"I want a story," she whined but was asleep before Sean could finish his first sentence.

Sean had a long chat with Kenny following breakfast the next morning.

Kenny ran straight to Annie.

"Sean and Corie are getting married!"

Annie smiled and patted the seat beside her hip. "Come up here and let's be talkin' about that. Does that make ye happy?" she asked as Kenny wiggled back on the seat.

"I guess so. But it means Corie won't have her own room anymore," she said, sounding sorry.

"I'm thinkin' that won't be makin' Corie too unhappy."

"But we never had our own rooms before."

"Well, not to worry," Annie said softly, tucking the girl under her arm. "Husbands and wives like to be sharin' things."

"My mama used to share her room with lots of people, and I could never go in there. But Sean said I can go into his room if I need to," Kenny said, playing with a bow on her dress. "I have to knock first, though."

"I'm thinkin' that's a grand idea," Annie said lightly.

"And Sean said Corie won't get cranky from sharing a room, like my mother."

"That's true, darlin'," Annie said sympathetically. What this poor child had been through, she thought sadly as she lowered her head and lightly kissed Kenny's brow. She'd had her doubts about Sean taking in stray children, until she had met McKenna. But Sean had proved himself once again to be a man of kindness, wisdom, and good fortune, just like his father had been. Annie could easily understand how his heart had been captured. In both instances, she decided.

It was a brief but touching ceremony witnessed by Jane Pringle, Annie Garrick, McKenna, and the Frasers. Jane had outdone herself with a scrumptious five-course meal, and Sean had purchased the best wines to be found in New Orleans; a crate had arrived by steamer only that day.

"To the bride!" Stephen cried for the fifth time that evening after dinner.

Sean cuffed him playfully on the shoulder. "Go toast your own wife."

"To my wife!" he called, raising his glass and winking at Catherine.

Corie giggled. "He's not really drunk, just happy," she said knowingly.

Catherine realized her new friend was probably speaking from experience, knowing half the men who resided in Natchez Under-the-Hill were continuously drunk. "Stephen is very fond of Sean. He'd do anything to see him happy."

"So would I," Corie said softly, smiling shyly at Catherine and then Annie.

"Aye," Annie breathed, "and I believe ye would."

"I finally have you to myself—and legally," Sean said as he turned his bride around and attacked the small buttons down the back of her dress. "No more blushing over my mother's accusations of my being a bad boy."

Corie giggled and pulled more pins from her hair. "She didn't?"

"She did, in a way."

"*You* didn't," she accused lightly.

"Blush?" he asked. "I certainly did. Just like a boy who had taken his first woman."

Corie thought that inordinately funny.

"My mother has a way of making people confess even before she has accused them," he said defensively, brushing the shoulders of her gown forward and down her arms. "She's uncanny, and that's a fact."

"I think she's wonderful," Corie said sincerely as she stepped out of her gown and petticoats.

"I think so, too," he said and moved away to rid himself of his own clothes. Normally a neat and careful man, Sean abandoned his former habits and threw his garments over a chair. Naked, he turned and walked across the room toward her. "Come here," he said, his eyes roaming her slender body, which was masked only by a sheer shift. He met her by the double chest of drawers and pulled her immediately into his arms, his mouth finding hers unerringly. "God, I love you, Mrs. Garrick," he muttered, and then his lips returned to hers, his hand cupping her chin, coaxing her to open her mouth.

Corie had been anticipating this for several hours, silently praying for his mother and the Frasers to make their way to their beds and leave her alone with him. The result of the wait was almost embarrassing as she moved against him, urging Sean not to delay even as his tongue teased hers. She felt his hands slide down her hips to her thighs as he pressed her against the chest at her back.

Sean dragged her shift up to her waist, pressing himself urgently against her.

"Let's go to bed," Corie whispered as his lips moved toward her ear.

"Can't," he breathed.

"Sean, I—"

"Do that again," he said huskily. "What you did a moment ago."

Corie wasn't certain she understood, but moved her hips tentatively. And then he was lifting her, balancing her buttocks on the edge of the chest just before he entered her.

"That's better." He sighed, raising his head to study her as he pressed home.

With a gasp of surprise Corie's eyes widened. "We can't do it like this," she managed to say.

"We'll manage," he said and very slowly eased his hips away from hers.

Corie's head fell back and she closed her eyes, concentrating on the incredible sensation of his withdrawal. "Don't leave me," she whispered raggedly.

Sean slowly moved toward her again. "Why is it that every time I take you just makes me want you more? I thought this day would never end."

"Me, too," she breathed as his lips roamed down

her neck. "It was a lovely day, Sean. Thank you," she moaned.

"Welcome," he breathed, pressing deep within her and halting there.

"Yes, you are," she whispered.

Sean moved his head back, staring into her eyes as he grinned. "What are we talking about?" he asked huskily.

Corie's arms tightened around his neck, and she pressed her cheek against his. "You're *welcome*," she said shyly. "Here. Like this. Inside me."

And then there was no more breath for talk as their hands and lips discovered each other all over again. Corie thought that every time was like the first time, and even better, if that were possible. She was completely unabashed and uninhibited with him, giving all he wanted and taking all he offered. It was a free and glorious sharing, this loving between them, and she was confident it was right.

Sean quickened his pace as he felt his climax approaching. And then he buried himself deep within her, holding her tight as he rotated against her, bringing her shuddering against him seconds before he poured his seed into her. He clung to her because he wasn't certain his legs would support him. With his breath still harsh in her ear, he began to chuckle between gasps of air. "I don't believe what you do to me," he said. "I'm like a bloody caveman, taking you on the furniture."

"And putting a crease in my backside," she murmured lightly.

He managed to raise his head then, grinning sheepishly. "I'm sorry, darling."

"Don't be," she said, smiling as she stroked the hair at his temple. "Where shall we try next?"

Sean laughed, wrapped her legs around his hips, supporting her back with his arms as he lifted her off the chest. "How about the bed?" he suggested, then lightly smacked her buttocks when she flashed a suggestive smile. "For a rest," he added pointedly. He eased her down on the mattress and rolled her onto her stomach, his hand massaging the crease in her upper thighs, as he sat beside her. "I promise I won't do this to you again."

"I'm not complaining, Sean." She sighed, her cheek resting against the arm under her head. "In fact, I like the attention I get after you bruise me."

He laughed shortly, his hand working up the length of her back. "I think you're insatiable."

"Whatever that means."

"It means you can't get enough."

"Do you think so?" she asked, suddenly worried that there was something wrong with her.

Sean sensed the true meaning behind her question and sought to reassure her. "I think it's true, but I also know it's natural, Corie," he said, his hand slowly caressing down toward her buttocks again. "I feel the same way, pet. It's just that women have a greater capacity than men when it comes to this. And, eventually, you'll want to move to a slower pace," he added wisely. "Once the novelty wears off."

"I don't think that will ever happen," she muttered as she looked back over her shoulder, frowning at him. "Is that true? You feel the same?"

"Absolutely," he said, smiling before bending to drop a lingering kiss on her shoulder. "And there's more than one way for me to make you feel good, my love."

It was several hours later before they both drifted

toward sleep. Corie, glowing from Sean's lovemaking, snuggled close.

But an uneasy thought found its way into Sean's mind; it had taken Marie years to get pregnant. She had been an emotionally loving woman but had not warmed to their love-play as freely as he might have liked. Marie had been more reserved, more dutiful when it came to this aspect of marriage. Corie was exactly opposite, and his instincts told him it would be different with her. Corie would likely come with child quite easily, if she weren't already.

The thought brought a mixture of pleasure and fear.

To celebrate the New Year, the inhabitants of Pearl Street attended the plantation owned by Stephen and Catherine Fraser, staying on for several days.

Corie was entranced and a bit in awe of the huge plantation house with its high ceilings and multiple rooms.

But McKenna was in another kind of heaven entirely as, for the first time, she was allowed to feed and care for chickens and *real* lambs.

When the time came for the Garricks to return to town, it took little coaxing on Catherine's part to convince Sean and Corie that Kenny should stay with them a few days.

"She's having a great time, and we're enjoying her so much," Catherine pleaded. "And you're newly wedded, you two. Wouldn't you like some time alone?"

"Except for the groom's old mother," Annie put in with a wry smile.

Catherine blushed heatedly at her faux pas. "I didn't mean—"

"I'm knowin' what ye meant, me darlin'." Annie

laughed. "And I'll be leavin' them tomorrow. You're right to keep McKenna here a few days." With that she kissed Catherine on the cheek and gave her a hug. "You write to me more regular than ye've been doin', me girl."

Catherine promised she would, knowing she wouldn't; she was the world's worst letter writer. Still, she was inordinately fond of Annie and gave the older woman a hearty hug before Sean helped his mother into the enclosed carriage Stephen had supplied.

Sean sat next to his bride, holding her gloved hand in his lap, as his mother smiled from the opposite seat.

"Ye'd best send out a few more duds for McKenna," Annie advised. "She'll be covered in God-knows-what every mornin' when she starts chasin' those chickens."

Sean laughed and nodded. "We'll pack up a few things and send them back with Stephen's coachman."

Annie looked at Corie then, watching the young woman's admiring eyes staring up at her new husband as he spoke. Annie had watched them together a little over a week, but she could clearly see that Corie fairly worshiped the ground that Sean walked on. It made her heart swell with happiness. They would do right by each other, and Annie was content. Now, if they would only give her a grandson. McKenna was lovable and dear, but Annie wanted to see her husband's fine name carried on forever.

"I'll be leavin' on tomorrow's packet," she said, repeating her earlier announcement. "I've me own life to lead, ye know."

Sean smiled at the familiar statement, knowing she said it to make him think that she was content to be alone. Knowing, also, that she was alone because she wanted to give him freedom to do as he wanted with his life and not be tied to her. "I know your friends have missed you over the holidays, Mother," he said. "Thank you for changing your plans and coming here. The holidays would not have been the same without you."

"I'm not certain you're meanin' that as a compliment, me boy."

Sean laughed, pulling Corie beneath his arm. "It is, love. I always enjoy having you here."

"You'll not be forgettin' it was me that hurried you're weddin', though, will ye?"

"That was a favor you granted me," he teased.

"A favor, is it now? I'm thinkin' you wouldn't have waited much longer anyway."

"True. But we would have waited long enough for my favorite girl to arrive from New Orleans. The wedding wouldn't have been quite so wonderful without you," he said sincerely.

"Pooh!" Annie said, reaching into her reticule. "I have something here . . . faith," she muttered, searching.

Sean and Corie's eyes met then, but he shrugged innocently.

"Here!" she said triumphantly, holding up a large ruby set in a heavy gold band. "It's the first ring me Joseph gave me," she said. Her dark blue eyes settled on Corie before she said, "I want ye to have it. It's me weddin' gift to you."

Corie drew in a deep breath as she stared at the ring. "But I couldn't take it," she said softly. "It's your ring from your husband."

"Aye, and mine to give," Annie said firmly. "I want ye to have something of the Garricks'." And then with a mischievous smile her eyes darted to her son and back to the younger woman. "In addition to me son."

When Corie seemed spellbound by the offering, Sean took the ring from his mother and placed it on the third finger of his wife's right hand. "Thank you, mother," he said softly and shared a secret, knowing smile with her.

Chapter 19

Her name was Sue Ellen Peachtree—a ridiculous name from her point of view but one she would cling to—and she was twenty-nine years old, pretty, and very spoiled. She had been married at age twenty and mysteriously widowed at age twenty-one. She was sweet-smiling, bad-tempered, hated most men, and loved many women. She was also very bored, unless she had a new lover or a new game in which to concentrate her efforts; unbelievably, she had fallen upon both, quite innocently.

She chuckled silently as she thought about *falling upon* her new lover. It had actually been the other way about. And her new lover had suggested a wonderful new game, a challenge that Sue Ellen could not possibly refuse. And that is why she had watched the entrance to the mercantile, this mid-January day; the game was about to begin. Sue Ellen had not had to wait long and was smiling happily as she followed a young woman into the shop.

"I need a nickel's worth of sugar, please," Corie

said to the man behind the counter. "And the same of crackers."

"Right, Mrs. Garrick."

So, *this* was Corie Garrick, Sue Ellen thought as she moved toward the same counter. Perfect.

"You didn't bring the wee one with you," the man said, bagging the sugar.

"It's very cold today," Corie said pleasantly. "I didn't think Ken—oh!"

"Oh! I'm so sorry," Sue Ellen cried earnestly. "Look what I've done!"

Corie fanned out the skirt of her new blue-and-white striped gown, wiping uselessly at the smudges on the hem. "It doesn't matter," she said.

"But it does," the other woman said. "I feel terrible, tripping into your skirt like that. I was so busy looking at . . . well, that's no excuse."

"Please," Corie insisted, looking up and smiling at the frowning woman. "It will wash out."

"With a great deal of work," she said sagely. "At least let me make amends by taking you to lunch."

"I have to get back. But thank you," Corie said graciously.

Sue Ellen turned on her brightest smile. "Now, I won't take no for an answer. And we won't be long. Let's just skip over to the hotel and . . ." She left the remainder unspoken as her hand covered her heart. "How silly of me," she said. "My name's Sue Ellen Peachtree. And you are . . . ?"

"Corie. Corie Garrick."

"Garrick," Sue Ellen said thoughtfully. "That sounds familiar."

"My husband owns—"

"The cotton warehouse! Of course. Well, I've never met him, you understand," Sue Ellen explained as she snatched up Corie's parcels and turned toward the door, "but I know of him, so to speak. Let's at least have a cup of tea," she said and exited the store.

Corie shrugged and turned to smile at Mr. Masters. "I guess I'm having a cup of tea."

"Looks that way," the man said with a chuckle.

Corie hurried from the shop and raced to catch up with the other woman and her parcels. "Let me take those," she offered.

Sue Ellen ignored her as she marched down the street. "I can't believe I was so clumsy," she muttered, ignoring Corie's comment. She flashed a brilliant smile then. "It's just as well, you know? I'm starving and it will be very nice having company over lunch."

Lunch, Corie thought. *I'm having lunch*. This woman had more gusto than a steamship.

Once they were seated in the hotel dining room, Sue Ellen took the helm again. "They make a very nice chowder here. Would you like some of that? Yes," she said, giving Corie no time to answer. "Chowder and we'll share a plate of those little sandwiches they do so well." So saying, Sue Ellen ordered their meal. "There!" she said, sighing. "Now we can chat."

Corie wasn't certain what they could *chat* about, but then, she needn't have given the matter a moment's worry.

"How long have you been married to Mr. Garrick?" Sue Ellen asked. "I haven't seen you about, and I know almost everyone in town. Well, everyone who cares to be known," she added with a bit of cattiness Corie failed to grasp. "You must be new to the town."

"I'm . . . ah . . . new to Natchez," she said

cautiously, considering Under-the-Hill to be another world entirely.

"Well, however did you meet Mr. Garrick? I mean, if you had met at someone's party, I would have seen you together, surely."

Corie understood then that this woman considered no one would dare to have a party and not invite her. Still, there was an impulsive excitement about Sue Ellen that she liked. "I met him in the neighborhood," she said uneasily.

"A neighbor introduced you?"

"Something like that."

Sue Ellen chuckled at that. "How evasive you are. Surely there was nothing untoward about your meeting?"

"A . . . ah . . . child brought us together," Corie said and immediately bit her tongue.

"A child! Good heavens!"

"Not *our* child," she returned hastily. "It was my younger sister, you see. She knew him and . . . Oh, let's change the subject."

The subject was changed. But Sue Ellen had a sackful of topics in reserve and chattered nonstop throughout the meal.

Corie had struggled to learn the art of making flaky pie crust since coming to the house on Pearl Street. She was trying her hand at it again when she said, "Sean doesn't like you eating alone in your cottage, Mrs. Pringle. And I don't, either."

"You need more flour on your work area before you roll that out," the woman said before turning back to the stove. "And McKenna will be home in a day or two. I'll take my suppers here again when she's back. I think it's important that you and Mr. Garrick have a few evenings alone together since you're not taking a wedding trip.''

Corie raised the wooden rolling pin and smiled at the woman's back. ''Why, Mrs. Pringle . . . you're a romantic,'' she teased.

''Umph! I'm not so old I don't remember how special it is to a woman to have some time alone with her man.''

Corie's smile melted into a look of gratitude, and despite the fact that she heard someone entering at the front of the house, she moved to the woman's side and pressed her lips lightly against Jane Pringle's cheek. ''Thank you, dear friend,'' she whispered and hurried from the room.

Sean removed his outer coat and had only time enough to hang it on a peg before his wife catapulted into his arms. ''Hello!'' he said, laughing. ''Do I take that as a sign that you've missed me?''

''Maybe,'' she offered.

''Only maybe?'' he asked, arching a brow.

''I don't want you to become too cocky,'' she said, smiling up at him warmly.

''I think you missed me,'' he murmured and bent his head, his lips claiming hers firmly, possessively. ''I admit freely that I missed you,'' he added quietly, pressing against her.

Corie arched her back and grinned as she hung suspended, her arms about his neck. ''I thought about stopping to see you when I went to the shops. It's a very long day with you gone.''

''It's probably just as well you didn't,'' he teased, nipping at her ear. ''It would have been a bit embarrassing, taking you amongst the cotton bales.''

Corie laughed and cuffed his shoulder. ''You would not!''

"I might have," he said, stepping back and tucking her small hand into the crook of his arm. "I found it to be a long day as well. Will you join me for a drink?" he asked, leading her toward the door of his study.

Corie looked a bit unhappy as she shook her head. "I'm making you a pecan pie. But I won't be long."

Sean let her go, entering his study as she walked beyond to the kitchen. *Pecan pie*, he thought with a sigh. He dearly loved his young wife, but he could not say the same about her pie crust.

He had a fire started and was in the act of pouring brandy into a glass when Corie joined him. "Some wine?" he asked, reaching for a crystal decanter.

"A little," she said, walking to his side and leaning against his arm while he poured.

Corie was understandably cautious about spirits of any kind, and Sean seldom poured a full glass for her. "Pie in the oven?" he asked, handing her the glass.

Corie nodded and moved toward what had become *her* chair. "Don't let me forget it."

Heaven forbid, he thought and smiled as he sat in the chair beside her. "How was your day?" he asked; it was the first full day since their marriage that he had left her alone while he worked.

Corie watched him press tobacco into the bowl of his pipe; she loved to watch him do this. "I was lonely here with both you and Kenny gone," she said. "I'm glad Mrs. P. and I get on well."

"Perhaps it won't be long before we can add another small body to the family," he said hopefully. "I venture you won't have time to be lonely then."

Corie knew exactly what he was talking about and just how much he wanted a child. He loved Kenny to distraction, but a child of his own was something Sean had wanted desperately, and he had plenty of love in his heart for a large family. And Corie wanted whatever would make him happy. "I hope it won't take long," she said softly.

Sean laughed gently. "Are you really all *that* lonely, my pet?"

Corie shook her head and set her wineglass aside. "I just want to give you a son."

A look of complete adoration stole across his face as he reached out a hand toward her. "Come here," he said softly, pulling her from her chair and onto his lap. "You've given me a great deal already, Corie. I want you to know that I'm a happy man." And secretly he was frightened to death of her becoming pregnant, although he understood that his fears were probably unfounded. Corie was physically a much stronger woman than Marie had been.

Corie snuggled down, settling her back against his chest as her head dropped to his shoulder. "It's funny," she said softly, "but I don't think I ever thought about female things until I came to live here. All the years I was wearing boy's clothes, it was like I was sexless."

Sean's chest heaved upward as he chuckled at that. "You are talking to your *husband*," he said. "I know better than *that*."

"But I was," she said, smiling at his suggestive tone. "I remember when I decided that I would one day find a husband who would be faithful to me forever and never leave me. But I thought of that person as . . . a sort of companion, I guess. I don't remember ever thinking of love as part of a relation-ship."

Sean's hand slowly stroked her hair as he listened to

her thoughtful words. "Perhaps you didn't understand what *love* was, my darling," he said softly.

"That's true," she said with a hint of bitterness. "I hardly had an example to follow."

"That's all behind you now."

"I know," she said, briefly turning her head enough to lightly kiss his cheek. "But what I'm trying to say is, I don't think I ever pictured myself in the role of a wife."

"Well, you fit the part beautifully."

"And I've never thought about carrying a child. That was just too *female* a thing for me."

"I've thought about it," he said, nudging her temple with his lips as one hand began to caress her breast. "But I must confess, I've thought more about what it takes to get you that way."

Corie laughed and tipped her head back to look at him. "Is there such a thing as a man being over-sexed?"

"I'm only that way with you. It must have something to do with the fact that you're an extremely sensual *female*," he teased.

"You make me that way," she accused.

"Do I, indeed?"

Corie wasn't certain how to explain her feelings to him, so she said simply, "Every time you come near me, I get hot."

Sean threw back his head and laughed before hugging her with delight. "It's that way for me, too, darling," he said easily as he turned her toward him, draping her legs over the arm of the chair. "That's better," he said as his eyes focused on hers. "Has Mrs. P. left the house, do you think?"

Corie nodded, swallowing heavily in anticipation as his fingers began to unfasten the buttons at her throat

"I need to taste a bit of this," he murmured as his lips moved along the soft, slender column of her neck. "So sweet."

Sweet!

"My pie!" she cried.

That night, after dinner, they feasted on each other instead of dessert.

Sean had never been so rough with her, so demanding. "Well, you took my breath away that time, Mr. Garrick," she murmured.

Sean pulled the quilts up over them and settled her against his side. He hadn't hurt her, he knew. Far from it. "That's what you get when you arouse me and then make me suffer through supper."

Grinning against his shoulder, Corie offered, "I must remember that."

Sean's hand connected lightly with her buttocks. "Who's insatiable?"

"Insatiable?"

"I think you referred to it as being oversexed."

"You make me . . ."

"I know . . . I make you that way."

Corie's fingers played with the hair on his chest as she savored the warmth of him next to her. "I made a friend today," she said, after a time.

"Did you?" he asked, pleasantly surprised. "I'm happy for you, darling. Do I know this person?"

"I don't think so. She says she knows of you, but she doesn't think you've ever met. Her name's Sue Ellen Peachtree."

It didn't take Sean long to acknowledge that he had never heard the name.

"She's a bit strange, Sean," Corie confessed. "Not *strange*, perhaps, but . . . I don't know . . . she has so much energy, she wore me out. I had lunch with her at the hotel, when I'd had every intention of coming straight home.'' To bake him the pie that she had burned beyond recognition. But she had learned a lesson today; from now on, her baking would be done long before Sean was due to arrive home.

''You don't sound terribly certain about wanting this friendship to continue,'' he observed.

''Oh, I think Sue Ellen is probably a very nice person. She just takes some getting used to. I found myself following her across the street to the hotel before I knew whether or not I even wanted lunch. I'm not used to women like that.''

''Overpowering.''

''I suppose that's the word.''

''Is she married?''

''Widowed.''

''Really?'' he asked, capturing the slender fingers that insistantly, if unconsciously, played across his chest. ''Why not invite her for dinner one evening? Perhaps she's lonely and that's why she was so insistent about your joining her for lunch.''

Corie felt a strange sense of foreboding when she thought of bringing Sue Ellen into the small house that was her haven, and yet she could not identify why she would feel that way. Shrugging off her hesitation, Corie nodded her head. ''We agreed to have lunch together next week. I'll ask her then.''

Faye Doherty waved the servants out of the dining room before turning to her guest and broaching the subject most dear to her heart. ''You had no difficulty identifying her?''

''None. Your description was quite accurate. Although I found her to be prettier than you indicated.'

Frowning, Faye's eyes narrowed upon the younger woman. "You're not catting after a mouse, Sue Ellen. We have an agreement."

Sue Ellen laughed, dabbing at her mouth with a linen napkin. "How delicately you put it." She loved to annoy Faye. It always made their evenings so much more enjoyable. Choosing now to placate the woman, Sue Ellen reached across the table and placed her hand over Faye's. "Not to worry," she said softly. "I think I'm going to enjoy playing out our *agreement*."

"See that you do," Faye said firmly before devoting her attention to her meal. "When will you see her next?"

"Lunch. Tuesday," Sue Ellen said, cautiously dissecting her fish fillet. "Corie is quite obviously mad about this man of hers, Faye. In fact, that's about all the twit can talk about. It's rather boring, really." She chewed thoughtfully for a moment before smiling. "And it's occurred to me that you're going to a lot of trouble because of this Sean."

"My reasons for teaching him a well-earned lesson are none of your concern."

"Unless you're planning on taking him back after you're rid of Corie. That, dear, *would* be of concern to me."

Slowly lowering her fork to her plate, Faye glared pointedly at Sue Ellen. "Don't you *ever* talk to me in that tone."

After a moment's visual wrestling, Sue Ellen's smile broadened evilly. "He must be quite a stud."

"That's enough."

"I don't think I care to share you with the likes of Sean Garrick, Faye."

"Really, darling? Think about all the possibilities," Faye said evenly. "Think about it."

Raising a questioning brow, Sue Ellen stated happily, "I think this little game of yours is more in depth than I've anticipated, Faye. This isn't about teaching that man a lesson, is it? You want that girl out of your way."

"She's a little whore from God knows where. And yes, I want her out of the way and *Sean* back with me."

"In your bed," Sue Ellen said pointedly.

"No offense, darling."

But Sue Ellen wasn't offended. The game was proving to be more fun than she'd had in a good many years. And she was thinking about the *possibilities*, as Faye had suggested.

Chapter 20

"It's me!" Kenny cried, winding up to race to the rear of the house.

Catherine laughed. "Come take your boots off!"

"Who's *me*?" Corie called, walking quickly from the kitchen.

"Me. Your sister," Kenny said, shrugging out of her coat and leaving it dangling from Stephen's hands. "I'm home."

"I'm glad your home, baby," Corie said, dropping to one knee as she hugged the girl. "We've missed you," she said before pushing Kenny away slightly so the child could see her happy smile. "Did you have fun?"

"We did," Kenny said, nodding her head vigorously. "There's so much to do on a farm, Corie. I took care of the chickens."

"Well, good for you," Corie said sincerely. "I'm very proud of you." She stood then, greeting Catherine and Stephen as the sound of Sean's booted feet approached from behind.

"Sean!" Kenny cried, hurtling herself toward him.

"Hello, moppet," he said, lifting the girl in his arms and hugging her.

"I missed you."

"I missed you, too."

"Catherine's got a baby rolling around in her stomach."

His eyes gleaming with delight, Sean nodded his head. "Yes, I know. What do you think of that?"

"I think it must hurt," Kenny whispered against his ear.

"I don't think it hurts her, sweetheart."

"That's what Catherine says."

"Well, I think you can believe her. Let me say hello to Catherine and Stephen, all right?" Balancing McKenna on one arm, Sean turned and shook Stephen's hand before bending slightly to kiss Catherine's cheek. "You heard that, I take it."

Smiling, Catherine ran her hand lovingly down the length of McKenna's arm. "She's been quite curious about it all."

"Oh, we know how that can be." Sean laughed, having answered hundreds of questions when the curious child latched onto a new subject. "Let's get you into the parlor and warmed up," he said to Catherine and then, setting McKenna on her feet, asked, "Do you want to run and say hello to Mrs. Pringle? I think she's baking something special to welcome you home." His eyes followed the running child, even as he reached back for Corie's hand. "I'm glad she's back," he said quietly and then led his wife into the parlor behind their friends. "I'll wager you've had enough of our curious, energetic little miss by now?" he asked of Stephen.

"Not at all. It was fun having her about the place."

"Liar." Sean laughed affectionately. "But we thank you for having her. As much as I love McKenna, I think it was good for Corie and me to have some time alone."

Catherine's eyes glinted with mischief as she turned on Corie. "Perhaps I should start teaching you how to make tiny infant clothes," she said.

Corie's complexion pinked slightly, in view of the fact that the two men were intent upon her reaction. "Perhaps you should," she said boldly, winking slyly at her husband. "And I think I had better learn quickly."

McKenna interrupted the adult laughter by darting into the room and going straight to Catherine. "Are you going to stay for dinner?" she asked eagerly.

Catherine smiled, placing a hand on the child's shoulder. "I don't think so, darling."

"We haven't had a visit at all," Corie protested. "Surely you could stay?"

"We were simply waiting for an invitation," Catherine teased.

"I'll tell Mrs. P.!" McKenna called, racing from the room.

Sean winced at the girl's disrespectful reference to the housekeeper. "I know she gets that from me," he said. "I'll have to watch my tongue."

Stephen enjoyed this immensely. "Ah, another change from your old bachelor ways."

"You'll have your share of changes soon enough," Sean returned and winked at Catherine as he walked toward the door. "I'll fetch some drinks."

Catherine had pulled Corie down beside her on one of the settees and now turned her attention on the younger woman. "Are you happy, Corie?"

"Very."

"Sean is, too, I can tell. We're very pleased, Stephen and I. I want you to know that. I think we shall all be great friends."

Those words meant more to Corie than anything else the woman could have said to her. These were her husband's dearest friends and they were readily accepting her into their midst. It was another important segment of a life she had never thought to have.

Sean returned with a selection of drinks and the men fell into serious conversation across the room from the two women.

"I had drinks with Royce Freeman at the club last night," Stephen said. "It appears he's on the brink of financial ruin."

Sean nodded before sipping his brandy. "I know. I've offered him a way out, but the man's being pigheaded and won't accept my help."

Stephen wasn't surprised to hear that Sean had offered aid to their friend, but he was amazed to learn that Royce had not accepted. Sean was an astute businessman, and anyone would be wise to follow his counsel. "Perhaps I can help persuade him, then. What are you offering?"

"I've offered him shares in two ventures I've been working on for months. I've told Royce he could buy in his share from the profits, but he's understandably afraid of incurring any further debt. And, I suppose, he doesn't want to be indebted to friends," Sean added thoughtfully. "But, dammit, he can't lose and he will easily be able to pay me his buy-in share after the fact and still earn a handsome profit."

"His creditors are hounding his door, Sean," Stephen said softly.

"Creditors be damned!" Sean returned heatedly.

"I've offered to help hold them off until he receives his share of the profits."

Across the room Corie started at her husband's near shout.

"Goodness," Catherine said softly, equally shocked.

Corie frowned as she stared across the room and watched Sean in heated argument with his friend. "Catherine, what does *creditor* mean?"

Nervously smoothing her gown over her swollen belly, Catherine hesitantly supplied the information. "A creditor is a person, ah, to whom one owes a debt."

"Does that mean that Sean owes debts?" she asked, her eyes never leaving Sean's anxious face.

"I doubt that," Catherine said lightly. "Stephen says Sean is one of the keenest business heads he knows. They're no doubt talking about someone else, Corie."

"Sean seems very angry. Would he be that angry over someone else's problems?"

"Oh, yes." Catherine quickly tried to reassure her friend. "He takes everyone's problems quite seriously, you know. Sean is like that."

"Yes, I remember," Corie said, thinking of the young apprentice barber.

But she remained unconvinced.

The inhabitants of the house on Pearl Street easily returned to the evening routines set long before the marriage of Corie and Sean. Corie had long since returned to the study for the favorite storytime. She now actually thought her previous attempts to avoid being in Sean's presence quite amusing. Now the

opposite was true; she wanted to be with him every
minute of every day.

And tonight it all seemed new and different. Perhaps it was her heightened awareness of her husband's
strong, deep voice as he spoke the words from some
child's book; a voice that soothed, making her feel
warm and protected. Corie rotated her head on the
back of her chair and watched his long fingers with
their sprinkling of dark hair smooth the page he
turned. Kenny was curled up on his lap, her head
under his chin, and Sean had the small book propped
on the child's knee. It was a sight that would warm the
heart of the most callous individual and a scene Corie
had never thought to share in her lifetime. Surpris-
ingly, it brought tears to her eyes, and she watched
these two people she loved through a blur of moisture.

This was the kind of happiness one seldom believed
one deserved. A happiness so total, so complete, that
it could foster an impending sense of doom; that it was
too perfect to continue, and some wicked hand of fate
would suddenly snatch it away from the possessor.
Corie had felt that impending sense of doom since
learning the meaning of the word *creditor* earlier in
the day. She feared, not that they would be poor—she
could easily live with Sean and be happy in poverty.
She feared more for him.

Sean stopped reading as he became aware that
McKenna's small body had gone limp against him and
her breathing was now deep and even. Ducking his
head, he smiled at the closed eyes and set the book on
the table beside him. "You've had a busy day,
moppet," he whispered, stroking a small wisp of hair
back off her temple. He turned his head then to find
his wife curled up in her own chair, watching intently.
He did not fail to see the tears hovering on the edge of

her lashes, but as he stared at her, Sean thought perhaps he understood the reason for them being there. Silently he reached out and took her hand in his, watching her and loving her from the small distance between them.

From his place before the fire Thor raised his head at his master's movement and seemed to grant his approval before he dropped his head back down onto his paws.

Corie thoroughly enjoyed her luncheon with Sue Ellen the following week, although the woman declined her invitation to dinner, claiming a prior engagement.

"Now, you must let me treat," Sue Ellen said, searching her reticule for coins.

"You paid last week," Corie protested. "Sean has given me money for our lunch."

"Darling girl," Sue Ellen said sympathetically. "I'm sure your husband is a generous man, but one should never take advantage of another's financial situation."

Corie thought that an odd thing for the woman to have said and puzzled over it until that night when she climbed into bed beside her husband.

Sean enjoyed reading in bed for a short time each night, but he always welcomed Corie by pulling her against his side, even as he read. And she was normally content to lie there with her head on his shoulder until he dowsed the lamp beside him. Not so tonight.

"Sean, are these bad times in Natchez?" she asked softly.

Sean turned his attention to her, his eyes dropping

down to the top of her head. "Bad? In what way, pet?"

"Are there a lot of people with money problems?"

"There are always people with money problems, love. But not as many as a few years ago, I expect." Curious, he set his book on the bedside table and turned on his side, facing her. "What brought this on?"

Corie managed a casual shrug, but she couldn't quite keep the troubled thoughts from being reflected in her eyes. "I guess it's because I have new friends that I'm hearing things I never heard talked about before. Things I don't understand."

Running his hand lightly from her shoulder to her wrist, Sean smiled patiently. "What kinds of things, sweetheart? Maybe I can help."

"Well, a few days ago you became very angry when you were talking with Stephen about creditors."

"That's true, I was angry because a mutual friend has refused my help," he explained. And then, arching a questioning brow, he asked, "Do you understand about creditors, Corie?"

"Catherine told me."

"Good," he said absently while he studied her frown of concern. "Did I frighten you somehow, darling? I know I raised my voice but—"

"No. It wasn't that . . . it's just . . . I thought . . ."

"Thought what, Corie? Tell me."

"And Sue Ellen said a very strange thing," she blurted. "When I wanted to pay for lunch today, she said we should not take advantage of your financial situation."

Sean was visibly taken aback by that comment. "What would she know of my financial situation?"

"I don't know, Sean," she said unhappily.

"What nonsense," he said lightly, but his pride was stung. "I can certainly afford to treat my wife and her friend to a simple lunch. A dozen of your friends, for that matter."

"Don't be angry, darling."

"I am angry. I resent people discussing . . ." His eyes rounding, Sean suddenly had another thought and sat up in the bed, frowning down at her. "Have you worried about my tirade with Stephen all this time?"

"Well, no, I—"

"And after this ridiculous comment Sue Ellen made today . . ." Running agitated fingers through his black hair, he accused, "You're afraid I don't have the money to support you."

"That is not fair," Corie said fiercely, kneeling to face him with total disregard for her nakedness. "I don't give sailor's spit for money!" she hissed, reverting to her past. "I've been worried for you!"

"Oh, you have?" he raved.

"I have, Sean Garrick! I can't believe you're acting this way when you know all I care about is you and Kenny. I think you're a . . . an impossible . . . a . . ." There was a moment of intense sputtering as she sought a name mean enough to suit him.

But Sean had already realized he had been defensive and unjust. "Try *cretin*, darling," he offered softly.

Corie gasped to a halt as she stared at him. "What does that mean?" she snapped.

"Fool, dolt, and a few other unpleasant things," he explained quietly, reaching for her hand.

Corie moved back, unwilling to have him touch her. "You're all of those," she accused.

"I agree," he said pleasantly.

"And I don't like it when I'm angry and you're not."

"We've just had the first argument of our marriage," he said with a smile.

"I only wanted to understand," she said miserably. "I can be careful with money, Sean." She'd never had much, but in the past when she got her hands on a few coins, Corie could make the money stretch.

"Listen, my little ninny, I want to tell you something." But when he reached for her, Corie backed farther away. "I'm sorry for my stupidity, darling. I apologize. And I wasn't really angry with you. Come here and let me explain."

"You can explain," she said, unmoving.

"Are you really one of those unforgiving wives?" he teased. "A man's sense of pride can sometimes make him say or do stupid things. Are you never going to forgive me?"

"I want you to understand, Sean. I don't care what happens as long as we're together. I'm on your side whether it's for good or bad."

"I know," he said and lunged, easily taking her down onto the mattress and pinning her beneath him. "I know, love," he said, all hint of teasing gone. "It's the same for me. For good or for bad. And starting tomorrow, I'm going to teach you about my business because you have a right to know and not be worried about off comments some person might make. If you understand, then you won't be defenseless. I have no creditors, love, I swear. And we won't starve. Ever."

"Then why would Sue Ellen say such a funny thing?"

"I don't know, darling, I truly don't. Perhaps she didn't mean the remark the way it sounded."

Corie thought about that for a moment while Sean

studied the play of emotions across her face. He could even distinguish the very moment she had decided to give her friend the benefit of the doubt.

"If she ever says such a thing again, I will ask exactly what she means."

Happy that the matter was settled, Sean grinned as he made himself more comfortable on her body, careful not to burden her totally with his weight. "There is one more matter I need to explain, Corie."

"All right," she said and waited.

"This may have been our first argument, but I doubt it will be our last. There is one rule I want to set between us here and now, and that is we will never, *ever* sleep on our anger. I don't ever want to lie beside you and wake up to any bitterness between us. We'll resolve our differences or we won't sleep. Will you agree?"

Smiling, loving him more by the moment, Corie nodded her agreement.

"And there is one more thing," he said.

Corie laughed lightly. "You're passing out a lot of orders tonight, my friend."

"Whenever we argue," he said, ignoring her comment, "we will make up in only one way."

"Oh?"

"My way," he said, his head lowering toward hers. "The best possible way."

"This way?" she said, raising her lips to meet his.

Over the course of the next hour, Corie conjured up at least a dozen topics which could easily lead to arguments between them.

Chapter 21

Sean was good to his word, and Corie accompanied him to his office the following day. The fact that Corie could neither read nor write did not interfere with her ability to understand the intricacies of the business as her husband explained them. She was also rather amazed by her ability to retain much of what Sean told her.

While Corie was with Sean, the young apprentice barber arrived to make a further installment on the debt he owed Sean.

"I thought you'd never see your money again," Corie confessed.

"There are people worth a risk, pet," Sean said. "It's a matter of determining the ones that can be trusted."

"But you didn't know him."

"I didn't know you either, Corie. And I should have been more suspicious of your motives in the beginning. But, somehow, I wasn't."

"You trusted me?"

"I did. Well . . . warily," he confessed with a grin.

Corie cuffed his shoulder.

And so their first disagreement had not been without merit; Sean now possessed an awareness of his wife's needs, in addition to her right, to understand this side of his life, and Corie learned a valuable lesson in the worth of investigating a matter before allowing herself to worry. But aside from these things, they both learned that putting an argument behind them could be the most splendid lesson of all.

Corie had agreed to meet Sue Ellen again the following week for luncheon, but this time she found herself not quite so willing a participant. It was nice having female friends for the first time in her young life, but a hint of sourness lingered in Corie's senses. She was definitely anxious by the time she joined the other woman at the hotel.

Their time together proved congenial enough, however, and Corie managed to relax long before they reached the dessert course. But with the arrival of their second cup of tea, Sue Ellen again made a veiled remark about Sean.

"Why do you talk about my husband's finances?" Corie asked reasonably.

With apparent surprise Sue Ellen set her cup down. "I wasn't aware I had."

"That's the second time," Corie pointed out. "And I don't think I like it."

Sue Ellen immediately became the picture of sympathy. "I'm certain you don't, dear girl. It must be awful."

"What must be awful, Sue Ellen? I wish you'd explain yourself."

"Well, I wasn't certain you were aware, you understand? And I am your friend, Corie. I didn't want to be the one to tell you."

Of course not, Corie thought snidely and with growing anger. "Why don't you explain it to me," she offered, "just to be certain that we both fully understand."

"I hardly think *details* matter at this point, do you? I mean, I've been frantic, wondering if you're starving."

"What?" Corie asked in hushed wonder.

"Why do you think I bring you here to lunch, dear girl? I'm certain it's the only decent meal you get all week."

Corie actually started to laugh. "What are you talking about?" she asked after calming herself.

"Why, ah . . . it's common knowledge that your husband is in grave financial difficulty."

"Indeed?" she said, imitating Sean's ability to use the word as an accusation. "Cow chips, I say."

Gasping, Sue Ellen's hand flew to her breast. "I beg your pardon?"

Corie's eyes narrowed as she leaned across the table toward the other woman. "I don't know why you act as my friend, Sue Ellen. Maybe it's because you thought you could uncover the truth about the gossip in this town. But I don't feel as if I want to be *your* friend after today. As a parting gift I'll throw some little tidbits your way, though, and you can do whatever you want with them. Sean talks to me about his business ventures, and I've seen his books." God help her if this woman learned she could not read, Corie realized as she spoke. "My husband has no financial worries, and even if he had, it's none of your damned business. Or anybody elses." Standing hastily, Corie threw money onto the table. "Lunch is *my* treat," she said and walked away.

"You fool!" Faye Doherty raved. "I ask you to perform a simple favor and you destroy everything."

"Hardly a simple favor," Sue Ellen returned snidely. "Corie Garrick has the temper of a hissing cat, and she's as quick to anger. If you're so clever, *you* deal with her."

"Oh, I shall, my dear," Faye said smoothly. "I shall. And with my usual finesse."

But it would take time. And Faye was growing impatient.

Spring began to make promises of its impending arrival before Faye could properly time her first encounter with Corie. The buds on the trees were easily visible, and multicolored perennials had poked their delicate heads through the earth the day Faye entered a shop to find Corie Garrick in attendance. The second person to catch Faye's attention was McKenna.

Corie was at the counter, intent upon matching the number of items of Mrs. Pringle's list to the number of items going into her basket. She could not match the goods with their written names, of course, but she had easily devised a scheme for ensuring she purchased all the things Jane needed. The list was given to the clerk and the items were dropped into a basket. Corie would then take the list back and simply score off a word on the list to match the number of articles in her basket. If there was ever a discrepancy, she would make the poor fellow start again.

Corie had also managed, with Jane's help, to memorize the costs of common household goods, and by ordering in pennies and nickels, instead of by weight, she could hope she would not be cheated. But it all required intense concentration. Sometimes she felt life had been easier when she had simply pilfered what she wanted.

"That's a very pretty toy," Faye said to the intensely curious child. "Do you know how it works?"

Kenny looked up over her shoulder, her smile quickly disappearing. "It's a top," she said reluctantly.

"Yes, I know. Do you remember me?"

"Yes."

"Would you like to have that top?" Faye asked, managing to maintain a civil smile.

"I already asked Corie. She said I couldn't."

"Oh? Perhaps I could persuade her. Perhaps Corie would let me buy it for you."

Kenny's eyes took on a decidedly friendlier glow. "We could ask her."

"Let's just take this pretty top over to the counter, shall we?"

Kenny followed the woman like a lost puppy.

"Hello, Mrs. Garrick," Faye said quietly.

Corie turned in the woman's direction and frowned when she saw the top Kenny had been admiring. "Miss Doherty."

"It's *Mrs.* Doherty," Faye said pointedly, "but that hardly matters, I suppose. Your sister and I have been having a chat about this toy. It appears she would very much like to own it."

"I've told Kenny she can't have the top, *Mrs.* Doherty."

"It does seem a shame. Surely such a pretty child deserves a toy or two?"

"The *child* has a room full of toys, Mrs. Doherty."

"My, we are hostile."

"*We*?" Corie questioned. "I'm afraid I can't let you do this. Kenny knows she can't have everything that catches her eye."

"It seems I've committed an error, then. I offered to buy the top for her."

"Well, you can *un*-offer. I would buy the top if I wished Kenny to have it, but I won't have her spoiled." There was also the fact that the top was beautifully made, and Corie had been certain the thing would be costly. She had felt compelled to refuse to buy it.

"But she promised me, Corie," Kenny whined.

"Hush," Corie said, frowning at the girl.

McKenna started to cry.

"I am sorry," Faye said. "My intentions were good, I assure you." With that she turned, leaving the toy on the countertop before she walked away.

"Good *intentions*, my foot," Corie muttered under her breath.

"She promised!" Kenny wailed.

"Stop!" Corie hissed, snatching up her basket and Kenny's hand in one angry action. "Sorry, Mr. Marsh," she mumbled and fled the store.

"Where are we going?" Kenny cried, trailing with difficulty in her sister's wake.

"To the warehouse."

"Why are you mad at me?"

"I'm not."

"Yes, you are!"

"Kenny!" Corie said in a fierce whisper as she stopped and faced the child. "I'm not mad at you. Now, please stop crying."

"I want the top, Corie," the child sniffed.

"Well, I want lots of things, too, and I can't have them. Now come on. I have to see Sean."

Once at the warehouse Corie left Kenny in the outer office, entered Sean's inner sanctum, and slammed the door behind her.

"I want you to teach me to read," she said heatedly.

Sean stared at her from behind his desk, recognized righteous anger when he faced it, and said simply, "All right, darling."

"We'll start tonight," she said.

"Fine."

Corie nodded once, turned, and led Kenny from the building.

Sean walked to the door of his office, staring silently into the chilled void his wife had left as he leaned against the open door.

"Whew!" Daniel said softly from his place at his desk.

"Right you are," agreed Sean.

Nothing seemed amiss when Sean arrived home that evening. Corie was there to greet him with open arms and apparent happiness. Kenny was a bit whiny, but that was overcome with a little attention from Sean. He waited through a pre-dinner drink, through supper itself, and through storytime; still Corie offered no explanation for her earlier behavior.

When she returned to the study, having put Kenny to bed, Sean was more than ready.

He carefully filled and lit his pipe as Corie looked round the room, wondering why he had not gathered books in preparation for her first lesson.

"Where do we start?" she asked.

Sean drew deeply on his pipe and motioned toward

her chair. "With an explanation, I think, my pet. Have a seat."

He deserved an accounting, of course. Corie had simply failed to come up with a plausible excuse for her actions. "I'm sorry for the way I acted, Sean," she said, making herself comfortable. "I lost my temper because I'm stupid. It's time I did something about it."

"You are hardly *stupid*, Corie. And most particularly not because you've had no opportunity to learn to read. Illiteracy and stupidity are hardly synonymous. What set you off today?"

"Kenny wanted a toy and I might have bought it for her except it looked like it would cost a lot. She started to cry when I said no and I felt terrible." A half truth was better than no truth, she decided. "I know she can't have everything she sees and wants, but it was a pretty little thing and I just couldn't bring myself to ask Mr. Marsh the price when there was something marked on it." Shrugging in resignation, she added, "I got angry at myself, that's all."

Sean could understand her frustration, and he sympathized because he just could not imagine his life without the written word. Reading was not only necessary for his business, it was something he enjoyed in his private life. He just could not imagine life without reading. "Let me gather a few things we'll need," he said, going to his desk. "We'll work at the table in the dining room."

"Thank you, Sean," she said eagerly, following him across the room. "I know you must be tired afte working all day."

"I'm never tired when I'm with you, Corie, n matter what we're doing." He looked up from gath ering pens and paper and grinned lasciviously. "Pa

ticularly when we're engaged in certain activities over others.''

Corie laughed and whirled away when he reached for her.

''And husbands help wives and wives help husbands. That's part of the fun of being married,'' he added more seriously.

Catherine proved a bit stubborn when it came to birthing her child and delayed the moment until early April.

Corie could wait no longer than a full day after hearing the news before she was hounding Sean to take her to see the new baby.

''Catherine might like a chance to rest before she starts receiving visitors,'' Sean pointed out logically.

''But we're their best friends, Sean. Jane and I picked out a gift for a boy, and, besides, I want to see him.''

''Aha! It's not Catherine you want to visit at all,'' he teased. ''Very well. I'll rent a rig and we'll all go out there after lunch.''

Catherine showed no signs of the prolonged labor that had taken place less than forty-eight hours previous to the arrival of the Garricks. She was sitting up and smiling when Sean and Corie entered her room with Stephen and McKenna on their heels.

''Is he sleeping?'' Corie whispered, her eyes darting to the lace-covered basket beside the bed.

Catherine nodded, looking very pleased with herself.

''I'm so happy for you,'' Corie said, hugging the woman cautiously before turning her attention to the baby boy. ''He's not sleeping. He's waving a fist.''

"Lift him up," Catherine said. "You can hold him."

"Not me," Corie said, backing up and colliding with Sean's chest. "He's too small for me."

"Don't be silly, darling," Sean said quietly. "McKenna must have been that small when you cared for her."

"I don't remember her ever being *that* small."

Stephen solved the problem by bending and scooping his son up in two hands. "He's a Fraser," he said. "He's tough enough to handle."

"Just like his father," Sean offered.

"I wanna see!" Kenny cried.

"Ssh!" Corie said. "Don't jump up and down, Kenny. You'll frighten him."

"Why?"

"Well, he's small. He's not used to strange noises."

"I don't make strange noises," she muttered but grinned when Stephen lowered the baby to a reasonable height. "His face's all bunched up."

Catherine laughed and reached for her son as he began to wail. "He had a hard time getting here, McKenna. He'll be pretty in a day or two."

"Boys don't get pretty, do they, Sean?" she asked, looking up at her idol.

"Most babies are pretty, moppet, and this little fellow will probably be quite beautiful," he said diplomatically. And then he noticed a silent communication take place between his friends and reached for McKenna's hand. "Let's see if Stephen can find us a nice drink," he said.

"I want to stay with Catherine."

"You'll see Catherine again before we leave."

"Corie's staying," Kenny said, her small voice pleading.

"Corie and Catherine want to visit."

"Me, too."

"Alone," Sean said pointedly, leading the child from the room.

"Can we get a baby for our house, Sean?"

"One day, moppet," he said.

"But I want one now."

Cautiously aiding McKenna's progress down the circular staircase, Sean smiled down at the child. "It takes a bit of time, McKenna, but Corie and I are going to work very hard so we can have a baby at our house."

Walking beside Sean, Stephen seemed to choke mysteriously.

McKenna stopped a step above Sean. "You have to work?" she asked, her brow furrowed thoughtfully.

Sean nodded his head.

McKenna immediately turned on the step and started back up.

"Ho, now!" Sean laughed and reached for her hand. "Where are you going?"

"I have to see Corie."

"Later, McKenna."

"But don't you think I should tell her I can't help her dust the tables anymore?"

Sean cast Stephen a puzzled look to see if his friend had understood. He hadn't.

Bending at the waist so that he was closer to the girl, Sean asked, "Why can't you help Corie, sweetheart?"

Exasperated, Kenny frowned at him. "Corie's got o work harder, Sean, so we can get a baby faster."

Laughing, Sean scooped the girl up in his arms.

"Nice try, McKenna. But I think you could still help Corie and we'll get a baby just as fast."

Flashing Corie an embarrassed smile, Catherine held her son close to her breast. "I'm a bit awkward at this yet. My milk came in just today."

"It must be wonderful," Corie observed, but a small laugh escaped her when Catherine started. "Maybe not so wonderful?"

"He's a bit greedy," Catherine said, sighing softly as the babe settled and began to suckle. "We've named him Andrew," she said, her eyes meeting Corie's. "I can't begin to tell you how I feel, Corie. But you'll understand once you and Sean have a child."

Blushing profusely, Corie smiled. "I don't think it will take us too long."

Chapter 22

There was one fear that Corie could not seem to shake. She was concerned that she might somehow embarrass Sean in front of people who mattered to him in his business and his life in the community. She had studied Catherine and Jane for months, hoping to copy their more graceful movements and manners. She fretted over the harshness of her voice, when genteel ladies always seemed to have whispery-soft voices. And her lack of verbal eloquence drove her to the point of almost constantly harassing Sean for meanings of new words and explanations as to their usage. She was determined that people meeting her for the first time would never guess at her origins, and she was going to achieve this by being acutely aware of everyone, every movement, and every word spoken around her.

She was doing it for Sean, but she understood that she was doing it for herself as well. Never, ever would he be ashamed of her and, therefore, never, ever, would she lose him.

Still the third week of April, and the evening Corie was to attend her first dinner party, threatened to shatter the sense of security, that sense of believing in herself, that she had been working so hard to achieve. As she stared at herself in the cheval glass in the bedroom, Corie began to doubt that she could survive the evening without embarrassing Sean and herself.

"I can't do this," she whispered.

Jane moved behind her and fastened a final curl in place. "You can and you will," she said firmly. "Do you want Mr. Garrick going off on his own? There will be other women there tonight willing to keep him company, I imagine."

"You know, Jane," Corie said affectionately, "sometimes you play dirty."

"I beg your pardon?" Jane returned, obviously affronted.

"You're right. There will be other women there tonight, and with me beside him, Sean will have a chance to compare me to them."

"What nonsense."

"It's true. Oh, I know he loves me," she said, turning to face the other woman. "But we've never been in a position like this before where we'll be surrounded by ladies who are smart and speak better than I do."

"There is *nothing* wrong with the way you speak," Jane said firmly. "And I will tell you something else, Corinne Garrick, you are more intelligent than the empty-headed twits who live in this town and fancy themselves superior to half the world. And if you want to convince Mr. Garrick that you're not good enough for him, you just keep on thinking the way you've been thinking. You'll convince yourself *and* him! You just remember that he knew where you came from and how you had to live, and still he wanted to marry you. You just remember that.''

"I didn't know you had such a temper," Corie said, a slow smile tipping the corners of her mouth. "And thank you. I guess I needed to be reminded of a few things."

"I *guess* you did," the older woman said. "You look exceptionally beautiful tonight. You remember that as well."

"I will."

"Now, go down there and show Mr. Garrick how truly lucky a man he is."

Beaming now, Corie bussed Jane's cheek. "Thank you," she said softly.

It was one of those evenings in early spring when one could *feel* things growing; it was a sense that everything on earth was renewing itself, and Sean was one of those rare people who never failed to notice. Warm spring evenings seemed to lure him outside after darkness had descended, and that is where Corie found him. He was seated with McKenna on his lap, on a white bench at the end of the walk that led through the gardens. Wearing black evening clothes, he should have looked ridiculous, surrounded as he was by freshly turned gardens. But he didn't. Far from it.

"See, moppet? Look over there by the big oak. Look high."

"I don't see anything," Kenny said disappointedly.

"There!" Sean said, pointing off into the near distance. "See all the tiny lights?"

"I see!" she cried. "Fireflies!"

"They look like they're dancing, don't they?"

"Yup."

"Yes."

"Yes," Kenny said dutifully.

Corie smiled as she entered the ring of candlelight cast from the table near Sean's back. "Chasing fireflies?" she teased.

Sean turned at the sound of her voice, bringing her into view for both himself and McKenna. "Oh, look at you," he said softly as his eyes traveled her length.

He didn't have to say another word as far as Corie was concerned; his eyes told her he was pleased.

"Corie, you look so pretty," Kenny said in awe.

"Thank you, baby."

"*Pretty* is hardly the word, McKenna," Sean said, setting the small girl on her feet. "Your sister is absolutely the loveliest creature I have ever seen." He stood before his young wife then, taking her hand and bringing it to his lips.

"Ah, mushy," Kenny drawled, obviously disgusted.

Sean grinned, his eyes never leaving Corie's. "Mushy? Is that a word for us?"

"I guess it is to Kenny."

"I think I would rather stay home tonight and be *mushy* with you. I don't think I want to share you with anyone else."

"Me, too," she said hopefully. It would be just fine by her if Sean changed their plans for the evening.

"But I suppose I can't be that selfish."

"You can be as selfish as you want," she returned

"You do look beautiful, my darling," he said catching her hand in the crook of his arm. "I suppos the carriage will be here by now. Come alon McKenna," he added, turning briefly to see that th child was there. "It's time to go inside."

"Can I have a story, Sean?" Kenny asked as she skipped ahead of them along the stone path.

"I've read you one story tonight, moppet. That's it, I'm afraid. Corie and I will be very late if we don't leave soon."

"Could we play the *alphabet game*?"

"McKenna," Corie pleaded.

"Just half the alphabet," she pleaded. "Real fast."

"We could play a bit while you walk us to the door," Corie said, taking her sister's hand. "You start."

"My name is Alice Adams and I sell apples," Kenny piped with a grin.

Corie also liked the game now that her spelling had improved. "My name is Betty Brown, and I sell buns."

"My name is Ken—"

"No, Sean! *Ken* starts with *k*." Kenny loved to correct him.

"All right. My name is Carl Campion and I sell candles."

All too soon McKenna was having to say good night. "Can I come?" she asked as Corie bent to hug the girl.

"No. We've talked about this," Sean said patiently.

"When I get big?"

"When you get big," he agreed, hugging her fiercely.

Rosalie, home of Peter Little and his family, was located on the Natchez Bluffs at the southern end of the Spanish promenade and overlooked the Mississippi River. Corie had passed the stately mansion many times but had never thought she would be attending a gala evening, arriving with considerable flourish at Rosalie's front door. The mansion appeared to be almost cubical, crowned by a hip roof with balustrade and graced at the front by a porch resembling a two-story-high classical temple. Its stately white columns reflected warm yellow light that flowed from every window across the front of the building and welcomed all who had passed through the iron gates to the grounds.

Sean descended first from the carriage and turned to assist his wife.

Her head tipping back in order to admire the high front of the mansion, Corie clung tightly to Sean's hand. "If you had asked me months ago what I thought of a place like this, your ears would still be ringing," she said. "Now I'm about to go inside and have supper."

Sean thought he understood. "Are you frightened, my love?" he asked quietly.

Corie's eyes moved to his. "Would you expect fear from me?"

"Under normal conditions, no. But tonight, I think, might be a little different."

Smiling wryly, she admitted, "I am. I'm scared to death."

"There are only people in there. Just like you and me."

"You're wrong, Sean," she said quietly. "The people in there are not nearly so good as you, and they are certainly *not* like me."

"That's true," he said, "I stand corrected. You, my darling, are better."

Corie laughed at the ridiculous statement and walked gracefully by his side as they mounted the steps to the front porch.

"What you fail to realize," he said for her ear

alone, "is that you are beautiful, willowy, graceful, intelligent, witty—"

"Stop!" She laughed again. "I know what you're doing."

Sean stopped walking and turned to her on the top step. "There is only one thing you have to remember, my pet," he said earnestly. "You are mine. I love you and I'm very proud that you are my wife."

Corie shared a few silent words of thanks as she stared into the darkness of his eyes. Then she tipped up and lightly kissed his cheek. "I do love you, Sean Garrick."

Sean turned toward the door, taking her with him. "And if I catch you dancing more than twice with the same man, I'll beat you," he teased.

"The way I dance?" She laughed. "Once should be enough for any man."

"Are you suggesting I'm not a master dance instructor?"

"No, my darling. I'm suggesting I'm not a *master* student."

Sean introduced his young bride to many people that evening but carefully chose those with whom they spent any considerable length of time. He tended to be cautiously polite and businesslike to particular members of the gathering. There were many couples who possessed a sense of humor and gentle manners, however, and these were the people he chose as their companions for the evening. The Littles had good taste in friends, but there were some Peter could not afford to snub by withholding an invitation to an evening that was considered one of the major events of the spring season. And Sean had attended enough of these affairs to know into which corner the cats

were drawn. He would not have Corie subjected to
that side of Natchez aristocracy. He remained close to
Corie's side, keeping her hand firmly tucked into the
crook of his arm, until he realized she had begun to
relax and was actually sparring gaily with a young
woman who stood next to her.

"Are you enjoying yourself, love?" he asked when
the young woman had moved away.

Her eyes were bright when she turned his way.
"We were laughing about the man whose wig has
gone askew."

"Really?" Sean grinned. "Where?"

"Over there," she said, her eyes darting fleetingly
across the room.

"Oh, my God," he breathed. "Hartly *will* be in a
tizzy when he discovers that. He fancies himself quite
a ladies' man, you see."

Corie giggled in surprise, gripping his arm. "I've
never heard you speak like that before."

"That's my Hartly impression," he teased.

Suddenly Corie's eyes widened, and her laughter
came to a halt. "I think I've had too much punch,"
she said. "I need to find—"

"If you go upstairs, I believe they have set aside
a . . . ah . . . ladies' retiring room."

"A retiring room?" she asked, her nose crinkling.
"Whatever happened to good old-fashioned words
like *privy*?" she whispered.

"They no doubt have one of those as well," he
whispered in return. "Hadn't you better march up
those stairs?"

"Yes, sir!" she said smartly and turned from him

Sean watched her go, grinning stupidly as he
watched her make her way through the crowded room
He was pleased that she seemed to be having fun

He'd been concerned that she would never relax when she had refused so much as a glass of wine, preferring to drink the nonalcoholic punch instead. But she had come around and seemed to have her confidence back in place. She was funny that way, he realized, never speaking her concerns openly. But he knew instinctively when her self-esteem was low. It was something she couldn't hide from him. And because he knew that about her and understood, he was secretly filled with pride every time she overcame another hurdle. She was quite a woman, his Corie. As young as she was, he'd never met another woman who possessed quite the same amount of courage.

Corie found the *ladies'* room with the help of a maid and was checking her appearance in a glass when she heard the door open.

"Well, we meet again, Mrs. Garrick," the woman said. "Hello."

Corie turned and faced Faye Doherty, determined to appear polite and then get away from the woman. "Good evening," she said.

"I'm very glad to see you out and about. I've only just arrived, but I saw Sean downstairs and wondered if you had accompanied him."

"Don't wives usually accompany their husbands to these affairs?" Corie questioned, fighting to keep her voice unaffected by her emotions; why was it she hated to hear Sean's name on this woman's lips?

"Not always, my dear," Faye said, smiling as she approached the mirror. "I do love your gown," she added in a tone that made the remark seem like an afterthought. "Despite everything, Sean still spares no expense when it comes to appearances."

Frowning, Corie's eyes met Faye's in the mirror. "I don't understand."

"I wouldn't expect you to, dear," Faye said, completing her perusal of her appearance and turning to face Corie. "He's so very stubborn. Did you know that?"

Pricked by the suggestion that Faye knew Sean better than she, Corie's spine stiffened. "He can be stubborn. Yes."

"I offered to help, but he refused. I suppose that's why I felt compelled to offer to buy that toy for your poor little sister."

Exasperated, Corie folded her arms under her breasts. "Mrs. Doherty, you're not making one *lick* of sense."

"My, you do have a way with words," Faye said, strolling to a boudoir chair and carefully arranging her skirts as she sat.

Angry now at this high-handedness, Corie snapped, "If you want me to understand, then speak the words plainly. If not, I'm going back to the party." She began to move toward the door until Faye's words stopped her.

"I suppose I've veiled my words in order not to hurt you."

Turning, Corie laughed bitterly. "Faye," she drawled disrespectfully, "I don't believe you'd give two hoots about not hurting me. I'm really not fooled by you. Now, if you have something to say, say it."

Faye Doherty was hardly familiar with bluntness and lack of respect when people addressed her, and her glowing pink complexion told Corie as much.

"Very well," she shot back. "I did offer to help, but Sean was too proud to take money. I think you should know that you are helping to ruin him."

Stunned, Corie literally rocked backward. "What are you talking about?"

"He's almost bankrupt, you silly chit," Faye said heatedly. "And he continues to buy you the most expensive gowns. You must be very selfish, *Mrs. Garrick*, if you demand the best for yourself and would not even buy a child a simple toy. I imagine that's a blessing for Sean, when I think about it," she said derisively. "At least you're not adding to his indebtedness for your sister's sake."

Corie thought about the many gifts, the continuous stream of new clothes that Sean insisted she purchase, and a boulder landed in the bottom of her stomach. It was true, he had showered her with many new things, but he had done the same for Kenny. But these other charges?

And then, in the midst of growing anxiety, Corie realized she had lived through this particular scene before. With a different woman, perhaps, and the accusations were new, but the subject of Sean's finances had surfaced again, and that made her suspicious above all else.

Regaining control, Corie asked tightly, "How do you know of Sean's business matters?"

"He's confided in me," Faye said primly, her gaze not wavering an inch.

"When did this *confiding* take place?"

"Oh, I don't think you want to know about that, my dear." There was another veiled meaning there.

Corie took a moment to grind her teeth, her fists clenching. "All right. *Where* did this happen?"

"At my home."

"Really? Recently?" she asked shortly, her fingers itching to be buried in the woman's hair . . . and pull.

"Quite recently. And for some time now."

Corie paced away, her arms gripping her middle as she turned and faced the woman squarely. "What you haven't counted on, Faye, is that Sean shares things with me about his business. I happen to know he is doing just fine financially. I've even seen his books. So now I have to ask myself why you are doing this."

Faye was not ready to give up just yet. "You've seen his books?" she asked. "*You* read? Come now, my dear."

"I do read," she said angrily.

"Books can be altered to show many things," Faye returned with a casual shrug.

Corie could see she was not about to win over this woman who obviously had the advantage of experience in games of this nature. And her anger was not going to aid her cause. Faye was remaining calm, while Corie could barely think straight. It was time to retreat and leave the woman frustrated, she decided.

Smiling she forced her body to relax and she stood proudly. "So, my husband is bankrupt and he's coming to you for comforting? Is that what you would have me believe?"

"Believe what you must, my dear."

Her smile growing, Corie said happily, "You're a sick woman, *Mrs*. Doherty." And with that she turned and glided from the room.

Chapter 23

That night Sean's most tender embrace seemed painful as Corie found herself *enduring* his touch instead of reveling in their lovemaking as she normally would. She did not believe he was seeing Faye again. But the woman had spawned just enough doubt that Corie was forced to mentally remind herself that Sean loved her. She was so busy casting mentally about for reassurance that she had little inclination for lovemaking.

Sean rolled onto his back and away from his wife's inert body, frowning as he turned his head in her direction. "What is it, Corie?" he asked softly. "What's wrong?"

"Nothing is wrong," she said quietly, rolling onto her side away from him. "I'm just tired from the party."

"You've never been too tired before," he teased, raising up and looking over her shoulder.

"I'm not used to being up so late," she explained in a husky voice.

Sean moved his head farther over her shoulder, his hand on her arm. "You're crying," he said in wonder, rolling her onto her back. "Sweetheart, tell me what's wrong."

"Nothing."

"For heaven's sake, Corie, something must be wrong. You never cry," he said with growing concern. "Are you feeling ill?"

"I'm fine," she choked.

"Dammit, Corie," he said in frustration and the dam burst.

Corie's tears flowed in earnest then. "Could you hold me?" she managed to gasp.

"Of course I'll hold you," he whispered, pulling her fiercely against himself. He let her tears wash down her face and over his chest for several moments, holding her tightly. But then, suddenly, he thought he could stand it no longer. "Corie, let me help you. I hate to see you like this. Tell me what's wrong."

Corie rotated her forehead against his chest.

Sean searched his mind for possible explanations for this behavior and could come up with only one. "Darling," he said as her crying began to soften, "do you think you could be pregnant?"

Corie managed to pull her head back and look up at him. "What?"

"A child . . . I thought . . . well, women sometimes become weepy when . . ."

That produced a new flood of tears.

"Do you think it's possible?" he asked, half hoping he had arrived at an explanation; otherwise he was stymied.

"I don't know," she cried. "I haven't had time to think about it."

Smiling at her pathetic little voice, Sean wiped tears

from her face with the pad of his thumb. "Do you think we could *think* about it?" he asked. "It's been quite some time since we couldn't make love."

Sniffing ungraciously, Corie looked at him again. "Has it?"

Sean was truly quite concerned about this lethargy that had appeared so suddenly. "Tomorrow I'm going to speak to Kevin Thatcher," he said. "Obviously there is something very wrong."

"I don't need a doctor, Sean."

"Unless you give me an explanation for this sudden unhappiness, Corie, you are going to see Kevin tomorrow."

Sighing, Corie rolled onto her back and stared at the ceiling. "Perhaps there is a child," she said quietly.

Doubtful now about this as a possible solution, Sean could not bring himself to feel any pleasure. Staring down at her, he gently touched her cheek. "I hope that is the answer," he whispered.

"Faye, please stop pacing," Sue Ellen protested, raising a glass of wine to her lips. "I'm certain you've achieved all you were hoping for."

Whirling on the younger woman, Faye paced across the parlor and frowned down at her. "How can you be so certain?" she growled. "That stupid girl did not even flinch when I hinted that Sean had secretly been coming here to me. And she seems to have convinced herself that she knows everything about his business. She's too damned sure of herself. I'm not certain I've achieved anything."

"But we must have her wondering," Sue Ellen said logically. "A little time and all her doubts will fester and bring about a clash between them. But if she's not convinced that her husband has been lying and cheating, then perhaps you will have to be a little more aggressive in order to be done with her.''

Retrieving her own glass from a table, Faye frowned over its rim. ''Would you care to elaborate?''

Shrugging casually, Sue Ellen stretched slowly, graciously, and winked at her current friend. ''I happen to have a few acquaintances who live Under-the-Hill. I think they would be willing to help. For a price.''

''Really?'' Faye drawled, smiling with growing curiosity as she joined the younger woman on the settee. ''Pray, continue.''

Sue Ellen giggled with delight while Faye became an avid listener for once in their relationship. She had reconciled herself to having to share Faye with Sean once this was all over, but *share* they would. Faye would never dare to turn her away. Not after this.

The very next morning Corie dutifully announced her bleeding had commenced.

There was no child.

That announcement seemed to establish a sense of despondency between Sean and Corie.

Sean was worried. Corie's smiles seemed forced and her laughter even more so. Her small signs of affection were tarnished by what he interpreted as distant thoughts, and even Kenny appeared to receive less and less of Corie's attention. His young wife had drawn into herself, and Sean's attempts to seek an explanation from her or have her see Dr. Thatcher met with definite resistance.

Corie had little awareness of her husband's con-cerns and Kenny's growing unhappiness. Her thoughts were taken up primarily with a plan to help Sean save his business. He had worked too hard to have his success snatched away from him. The small nagging doubt that her husband had been seeing another woman received little attention as she concentrated her efforts on helping Sean. She was relatively certain Faye had lied about Sean's cheating, but Corie was not so certain Sean had not lied about his finances. There were too many coincidences surrounding the information she had gleaned about that.

Finally arriving at a decision a few days later, Corie waited for the heavy rains to stop. She would turn to Peter Kemper for help.

In a moment of desperation Sean ignored the heavy rains and set out from town in a rented rig. He was turning to Catherine Fraser for help.

"Catherine," Corie greeted the woman a few days later. "Whatever brought you out on a day like this?"

Catherine quickly entered the small house, giving Corie clearance to close the door against the rain. "I'm hoping for a cup of tea," she said, putting Andrew into Corie's arms. "I don't think this rain is ever going to stop," she said, fanning the water drops from her cloak. "My coachman is going around back to wait in the kitchen. I'm certain Jane won't mind."

"Of course she won't," Corie said, unwrapping the heavily blanketed baby. "Get your cloak off now, before you catch your death. And you haven't told me why you would come out on a day like this."

"I thought you would be happy to see me," Catherine said, reaching up to hang her cloak on a peg. "We haven't had a visit with each other for weeks it seems."

"I'm always happy to see you," Corie said, giving Andrew up to his mother. "What's the real reason for your visit?"

Catherine laughed shortly and led the way to the parlor. "You have a suspicious nature."

"True."

"All right," she said, sitting opposite her friend. "I'm here because Sean is very worried about you."

Frowning, Corie studied the stripes of her gown for a moment.

"What's wrong, Corie? He tells me you're very unhappy and distant. That's not like you. Is it because you're not in the family way?"

Corie's eyes found her friend's. "I'll set the kettle on for tea," she said, getting to her feet and evading the issue.

"Wait. Forget the tea and talk to me. Sean is almost out of his mind with worry. Did you know that?"

Corie merely shook her head.

"He says you've been different since the night you were at Rosalie. Did something happen there, Corie?"

"I think I could be pregnant," Corie said, ignoring the question.

"What?" Catherine asked, bolting back in her chair. "But Sean said—"

"I'm not certain. I've had some spotting but not the usual," Corie said uneasily. She wasn't accustomed to speaking of intimate things with anyone other than Sean. "I don't know what that means."

With a growing smile, Catherine laid Andrew on a blanket on the floor and sat beside Corie, taking her hand in both of hers. "No wonder you've seemed different, you silly girl. You're scared half to death, no doubt. Why wouldn't you talk to Sean or Dr. Thatcher—even me, if you preferred not to talk to a man about this? I could shake you," she added with affection.

Now that she had effectively turned the tide of the

conversation, Corie found she could not look Catherine directly in the eye. Although she told no lie, Corie was feeling guilty for being less than truthful.

"You really must see Kevin, Corie," Catherine insisted. "I've heard of this happening to other women during the early stages of their pregnancy, but you don't want to take any chances. Kevin might want you to keep to your bed for a few days until this stops. Would you like me to be with you?"

Shaking her head, Corie said, "I'll see him tomorrow."

"And you'll explain to Sean? You promise me?"

"Tonight. I promise."

But that afternoon, after Catherine left her, Corie braved the rains and went to find Peter Kemper.

Chapter 24

The world of Natchez Under-the-Hill had become a foreign place to Corie now, and she understood that was a result of the changes that had taken place within her. She seldom came here anymore, knowing she was not welcome by her mother. Knowing, too, that most of the people who had known her here would now resent her. They would, no doubt, be suspicious of any reasons she might have for returning. And while she often felt pangs of guilt over not seeing her mother, Sean had been as good as his word and had food delivered to Constance regularly. But he would not provide money; Constance would only use the funds to buy drink.

As Corie sloshed along the street toward Tim's Place, she wondered now if that was the only reason Sean would not provide money to her mother. Immediately on the heels of *that* thought, she chastised herself for not being charitable toward her husband; Sean was wise in placing his money when people needed help. She, above everyone, should understand that. He was not responsible for the welfare of Constance Alexander in any event. "You're turning yourself into a bitch," she muttered to herself.

Failing to locate Peter at Tim's Place, Corie hitched up her skirts and started the difficult climb up the steep, muddy hill toward the place where Peter and his father stored their stolen goods. She hated the caves. Had always feared them. But this was a desperate mission, and her fears would just have to be put aside. She fell more than once to her knees, her sodden clothing pulling her down and her footing uncertain. Eventually, knowing she was close to Peter's cave, she called out breathlessly. But the rains drowned out his name, and it was only when she fell into the open mouth of the cave that Peter heard her call for him.

Rushing to her, Peter helped her to her feet and moved her inside toward the lantern. "What the devil are you doin' here?" he asked.

Gasping, Corie dropped to her knees beside the small fire. "I need your help," she said.

"Can't that swell of yours give you all the help you need?" he asked resentfully.

"Please, Peter," she begged, wiping the moisture from her face. "I need help for Sean."

With a rude grunt Peter squatted beside her, staring into the fire. "And you come to *me*? Why should I help the likes of him?"

"Because he's been good to me?" she asked softly "Because I love him and he loves me?"

"You forget that I love you, too," he said, scratching the earthen floor with a stick. "I think you're witch for askin'."

"And you're right," she said with a small, w smile.

Peter stared at her for a long moment and th

laughed, shaking his head. "You've got more guts than brains, Corie, comin' out on a day like this." His eyes flashed briefly toward the mouth of the cave and the downpour of rain.

"I'm desperate," she said.

Sighing heavily, he nodded his agreement. "You might as well start tellin' me."

"I need a shipment of something very costly. What do you think you can find?"

"For chrissake, Corie . . ." he sputtered.

"And I need the goods put in Sean's warehouse one night soon."

"Jesus!" he muttered.

"You can do it, Peter."

"Of course I can do it," he said angrily. "It's a matter of if I *want* to do . . ."

There was a rumble deep within the bowels of the earth then and Peter's eyes shot upward only briefly before he dived toward her. "Down!" he screamed.

Sean returned from work late that afternoon in a hack, due to the downpour of rain. When he entered the house, Corie did not greet him as was her habit, and he wondered if Catherine had, in fact, come to visit. He entered the parlor and, finding it empty, proceeded to the kitchen, where Kenny was happily sneaking raw cookie dough from a bowl while Jane had her back turned.

"Hello, you two," he said and grinned as Kenny jumped from her stool and ran toward him. "Don't you dare put those sticky hands on me," he teased, and the child took a step away.

Jane turned from the stove and frowned at the child. "Not again," she admonished, reaching for a towel.

"If you keep eating that dough, you're going to get a tummyache, my girl."

Kenny allowed her hands to be wiped and looked appropriately chastised.

"Where's Corie?" Sean asked.

"She must be upstairs," Jane answered.

"Did Catherine come by today?"

"Yup!" Kenny supplied with a grin.

"Yes," Jane and Sean corrected.

Kenny chattered about Andrew's belching for a moment, but Sean's attention to the child was distracted at best. Turning toward the stove where Jane spooned dough onto a baking tray, he asked, "How did Corie seem to you today, Mrs. P.?"

Jane's eyes met those of her employer and then turned to Kenny. "Would you run upstairs and find Corie, dear?"

Kenny nodded, racing from the room.

"There is something wrong, then," Jane said, having instinctively felt the tension between husband and wife. "I've wondered."

Sean took two steps toward the table, pulled out a chair, and sat, obviously weary. "I don't know what it is," he confessed. "Corie has been unhappy for days and won't confide in me at all." He raised worried eyes and frowned at the older woman. "We normally communicate so well. At least I thought we always had. I didn't think there was anything that Corie and I could not share openly. But something is worrying her or hurting her, and she won't talk to me. She openly avoids responding to questions. At other times she's evasive. And she's obviously unhappy. I had asked Catherine to come here and talk with her, hoping Corie would open up to a friend if she feels she can talk with me. Did you notice any change in her after Catherine left?'' he asked hopefully.

But Jane was immediately shaking her head, joining him at the table. ''I haven't seen her since shortly after Mrs. Fraser left the house. She's been upstairs all this time.''

''Perhaps she's been resting,'' he said, getting to his feet. ''Perhaps she's not well and doesn't want me to know.''

But before Sean could exit the kitchen, Kenny returned.

''I can't find Corie,'' she said, clearly puzzled. ''I looked in all the rooms.''

Sean felt an alarming quickening of his pulse. ''Did you look in my study, moppet?'' he asked, moving around the child and hurrying toward the door.

Sean entered the empty room, turning in a full circle as Jane and Kenny watched from the door. ''She's got to be somewhere in this house,'' he said softly. ''She surely wouldn't go out in this rain.''

Sean raced from room to room, little noting that Kenny was on his heels every step of the way. When he had retraced his steps, returning to the study without a trace of Corie, Sean placed his hand on the back of her chair. ''Where are you?'' he whispered.

''Maybe she went to buy something,'' Kenny offered uncertainly.

Sean seemed to notice the child for the first time in several moments and placed his hand on the back of her head, drawing Kenny up against his hip as he stared at Jane Pringle. ''Why would she leave the house and not tell you?'' he asked, knowing that questioning the woman was futile. ''I don't like this,'' he muttered, stroking Kenny's hair. ''I'm going out to look for her.''

Nothing Jane Pringle could say would stop him, and Kenny, sensing Sean's fear, began to cry. But still he went, running the streets of Natchez like a madman. Storming into all the usual shops only to learn that she had not been there. His fear turned to panic when he realized that he had lost her; she had been despondent. But why? And then there was another question that begged an answer: How long had she been unhappy? And was *he* the cause of her unhappiness? If so, where had she gone and to whom? He refused to contemplate the possible answers to these questions as he hastily turned toward Pearl Street.

But Sean did not return to his home.

Not until the wee small hours of the morning.

The cry had gone up to the town above the hill . . . *landslide!* The caves had toppled.

Sean raced to the small, disheveled room above Tim's Place, but found Constance the only occupant of the room. Dashing down the steps and around the building, he entered the infamous bar seeking Peter Kemper.

Tim, himself, was not to be found, and few patrons stood about drinking this night. Most available and able-bodied men were frantically digging up the sodden hillside, seeking the lost.

Sean merely had to ask a single question before he was pointed in the direction of a corner table.

"There," some nameless drunkard pointed. "Peter's father."

"Where is he?" Sean demanded before he had reached Kemper's side. "I'm looking for Peter."

"So's half the people up there," Kemper mumbled into his tankard.

"What?"

"He's dead for certain. They's tryin' to dig him out."

Sean grabbed the front of the man's wet jacket and dragged him half out of his chair. "You're saying Peter was in a cave? Was he alone?"

Kemper squinted at his assailant, focusing through a haze of rum. "Don't know."

"Think! Goddammit! You must know. Have you seen Corie today?"

"Corie?" Kemper's head snapped back when Sean shook him.

"Corie Gar . . . Alexander. Could she have been with Peter?"

"Don't know."

"Son of a bitch! Get up! You damn well do know!" Sean pulled the old man to his feet, forcing him toward the door of Tim's Place. "You're going to show me where," he ranted, pushing Kemper by a steel grip on the shoulder. "You'll show me the location of your damned cave, or I'll kill you here and now!"

"We can't find nothin' up there," the man whined. "There's nothin' but mud up there."

Sean pushed Kemper onward but quickly found the man less than useless. And once up the Hill there were others to help him identify the approximate location of the one cave that he feared. A group of men were digging there, the rain forcing mud to run from above them and pool about their feet. Sean grabbed a shovel from one man's hand and began to dig as if he were born with the tool in his hands.

He worked frantically, even when men shouted through the rain that his efforts were futile. They were about to give it up. What little headway they made

God reversed with more mud and the ever-present
rain. And because Sean refused to quit, a few hearty
souls remained at his side.

He lost all track of time . . . lost all sense of
feeling in his arms and ignored the pain in his back.
He knew of no other place Corie could have gone, but
he refused to think about her reasons for coming here;
back to Peter.

At some point during that long night someone had
the foresight to construct a makeshift runoff of planks
above the location of the digging. Once the wooden
''roof'' was in place, the mud ran off to the sides and
the men began to make some headway.

Sean dug more frantically.

''Give me your shovel!'' a voice rose above the din.
''Rest a while!''

Sean turned his head toward the man who had
spoken . . . it was Stephen.

''Jane sent a boy to fetch us,'' Stephen explained.
''Give me the shovel.''

Sean could not rely upon words, but his eyes
thanked his friend for coming. ''Get your own
damned shovel,'' he said affectionately. ''We need
every pair of hands.''

''Are you certain she's in there?''

Sean shook his head and bent his back, digging
once again.

Stephen seized a shovel from the nearest man and
stepped up beside his friend.

If they had been any closer to the mouth of the cave
the rescuers would have found them both dead. As it
was, Peter's lifeless body had probably saved the
young woman he loved; had loved from the time she
was old enough to understand what *love* meant.

The cave was deep and contained enough air to support the needs of the unconscious Corie during the hours it took the men to find her. Sean scrambled into the first small opening they had made.

Stephen was right behind him.

"She's here!" he cried, racing toward the two fallen bodies.

Wooden beams that had been used to shore up the mouth of the cave lay shattered and broken around and over the two very still bodies. It was readily apparent that Peter was dead. Sean tore at the debris, throwing chunks of wood and clumps of earth in a wide circle and then, with Stephen's help, rolled the body of Peter Kemper off Corie.

"She's alive!" Stephen roared, gripping Corie's mud-covered wrist and pressing his shaking fingers into the hollow of her throat.

Of course she's alive, Sean thought, having refused to think any differently. As his eyes and hands scanned her body in search of injuries, the first thing he noticed was a protrusion of wood from her shoulder.

"She's got a fierce bump on her head," Stephen said.

"Here," Sean returned, pointing briefly to the wood with shaking fingers. His hands pressed along the length of her arms then, searching for broken ones.

"Her leg," Stephen said.

Sean's head snapped around, and he cringed at the grotesque positioning of her foot. "Jesus, Mary, and Joseph!" he breathed as he bent over Corie's legs. "It's her ankle, I think."

"We have to get her out of here," Stephen said, turning toward the mouth of the cave and the men gathered there. "Someone get us a carriage down below and a stretcher!" he called.

Sean could only stare, lightly caressing Corie's muddied wrist. "My lovely, sweet girl is broken, Stephen," he whispered.

Jostling about in the wagon bed caused Corie to cry out more than once during their arduous trip up the hill. But she did not fully awaken, and for that, Sean was thankful; her pain, obviously, would be tremendous.

During the trip, Stephen directed the driver of the wagon to fetch Dr. Thatcher and return him to the house on Pearl Street, paying the man handsomely for his trouble.

Once at Sean's home the two men carried Corie carefully up the walk and the steps, finding the door open wide as Catherine and Jane stood there waiting.

"She's alive!" Catherine cried, her hands covering her lips as hours of worry fulminated at last and tears rolled down her face.

"Pull out the table in the kitchen," Stephen directed as he and Sean carefully made their way up the steps.

Jane sprang into action and ran to the back of the house.

Catherine hesitated briefly, walking backward down the hall as the two men advanced with their burden. "Is she badly hurt?" she asked.

Stephen nodded and his wife whirled blindly, racing ahead of them then.

Jane Pringle had single-handedly pushed the wooden chopping block aside and dragged the large round table into the center of the room. The two men waited as the women pulled the table apart a dropped a wooden leaf into its middle; it would now support Corie's length.

"We'll have to ease her onto her stomach," Sean said as they lowered Corie first to her side and then gently turned her over.

Catherine's cry at the sight of her friend's shoulder brought Stephen about. "Fetch some linens," he said, "and then check on McKenna."

"I'm staying," Catherine said stubbornly, her eyes meeting Sean's. "You'll need help getting her out of those clothes."

Jane left the room to fetch the needed linens while Stephen hefted great kettles onto the stove, filled them with water, and built a blazing fire.

Catherine had found scissors and was attacking Corie's gown.

"I'll do that," Sean said.

Catherine's eyes met his, and she nodded. He needed to do this, she could see. "I'll rummage through your wardrobe for dry things for you and Stephen," she said, and Sean nodded.

The kitchen became a hive of activity as the four people who loved Corie so desperately set about to see her clean and as comfortable as possible. There was no thought given to Corie's nakedness as the two men moved her gently, stripping away every piece of wet and mud-covered clothing. Then Jane and Catherine moved in, washing Corie's battered flesh. Sean and Stephen held Corie slightly above the table, moving her as little as possible, as a blanket and then clean, fresh linens were eased beneath her. Finally settling her once again, she was covered with clean sheets. The temperature in the room rose as more wood was added to the fire in attempts to warm the unconscious young woman.

It was time then for the men to see to themselves. Jane fled the room, and Catherine directed her attention solely toward Corie. Sean and Stephen stood near the stove, stripped themselves of their wet garments, washed with warm water and donned the clothes that Catherine had brought to them.

"Where the hell is Thatcher?" Sean growled as he took a place beside the table and engulfed Corie's small hand in both of his own. "What if that damned driver took your money and didn't fetch the doctor?"

"Thatcher will be here," Stephen said quietly.

Catherine stood on the opposite side of the table and studied Sean's weary face. "She'll be all right, Sean," she said with quiet confidence. "She's a strong girl."

Sean continued to study the face of his wife as he said, "I'd already lost her, you know? But I don't want to see her dead."

"What?" Catherine gasped.

His eyes raised slowly to hers before he spoke. "She'd gone back to Kemper."

"No! Who is—"

"An old *friend*," he said bitterly. "I had been searching for her for hours, and she had gone back down the Hill to him," he added. "We found them together in that damned cave."

"That doesn't mean anything, Sean!" Catherine said frantically. "Think about what you're saying. There could have been a hundred reasons for her to go there. I won't believe you. It's impossible."

"Why is it so impossible?" he asked wearily.

"Because she loves you, you stupid man!"

"Catherine," Stephen warned as he stepped to her side.

"She does," she hissed, glaring at each man turn. "This is lunacy!"

Catherine was prepared to do battle with these men in defense of her friend, but the thoughts were lost and their dialogue interrupted as Jane Pringle returned, directing Kevin Thatcher into the kitchen.

All thoughts and concerns and conversations were directed toward Corie's welfare from that moment on. Dr. Thatcher examined his patient and then ordered Stephen to take Catherine from the room.

"I'm staying," Catherine said mutinously. "Corie is my friend."

Thatcher was a man not much older than Stephen, but he packed the authoritarian tone of an older, more experienced doctor. "You're nursing a young son, Catherine," he said. "I don't want you upset. Go with Stephen."

And that was that, as Stephen took his wife's hand and led her from the room.

Kevin Thatcher was caring, organized, and meticulous when it came to the treatment of his patients. Once he had cleansed his hands and his instruments, he bent over Corie's shoulder. "I'm going to hurt her, Sean," he said softly, "and there is nothing I can do to alleviate the pain even though she appears unconscious." The man seemed to pause over Corie, silently staring at his hands as if he was feeling helpless. "I want you to hold her," he said as Sean watched the strong, capable hands of his friend move toward his wife's torn flesh.

Sean moved around the table to stand at Corie's head and placed his hands on her upper arms.

Corie reacted almost immediately as wood and splinters were removed from her body.

"I know, Corie," Thatcher crooned. "You must try be still now."

"Sean!" she cried.

"I'm here," he said and lowered his head so she could see him. "You must try to be still, Corie."

"Oh, Sean," she moaned through her haze as Thatcher dug into her flesh with his well-honed surgical tools.

It was an agonizing few moments for everyone as Kevin worked with cautious efficiency, ensuring the wound was completely clean and free from debris. But Corie's pain had touched him. "Dr. Crawford Long has worked quite successfully with ether as a surgical anesthesia these past two years," he told Sean while continuing with his work. "But it seems to me a dangerous practice to put someone who is unconscious into a deeper sleep." He stood to his full height then and frowned at Sean apologetically. "I'm sorry for her pain, Sean, but with Corie slipping in and out of consciousness, I just hesitate to use the stuff."

Sean nodded his understanding.

Corie lost consciousness again during the procedure, but Kevin assured Sean that was natural and for the best.

Once the worst of her wounds were cared for, Dr. Thatcher attended to the business of straightening Corie's ankle and setting the broken leg, raising Corie to screaming consciousness once again. He then rendered the leg immobile with a temporary concoction of slats and harness straps well cleansed with lye soap. "I have a leather cast that I'll bring along tomorrow," Kevin said as he dried his hands. "The thing looks horrendous but it will stabilize this leg and be more comfortable in the long run. Now, let's ca' Stephen to help us get Corie up to her bed. It's time w attempted to find her a bit of comfort."

Dawn was nearing before Sean was left alone wi his sleeping young wife. Exhausted, he fell to l knees by her bed and covered her hand with his own. His eyes searched her face for some small hint of awareness, but she was sleeping the light sleep of one tortured. Occasionally Corie's lips would move, and she would moan softly as she tried, in vain, to find some more comfortable position. Time drifted by with Sean paying no heed to the hours lost as he knelt at her side. Eventually his weary head dropped to the mattress beside Corie's hip.

"Why?" he whispered.

Chapter 25

Corie lived in a haze for several days, and Sean remained at her side, sleeping in a chair beside the bed when exhaustion overtook him. It wasn't until Corie gained awareness of her surroundings that he quit the room, having first told her quite bluntly that Peter Kemper had died that night in the cave.

Between bouts of dozing, Corie would ask for Sean, but Jane Pringle and Kenny were afraid to pass along the request.

Sean alternated between fits of anger and attacks of melancholy, and no one, including Stephen, was prepared to suffer his wrath.

Only Catherine dared.

On the ninth day after her accident Corie awoke to find Catherine sitting silently in a chair beside her bed.

"It's such a wonderful thing," Corie whispered.

Catherine looked up from the face of her nursing son and smiled. "Hello. What's wonderful?"

"A mother nursing her child."

"It is, I promise you. And one day you'll be doing this, too."

Corie's head turned toward the window before she spoke. "I don't think so, Catherine."

"Of course you will," Catherine said quickly. "You might be pregnant even now. Remember?"

"I remember," she said, turning back to look unhappily at her friend. "But it's unlikely after what happened."

"Nonsense. If that baby was there and meant to be born, you've still got him."

"You're always so certain, Catherine," she accused, not unkindly.

"Not always. But there are some things I believe in quite desperately."

Smiling sadly, Corie asked, "Could you conjure up a little belief that my husband still loves me?"

"I don't have to tell you that."

"You do, Catherine. He seems to be angry with me, and I don't understand why. I know he doesn't like me to go down the Hill alone, but that would only cause him to scold me. There's something else and I can't even ask him what that might be. He won't come in here when I ask for him."

"He didn't leave your side for days, Corie," Catherine said softly.

"He hasn't been near me for days, Catherine. And he's moved his things to another room."

Catherine turned Andrew in her arms and settled him against her other breast. "He thinks you left him," she said quietly, watching Corie's reaction carefully.

First there was confusion. "What?"

"He believes you returned to Peter."

Then there was disbelief. "As in . . . I left my husband to go to another man?"

"Yes."

Then anger. "Well, isn't that just ducky! He has a lot of faith in me, my Sean!" she scoffed.

"Corie—"

"How *could* he?"

"He's hurt and confused," Catherine reasoned.

"Don't you stick up for him, Catherine Fraser," Corie railed. "How could he think I'd leave him? Doesn't he realize how much I love him?"

"I think if you both ever calm down, you might remind each other of that," she said softly.

"I can't if he won't even come near me!"

"Corie, settle down. You're not doing yourself any good."

And Andrew, alarmed by the raised voices, began to cry.

"I'm sorry," Corie whispered, raising her hand to her forehead. "How did this mess happen?" she asked when Andrew had quieted.

Catherine had questions of her own. "Why were you there, Corie? Why on earth were you with Peter Kemper?"

"I went there to get him to help me."

"Help? What kind of help?"

"I needed a rich cargo."

Catherine sighed, stroked her son's cheek, and walked across the room. There she settled Andrew in a large basket lined with fine linens and blankets.

When she had returned to her chair, she frowned at the woman in the bed. "Dare I ask *why* you would need a *rich cargo*?"

"To help Sean."

"Sean?" she asked with surprise. "Corie, Sean doesn't deal in stolen goods."

"He might not like it, but it's a way out. Catherine, Sean's bust."

"What?" she asked, clearly confused by the term.

"He's got financial difficulties."

"Sean? That's preposterous."

"It's true."

"Corie, you're being . . ." But Catherine stopped before she accused her friend of anything. "How did you discover Sean was . . . bust?"

Corie moved fitfully in the bed; she had only one arm with which to boost herself, and one leg was weighted heavily by the leather splint.

Catherine stood up and plumped another pillow behind her friend's back. "So, how did you find out about this financial difficulty?" she prodded.

"Do you remember when you and Stephen had dinner here and Sean became angry when they were talking about creditors?"

Nodding thoughtfully, Catherine frowned. "You asked me what *creditor* meant."

"That's the night. Shortly after that I met a woman who seemed to know about Sean's problems. In fact," she added reluctantly, "I know of two women who know. It appears we're the only ones who don't know Catherine. All of Natchez must know."

"Two women. Would one be this *Sue Ellen* I'v heard you talk about?"

"That's right."

"Well, who is she anyway, Corie?" she snappe "I mean . . . she might just be some gossipy ninny.

"I thought so, too."

"Then why on earth would you pay her a mind?"

"You've forgotten there was someone else," Corie said softly.

"All right," Catherine said, crossing her arms under her bosom. "Who else?"

"Faye."

Startled, Catherine sat forward in her chair. "Faye Doherty?"

"Yes."

"Oh, for the love of God, Corie."

"She knows."

"Of course she knows. She may have even started the rumors." The moment the words left her mouth, Catherine considered the comment as feasible. "That could be it, you know? I don't know what she would hope to achieve, but Faye is capable of such a thing. What if she wanted Sean back, Corie? Have you considered that? Or maybe she just wanted to hurt him. Or *you*."

"She said she offered him money. And other things."

"Such as a return trip to her bed?"

"Apparently."

"And you believed her?"

"No. Not the part about her bed." But tears had formed and clung precariously on her lashes. "Maybe I was wrong."

"You weren't, Corie," Catherine said quickly as she sat beside her friend and gripped Corie's hand. 'Sean loves you too much to go to Faye. He was done with her long ago."

"He was quick to think I wasn't *done* with Peter, and he knows Peter and I were never lovers. I was a virgin when Sean took me, Catherine. I can only think 's reacting this way because he's guilty of the very ings he's accusing me of."

"Oh, pooh!" Catherine got angrily to her feet and crossed the room. "You two are behaving very badly, and I think it's time you talked. I'm going to bring Sean up here."

"He won't come," she said softly, certain his anger would not permit him to enter the room.

Catherine found Stephen and Kenny with Sean in the study. Marching into the room, she stood directly at Sean's feet. "I think you should go up there and talk with Corie."

Sean's eyes narrowed. "Oh, you do."

"There's a lot you both don't understand, and you're never going to get over this if you don't talk about it. Ask her *why* she went to Peter, Sean."

"I don't need to be told that, Catherine," he said evenly.

"I think you do!" she said. "How can you be so damned stubborn?"

"Catherine!" Stephen barked.

McKenna, seated on the hearth rug beside Thor, leaned into the dog's heavy coat for comfort.

"Catherine . . ." Sean sighed, trying to be reasonable, particularly in McKenna's presence. "Corie had gone away from me days before she actually went down the Hill."

Clearly stunned, Catherine stiffened. "What?"

"She'd been miserable and unhappy for days. She even cried a time or two."

Placing her hands on her hips, Catherine asked in disbelief, "Did it occur to you that perhaps she wasn't well?"

"It did," he snapped, tired of being picked to the bone. "I asked her that. I even suggested she might be pregnant. She wouldn't talk."

"Well, perhaps she is pregnant."

"Then why in the name of all that's holy would she venture out in the rain? If she cared at all about the possibility of there being a child, surely she wouldn't risk her health?"

"Ohhh!" Catherine shuddered and dropped her hands against her sides. "She went because of you, you stupid man! And ask her who has been putting ridiculous thoughts into her head while you're at it."

"Catherine, I think you've said enough," Stephen warned, stepping to her side.

"I've only begun, if this friend of yours doesn't get up—"

"That's enough!" Stephen barked and turned her to face him. "Go and get Andrew. I think it's time we were on our way home."

"I won't go and . . ."

But Catherine did not have the opportunity to complete the thought. Three sets of surprised eyes followed Sean's weary body as he silently departed the room.

"Well . . ."

"No more," Stephen said. "I think it's time we left."

"But, Stephen, they're being silly."

"It's their problem to work through, Catherine," he said firmly. "I don't want you to interfere."

"I'm not inter—"

"Go!"

Now there were two sets of silent combatants.

Jane Pringle had decided very quickly that she did not like the way Sean was behaving and refused to eat at his table. Consequently, Sean was left with the sullen company of McKenna at meal times.

"Corie's so sick and you never go to see her," Kenny accused one night over supper.

"McKenna"—Sean sighed—"I've said we won't discuss this."

"If you make her sad, you'll feel bad, like I do," she said.

Sean lowered his fork and stared at the child. "What do you mean, moppet?" he asked reasonably.

"It makes me sad that Corie's hurt and sometimes I wasn't very nice. That makes me sadder."

For the first time in several days Sean's attitude softened. "Sweetheart, none of us can be *nice* all the time. But that has nothing to do with Corie getting hurt. What are you trying to say?"

"I think she went out in the rain because she thought I liked Faye better'n her."

"Faye?" Sean tried to puzzle this through but could not sort out her child's logic. Moving his chair back from the table, he gave his knee a pat. "Come up here, darling," he said and pulled Kenny up onto his lap. "I don't understand, McKenna. Tell me about Corie and Faye."

"Corie got mad when I was talking to Faye."

"When was this?"

"Long time ago. Corie wouldn't buy me the top, but Faye said she would and Corie got mad. She dragged me out of the shop."

Sean gave the child his full attention as he puzzled with the concept of Corie confronting, or not confronting, Faye Doherty. "What happened after that?"

"We went to see you at work." Kenny tipped her head and looked directly into his eyes. "You remember. That day when Corie was so mad and made me stay with Daniel."

The day Corie had demanded that he teach her

read. "McKenna, why wouldn't Corie buy you the top?"

"She thought it might cost too much."

"And Faye offered to buy it?"

"Yup."

"Yes," he corrected absently. After a moment's thought, he asked, "Why would you think Corie thought you liked Faye?"

"Because the day she went out in the rain, I heard Corie say, 'Damn, Faye,' when she was dusting your desk."

A child's logic?

"I thought she forgot about the top, Sean," Kenny said miserably. "I wasn't mad about the top anymore."

Sean hugged the child against his chest as his thoughts went into a spin. "I don't think Corie was thinking about the top, moppet," he whispered. But she *had been* thinking about Faye. Why?

"Maybe she's been sad all this time," Kenny offered.

After a moment Sean shook his head. "Or at least since the evening we spent at Rosalie," he speculated.

Corie had settled back against her pillows as soon as Jane had removed her supper tray. Her rest was short lived, however.

Sean stormed into the room with such force the door bounced back against the wall. "Was Faye Doherty at Rosalie the night we were there?" he demanded.

Stunned, Corie took a moment before she nodded.

Sean spun and left as quickly as he had come.

* * *

Sean's next entrance; a short time later, was equally as stunning as he stormed into the dining room where Faye and Sue Ellen were in mid-meal.

Clearly startled, both women frowned at the intruder for a moment. But Faye was quick to read Sean's obvious anger to her own benefit. "Hello, darling," she drawled, getting to her feet and moving toward him. "I've been expecting you."

"Have you indeed?" he asked, his eyes going to the younger woman.

"Of course," Faye said, resting her slim hand on his upper arm. "The entire town knows about your troubles, Sean. Really. How could she be so stupid as to have an affair with a man like that?"

Sean's eyes dropped to the woman at his side. "*She?*"

"That little whore you married, Sean. Don't let your anger make you dense, darling. Oh, I understand you must be livid, but think about it. You must surely understand that all of Natchez is aware that she was found in that cave with her lover from the past. It must hurt terribly, Sean," she added, tugging at his hand and moving toward the table. "But you're here with friends now. Come and sit. I'll pour some of that fine brandy you like so well."

Vibrating with rage, Sean nevertheless allowed himself to be quietly led and sat as directed. "You haven't introduced me to this lovely young woman," he managed to say with feigned ease as his eyes settled on Sue Ellen.

"Oh . . ." Faye turned from the sideboard with a crystal decanter and brandy snifter in hand. "How rude. This is . . . Susan."

"Susan," Sean repeated quietly as the drink materialized between his hands. "Susan. Or Sue Ellen?"

Sue Ellen Peachtree rarely revealed her emotions unless she chose to do so. Although she realized it was not wise to do so now, facing this man's particular brand of anger had her instantly flustered. She gave the game away when her complexion colored.

"I've thought it odd that a young woman would befriend my wife and yet choose not to come to our home. Additionally, that young woman made some very untoward comments that have had me puzzled. I believe, however, that I'm beginning to sort things out."

Faye, always confident, laughed lightly. "How mysterious you are when you're angry, darling."

Sean's perusal turned to his ex-lover then. "I was sorry that I missed you at Rosalie, Faye."

Faye blinked but took up the challenge. "Rosalie? You were there?"

With a sinister smile, Sean faced the woman squarely. "Did you really believe I would fail to escort my *whore* of a wife? I think not," he added, laughing shortly. "You knew I was there just as you knew Corie would be there. Did you hope to break apart my small family, Faye? Is that why you've conspired with this young woman? Or did you have something more evil in mind?"

"Really, Sean, I don't know—"

"Neither do I, *love*," he said derisively before downing the contents of his glass. "And furthermore, don't care to know. At least not from you." He stared from one woman to the other before dropping the next stone. "At this point I know only that I do not wish either of you ever to come near me or my family again. And that stands most particularly for Corie.

Should I ever discover that either of you has said so much as a word to her in future, I will see you both ruined in this town.'' He allowed a moment's silence before asking, ''Is that clear?''

Faye's complexion colored to livid red before she jumped to her feet. ''You seem to think very highly of yourself, Sean Garrick. Before me, you were *nothing*! You were just another struggling merchant.''

''Don't you see, Faye?'' he said forcefully as he stood to face her. ''That is all I've ever wanted to be. It was *you* who wanted more. And struggle as I might, I've earned a reputation in this town, and I've earned it on my own. The one thing that might have brought me low eventually was my association with you.''

''What an ignorant bastard,'' Sue Ellen threw in. ''You don't have the power to harm a fraction of this woman's reputation. You'll be laughed out of town, and I'll be happy to see to that.''

Surprised by the quiet but fierce tone, Sean stared at the younger woman for a moment before commenting. ''Indeed? You have a new champion here, do you, Faye?''

''Get out!'' Faye screamed.

''Curious,'' he said quietly. ''You always had a penchant for the extreme and the unusual. How far does that extend, I wonder?''

''Leave!''

Sue Ellen glared as Sean's smile grew to maximum proportions.

''Remember that my threats are not idle, *ladies*,'' he said quietly. ''Never, ever approach me or a member of my family again.''

After a mock bow to each of the women, Sean silently took his leave.

Chapter 26

The hour was late, but Corie found she could not sleep. Kenny had come to say good night and had babbled on about not liking Faye at all, and now Sean had been gone for hours. And after his mysterious, but brief, visit to her room. It was fair to say that Corie had been alarmed by his abruptness, not to mention the question he had posed. She was confused and she was worried.

Sean entered the house quietly, dropping his coat over the newel post as he made his way to his study. He was weary from his frantic musings since he had first talked with McKenna at supper. And his confrontation with Faye had brought little satisfaction. He still did not know the entire truth of it, but he knew others had interfered in his life. And the devil of it all was that they had triggered something desperate within Corie. Too many things stated this day had made sense, and too many thoughts did not; Catherine had tried to tell him, and he had not listened.

It had taken a child's logic.

317

Corie hadn't loved Peter, he reasoned again as he made his way up the stairs. They had been childhood friends, and she had come to Sean a virgin. And she hadn't run to another man that night but had been tormented and unhappy and seeking . . . what? *That* he would have to determine.

She was lying back against the pillows, staring at the ceiling. A low-burning lantern cast shadows about the room when he entered. The sound of his soft steps reached her, however, and Corie turned her head in his direction.

"I've brought you this," he said quietly and extended a glass of amber liquid. "Drink it slowly."

Corie frowned in confusion as she accepted the glass and watched him pull a chair close to the bedside.

When he was seated, Sean took a hearty pull from his own glass before bending forward and resting his elbows on his knees. "Why did you go there, Corie?" he asked softly.

"I didn't leave you, Sean," she said simply.

"I know that. Why?"

"To ask for help."

"What kind of help?"

Tears came again to Corie's eyes, almost rendering her speechless. "For you," she choked.

"What kind of help?" he pressed.

"You work so hard," she said as tears washed down her cheeks. "I couldn't stand to see it all taken from you."

"Corie," he said firmly, "what kind of help?"

"I know you're bust, Sean."

"Bust?"

"You have financial difficulties," she parroted.

Sean pressed his back into the chair. "Not this again? Still?"

"I thought it was true!" she cried.

"Because of something Faye said?"

Corie merely nodded her head.

"I told you about the business," he said flatly. "Did you choose not to believe me?"

"I did believe you!" she cried, frightened by his apparent lethargy; his *anger* would have been more welcome. "But that was before. I thought you were trying to protect me." After a moment Corie whispered, "She was lying, wasn't she?"

Sean carefully set his glass on the bedside table. "I don't know what she said."

"She said she offered you money and that you had been to her house. She hinted you had been there often."

"And you believed her?" he asked, growing angry that she could have so little faith in him.

Corie's left hand now covered her teary face. "Only about the money."

Sean reached forward and removed the untouched glass of brandy from Corie's hand; for the first time in his life he *needed* a drink. In fact, he thought he might need several more before this night was over. His disappointment was raw in the back of his throat. "The day you asked me to teach you to read . . . you'd seen Faye that day?"

Her brows drawn high over the bridge of her nose, Corie nodded in frightened hesitation; something was very wrong. "I went to Peter for help, Sean," she blurted anxiously. "Not because—"

"And Faye made some suggestion about my fiances, did she?"

"Y-yes."

"And, of course, there was your *friend* Sue Ellen. She played a part, too."

"I don't understand."

"No, I don't suppose you do," he said quietly. "And the evening at Rosalie . . . Faye spoke to you there."

"Yes. Sean . . ."

Pinching the bridge of his nose, Sean got wearily to his feet. Staring down at her, he said, "What I fail to understand in all of this, Corie, is why you would not speak to me. I worried for days. *Everyone* who cares about you was worried. I tried to talk with you. I wanted desperately to help . . . to comfort you. But you refused to confide in me . . . you had so little faith in me," he added in a pained whisper.

"No! Sean!" she cried, reaching out to him as he turned away.

Corie was too late in reaching out.

"Look, man, the last thing I want to do is interfere. But this thing between you and Corie has invaded my own home, for chrissake. I'm going to have a sick woman on my hands if we don't talk with you. Can you accept the fact that we mean well, Sean? I mean . . . we're your friends and we . . ." Stephen Fraser finger combed his hair in agitation and paced away. "Damn! This is ludicrous." Turning back, he stared across the room at his friend. "Catherine has been here visiting Corie while you're at work. My own wife has been harping at me for over a week now to come and see you. She's convinced Corie did not go down that hill to be with this Kemper fellow."

"I know that," Sean said quietly as he reached for his pipe.

Stunned, Stephen took a step forward. "You *know*?"

Pressing tobacco into the bowl of his pipe, Sean nodded. "She went there to get help for me. Or so she thought," he added ruefully.

"If you know that, then why the devil is this rift between you not mended?"

"How would you feel, Stephen, if Catherine would not confide in you . . . if she had little or no faith in you? If she wouldn't allow you to help with a problem? Or a *supposed* problem?"

Stephen joined his friend then, sitting thoughtfully in Corie's favorite chair. "I don't know. I suppose I would be hurt."

"Suffice it to say, I'm *hurt*, my friend."

"Sean, I don't think—"

"I also don't believe that lack of faith is a sound basis for a good marriage. Would you agree?"

"I think I'd better get Catherine down here," Stephen mumbled.

"Coward," Sean accused, smiling miserably.

"Maybe it was something impetuous," Stephen said hopefully.

"That she'd planned for several days?"

"Lord, I don't know," Stephen groaned.

"Well, I do," Catherine interjected as she joined them in Sean's study. "It's called blind love," she said, stopping before Sean's chair. "It's a willingness to lose everything . . . to risk anything . . . to help someone you cherish." Kneeling at Sean's feet, Catherine placed her hands on his knees. "That's what she thought she was doing, Sean. You can't fault her for that."

"No, I can't," he said, staring at her intently.